Dedicated to Life – you got to love it

AUTHOR'S NOTE

All the characters and events portrayed in this story can be considered fictional. Nevertheless, the tales are somewhat based on real experiences and real characters, just names, dates, locations and times have been changed completely, along with the facts.

CHAPTER ONE

Recognising Matatanisho

Both the 'why' and the '*how*' for Titus Tembo being proclaimed Africa's second-best photographer are very simple yet complex. It was as clear as mud to Titus Tembo! Confused? Well, that makes at least two of you! Let's be patient and together take the first steps on this journey of enlightenment with Titus Tembo.

The '*how*' is somewhat transparent yet intriguing. Conceived on the African continent in a foreign country, gives us the starting point. Titus Tembo's British mother being a mzungu, was dispatched from Ghana to the United Kingdom to give birth. This clearly added to his confusion later in life. This state of mind that his beloved Baba, Eng. M. J. R. Tembo, the father of Titus Tembo, referred to as his son's 'Matatanisho' remains with Titus Tembo even today. Being called a '*pointy*' in Kenya by his fellow African brothers and sisters due to his mixed race and carrying two passports, one of which was different to that of his Baba added to the '*Matatanisho*.' It was often the case that father and son took different lines on entering some countries' passport control areas together. Titus Tembo's British passport gave him different privileges to that of his Baba and his Kenyan passport. Titus Tembo spoke English as a first language and as we all know the problem with the English language is that it rarely sticks to its own rules. The life foundations of Titus Tembo were built on the instability of living in at least thirty homes in five different countries before the age of eighteen, when Titus Tembo declared his independence. Well, that is the number Titus Tembo could recall in terms of homes anyway.

Eng. M. J. R. Tembo would hire nannies, maids & tutors or all in-ones to see to his son's needs. Each woman would come into their home put her stamp on the household and then do the same for Titus Tembo. Her replacement would come with her own ideas, be they based on her country of origin, parental upbringing, training or just tribal beliefs. Living on the equator meant the sun went down at 6.00pm and twilight lasted less than 30 minutes. One woman would ensure they ate dinner before 6.00pm, insisting she would not cook in the dark like a wizard. Another woman would insist they ate after 7.00pm as they should not be eating dinner in the daylight as if it was lunch. Whatever the reason, Titus Tembo's understanding of what was normal changed as frequently as the household help.

The European forests turn red and orange just before they go into hibernation come Autumn. African rain forests display the exact array of red and orange colours just before they burst into life with fruits to feed the forest inhabitants. In the meantime, the result of all the colours in Europe is to see the dead leaves fall from the trees. Titus Tembo felt he was always somewhere between the two life cycles of European and African forests, yes 'Matatanisho.'

Titus Tembo suspected there were many small contradictions all helping a little in defining his 'Matatanisho' outlook on life; not remembering his mother, as she died when he was very young when they lived in Ghana, then moving around from country to country on the African continent, being given a first name of a Roman Emperor, and a British education. Indeed, looking back Titus Tembo believed his 'Matatanisho' contributed greatly to the three very successful yet short lived marriages he had experienced by the time he was rapidly approaching thirty-five years of age! Surely his indecision between an intrapreneurial or entrepreneurial approach to life and business was inherited from his beloved Baba? Titus Tembo believed he could definitely thank his beloved Baba, Eng. M. J. R. Tembo for his mindset which turned great ideas into at least three businesses that he no longer had any part in as of today.

Eng. M. J. R. Tembo had a passion for photography from an early age. A very basic Single Lens Reflex camera was put in the hands of Titus Tembo by his Baba as soon as his son was able to walk and talk a little. Yes, thanks to his hero, as most of all the 'how' or is it the 'why' or both, was down to his beloved Baba. Life can be confusing - all smoke and mirrors - but through the lens of a camera using mirrors and a prism system, you see it as it is, if only life was so simple.

Eng. M. J. R. Tembo gave his son lots of advice as they moved around Kenya and later on the African continent, from one of his exciting international postings, a new job, or down to a new business idea. There were also those special chats around the safari camp fire in the bush when Titus Tembo returned at the end of each school term from England. Titus Tembo will admit to you now, at the time much of this wisdom sadly fell on stony ground. Indeed, he was more interested in avoiding the insect bites and his ears were tuned in to the sounds of the bush night, like the roar of a male lion in the distance. After sitting in those cold British classrooms for a whole term, anything was far more interesting to Titus Tembo than listening to yet another grown up giving him even more advice. Nevertheless, Eng. M. J. R. Tembo persisted and remains today, the hero of his only son. Those were the days when Titus Tembo secretly put on his school uniform of an evening so as to keep warm in bed during the winter months. This would also allow him some extra time in bed on those cold mornings. His teachers at the boarding school would complain about how scruffy Titus Tembo was when the cool evenings came around, but they never guessed his special dressing secret. Titus Tembo was not sure if he would tackle his problems a little bit differently these days? Today the words of Eng. M. J. R. Tembo still guided Titus Tembo from beyond his grave. Indeed, many of his father's life's lessons struck a chord with Titus Tembo long after his beloved Baba departed this earth. It was many years later that Titus Tembo realised the full truth behind the mzee's words. Fortunately, as he faced up to his many small life crises, the lessons of life and some achievements, the latter that Titus Tembo could proudly say would make Eng. M. J. R. Tembo happy if he were alive today; he recalled much of the advice he shared with him. Today Titus Tembo's benchmark to decision making is *would it make Eng. M. J. R. Tembo happy, if yes then go for it.*' Nothing got Eng. M. J. R. Tembo down or for that matter over-excited. He often remarked, '*WE WILL ALL BE DEAD ONE DAY WHATEVER BEFALLS US*'. So, Titus Tembo recalled his beloved Baba's words of wisdom and just gets on with playing the game of life, using as best he can, whatever the cards he ends up with in his hands. Titus Tembo keeps on keeping on and continued the same journey after his beloved Baba passed on. Even in death Eng. M. J. R. Tembo saved his son one last time. But that is a story for another day.

Photography was always playing a role in their lives. They took photos of buildings, places, people, the wilderness, its wild animals, cities, the country side, their poor, everyday folk, big and small, tranquillity and conflict. Their photographic sessions just became their norm, Titus Tembo's beloved Baba and he, every day without question carried a camera and Titus Tembo does to this day. So, as the years of practice passed, Titus Tembo's understanding of the art, and the ability to capture the moment increased. Titus Tembo recorded the memories in pictures and saw a subject through the eyes of a supporter, a parent or lover or whoever the audience best suited that scene. A good photograph or video recording, he felt somehow, was showing it as it really was, that moment which was being recorded by him and as such it helped bring stability to what he would say was lacking in his early years.

Towards the latter part of his working life, Eng. M. J. R. Tembo left Africa to experience yet another culture in the United Arab Emirates. Eng. M. J. R. Tembo was plucked by some international recruitment consultant from a time of contemplation. He was treading water in his business life somewhere near the impenetrable forest in Uganda after discovering the wonders of a new simple and effective method of meditation. His beloved Baba had meditated for many years but this Transcendental Meditation taught to him by a Ugandan Asian guru became a life changing experience for his beloved Baba. None of this appeared on his Curriculum Vitae compiled some twelve months earlier. Eng. M. J. R. Tembo had registered his interest in a power plant project about to kick off in Tanzania but heard nothing back at the time. Then over a year later, the recruitment consultant wanted Eng. M. J. R. Tembo for something completely different. According to the recruitment consultant his beloved Baba was the ideal man for this opportunity in the United Arab Emirates, with his hands-on experiences in many different types of businesses and later in his career holding down Senior General Management positions, good schooling in Kenya, an Electrical Engineering honours degree from the University of Wales Institute for Science and Technology in Cardiff, Wales, Great Britain. His beloved Baba liked to insist naming in full the University when asked about his qualifications. This degree in engineering was backed up with a Master's in Business Administration from the leading South African University business school. In fact, it was an MBL to be precise; Master's in Business Leadership as opposed to commonly referred to Master's in Business Administration. This, his beloved Baba proudly obtained as a *cum laude*. For college graduates who haven't managed to squeeze in a Latin course or don't have a Latin-English dictionary handy, Titus Tembo's beloved Baba referred to it as '*with great distinction.*' Eng. M. J. R. Tembo claimed this learning was like someone switching a light on after he spent most of his career in the dark. In those camp fire talks the importance of life-long learning would be stressed to Titus Tembo by his beloved Baba. At the time it was just noise that went over the young head of Titus Tembo. Much later in his life he explained to his son, that a second light came to him in the form of Transcendental

Meditation that opened up a whole new way of seeing everything more clearly and being in harmony with nature and the universe. Unlike his beloved Baba in later life, for Titus Tembo until his beloved Baba left him for good, Titus Tembo was happy in his ignorance, in his darkness and accepted his '*Matatanisho*' as the norm.

Eng. M. J. R. Tembo had a track record of technical training covering electrical power distribution in the United Kingdom utility supply industry, he worked in the copper mines of Zambia, Central Africa, gold mines of Ghana, West Africa, refractory manufacturing and primary aluminium production, the latter albeit briefly in Southern Africa. As a starting point in the United Arab Emirates, Eng. M. J. R. Tembo, headed up a cable manufacturing company in the Emirate of Sharjah. Eng. M. J. R. Tembo, on being awarded this appointment, knew very little about cable manufacturing other than what he had read in recent months and many years ago as a graduate apprentice during his early United Kingdom based training. What he did know was people, and the managing of manufacturing businesses. It was obvious to Eng. M. J. R. Tembo that this cable manufacturer certainly had the staff that his leadership would provide to guarantee success for this business. These were boom times and cables and wires flew off the shelves. Eng. M. J. R. Tembo settled in his job in the Emirate of Sharjah and he established his new life in the Emirate of Dubai, taking a risk in buying a villa off plan on the man-made island of Palm Jumeriah. With Eng. M. J. R. Tembo at its head, the business could not fail to be anything but very profitable during this boom time in the United Arab Emirates.

The owners had their long-standing representative as their eyes and ears based in the office just along the hall from the desk of Eng. M. J. R. Tembo. Mr. Maher would be in the office at the cable factory most days, but not before late morning at the earliest. Eng. M. J. R. Tembo assumed wrongly that the family adviser had other business he was committed with at the start of the working day. In fact, since Mr. Maher sent his family, his wife and two girls, to Canada for schooling, he no longer kept family hours and needed the early morning to catch up on his sleep. This kindly man, Mr. Maher, was trusted by the family owners and was the one who had recruited Eng. M. J. R. Tembo in the first instance. How this was ever possible remains a mystery as Tembo spoke three languages, good Swahili with its Arabic influence, his tribal language as his first choice and perfect English; none of these languages Mr. Maher could understand. To be fair to Mr. Maher he did speak the sixth most spoken language on earth and the first language of the United Arab Emirates, but unfortunately

Arabic was the only language he spoke and it was not a language Eng. M. J. R. Tembo had yet mastered. Partly down to the language barrier, in reality the international recruitment consultant ensured the appointment. Mr. Maher rubber stamped the deal once he looked at the man in person. What he took in was a well-presented Eng. M. J. R. Tembo who had a genuine British education and training, enough to be trusted. Maybe this was the reason why the two men got on so well together as only very occasionally they used someone in the office to translate when they needed to discuss important business matters. There was no meaningful discussion possible between them on cars, sport, politics, religion, ethics, morals, current affairs, women, or for that matter anything they may disagree on when debating. Without any conversation between them, the Muslim Mr. Maher still managed to introduce, the Christian Eng. M. J. R. Tembo, to Middle East culture, even sneaking Eng. M. J. R. Tembo, a devoted Christian, into his Muslim place of worship one weekday evening. Mr. Maher during his time in the office, always insisted Eng. M. J. R. Tembo drunk many cups of strong Arabic coffee which he claimed was very healthy with its addition of cardamom. This latter ingredient gave the Arabic coffee a strong and unique taste, so different to Kenyan coffee, an intensely aromatic aroma that got Eng. M. J. R. Tembo drinking some ten small cups daily at work. On occasions Eng. M. J. R. Tembo was obliged to accept one of those fat Cuban cigars Mr. Maher loved so much. Despite just playing a role of cigar smoker and trying not to suck in the smoke, occasionally Eng. M. J. R. Tembo found his head spinning, and he would be forced to lie-down in the board room in order to recover fully. This was somewhat of a shock to Eng. M. J. R. Tembo as he'd never experienced anything like it, or saw his movie hero Clint Eastwood suffer those effects on the big screen in those 'Spaghetti Westerns' he liked so much when a student in Cardiff.

Eng. M. J. R. Tembo enjoyed those sudden, albeit infrequent and brief breaks when Mr. Maher jetted off to Canada. It gave him time to visit a movie house of an evening in Dubai and enjoy movies like the '*Last Samurai*'. Most of the movies were censored back then, but Eng. M. J. R. Tembo always remembered the turning point in the censorship when they showed the naked shoulder of the dead Samurai warrior's wife. The movie house was packed with men in their bright white clean designer branded kandura national dress, and to a man they all clapped unknowingly the lifting of the censorship that day. Several years later, society had moved on so rapidly in the United Arab Emirates that it had reached the point where movies of this nature were actually being filmed in Dubai and Abu Dhabi. Titus Tembo's beloved Baba played what he liked to call a star role as an extra in the movie *Mission Impossible Ghost Protocol*. He liked to tell his son occasionally how he acted in the movie with Tom Cruise. He was, however, most impressed with Jeremy Renner, who was more approachable than Tom Cruise. Mr. Tom Cruise was not allowing anyone to disturb his movie; after all time was money, and in the main his money was financing this movie. Titus Tembo's beloved Baba at the time never noticed the oh so funny Simon Pegg, but on the other hand he'd never forgotten how when the action started, Jeremy Renner changed into his role so completely he did not need to be in ear shot of the actor to understand what his character was to be. The movie was being made by one of Hollywood's own big five, but Eng. M. J. R. Tembo did not make a killing for his three days in the movie industry.

It turned out that officially Mr. Maher was living with his family in Canada and working full time in a Lebanese grocery store located in Quebec City. For whatever reason, Mr. Maher held two passports, one from Syria and one from Lebanon. This allowed Mr. Maher to have an official ghost working in Canada in order for him to eventually qualify for Canadian citizenship while living and working in the United Arab Emirates. It seemed a reasonable compromise to Mr. Maher as he was paying his taxes from the job he had in the Canadian supermarket, his family were there, and he was always ready to fly back to Canada at short notice on his Syrian passport when required.

The holy month of Ramadan came along and Eng. M. J. R. Tembo understood that unlike Kenya, there was to be strict adherence to the fasting by all people in public during the daylight hours. Well, it turned out in the end fasting was not as seriously enforced in the United Arab Emirates as it was by its neighbours in the Kingdom of Saudi Arabia. There, they often gave their expatriate managers time off in a foreign country to recover part of the way through the holy month! That was not necessary in the more liberal and westernised United Arab Emirates. Nevertheless, this would be a new experience for Eng. M. J. R. Tembo as in Kenya naturally it was just the Muslims who followed the tradition. The United Arab Emirates fell somewhere between the Kingdom of Saudi Arabia and Kenyan practices when it came to the holy month of Ramadan. Eng. M. J. R. Tembo had told his son that Mr. Maher appeared sensitive to his concerns as this was his first Ramadan in the Middle East. Titus Tembo's beloved Baba was ready to fast and just take some water from time to time to ensure he would be able to still work efficiently. However, Mr. Maher would hear none of this nonsense, and went ahead setting up a place for Eng. M. J. R. Tembo in the board room to drink his daily ration of coffee as Mr. Maher was insistent that Eng. M. J. R. Tembo carry on as normal, albeit out of sight during the daylight hours of Ramadan. It turned out that Mr. Maher was not so thoughtfully concerned with Eng. M. J. R. Tembo, but indeed wanted this room set up so he could continue to drink coffee and most importantly smoke his beloved cigars. The little Indian office boy would be let into the board room with the coffee pot as soon as Mr. Maher thought he had opened the windows long enough and sprayed sufficient air freshener to cover the cigar smoke smell.

The atmosphere in the United Arab Emirates during the thirty days of Ramadan reminded Eng. M. J. R. Tembo of the commercialism of Christmas he'd experienced while in the United Kingdom as a student all those years ago. Completely different to a Kenyan Christmas, when people went back to the villages to work their summer breaks away. He vaguely remembered as a child cleaning house or working in the fields over a Kenyan Christmas. Like a British Christmas, during Ramadan it was party time in the United Arab Emirates most evenings once the sun went down. Hungry Muslims would mix with the rest of the population to break the fast in public parks, or tents specially set up by five-star hotels or restaurants all keen to make a quick buck. Nearly everyone would over indulge each evening. The daylight hours shortfall in caffeine and nicotine intake was more than made up for during the hours of darkness. By the end of the holy month there were a lot of fatter and unhealthy-looking people in need of dieting and visiting the local gymnasiums. Maybe the morning traditional breakfast before sun-up, that Eng. M. J. R. Tembo had not experienced, was more refined? After the evening celebrations, Eng. M. J. R. Tembo expected there were not so many hungry mouths to feed but possibly some very tired people having difficulty sleeping well, this would be due to their feasting late into the night. What he did know for certain was that people were nothing like as efficient at their day jobs during the holy month.

Following the holy month, Mr. Maher insisted they went back to their regular routine in showing Eng. M. J. R. Tembo of an evening the famous sights. They visited places like the well-known Longs Bar situated in the basement of a Five Star Hotel along Sheikh Zayed Road. One of the first lessons Mr. Maher gave on their outings to Dubai, was to stress the importance of Sheikh Zayed to the United Arab Emirates. He, Sheikh Zayed bin Sultan Al

Nahyan was the ruler of Abu Dhabi for more than 30 years and he was the respected and much-loved founding father of the new nation named the United Arab Emirates.

When they stopped in any bar, there Mr. Maher would take a whiskey before rushing off to the next location, and he insisted that the alcohol would not affect his driving ability. It certainly put him at risk as there was a zero-tolerance policy towards drinking and driving in the United Arab Emirates. What Eng. M. J. R. Tembo agreed with was that in no way could it affect Maher's driving as it was already so bad it could get no worse with the addition of an occasional whiskey. The standard of his driving reminded Eng. M. J. R. Tembo of how bad the general driving became just before sunset during the holy month, in Mr. Maher's case his driving was even worse if that was possible! On their outings Mr. Maher seemed oblivious to the cars around him who he cut-up and the responding honking of the horns he did not realise were for his benefit! The evening outings became more frequent and Eng. M. J. R. Tembo did not want to cause offence by refusing the invites. What he did was sip on an energy drink in order to stay the course into the early hours and work the next day. Eventually the many coffees, an occasional cigar and nightly energy drinks had their damaging effect on the health of Eng. M. J. R. Tembo.

The doctor at the factory who examined Eng. M. J. R. Tembo was so concerned about his high blood pressure that he was not ready for them to leave the examination room until he got Eng. M. J. R. Tembo to commit there and then to immediately completely give up smoking, take only one of those energy drinks a month and a maximum of just one Arabic coffee a day. Due to this health scare, with immediate effect, Eng. M. J. R. Tembo went back to his own healthy lifestyle, returned to regular transcendental meditation, exercised most evenings and ate healthy foods. Mr. Maher accepted that his slightly older friend was not young enough and healthy enough to enjoy life as he himself did. For Mr. Maher a sprint on the spot in the shower each morning was deemed sufficient exercise to keep him fit. His smoking helped keep his weight down and the Lebanese diet kept him young. The regular Arabic coffee or occasional whiskey was an additional benefit to ensure he'd have energy to meet all that two jobs in two different continents demanded of him at any time.

The Saudi Arabian owners of this very profitable cable business were not the most generous of people, yet Eng. M. J. R. Tembo believed strongly in rewarding his team as they were the ones paying back the owners' investment many times over. Fortunately, the bonuses recommended by Eng. M. J. R. Tembo (and paid), were within the limits set for Mr. Maher to authorise without the knowledge of the family. There was nothing extra for Eng. M. J. R. Tembo in terms of a monetary bonus but for Eng. M. J. R. Tembo, he was happy enough in the short term to sell off his leave entitlement and work all year round. The United Arab Emirates authority had only recently moved from a five-and-a-half-day week, which in reality was a six-day week, to a more acceptable five-day week. So, for Eng. M. J. R. Tembo there were weekends for mini holidays, photo opportunities and occasional staycations. His hard work paid off in another form of recognition via a number of high-profile business awards.

Circumstances worked in the favour of Eng. M. J. R. Tembo as the family owners from the bordering country vied between the brothers for control of their United Arab Emirates investment in the cable business. Eng. M. J. R. Tembo stepped out of the business before he was pushed out by the family owners. He spent some weeks enjoying working on his golf game and desert photography during the cooler winter months. He had the opportunity to snap the foxes at play on the Nad Al Sheba golf course, and a horned viper when on desert safari. The latter experience involved the police airlifting a local out of the desert by helicopter. The man had got too close and the snake was not at all pleased, resulting in the man being bitten by the viper. For Eng. M.J. R. Tembo, he faced more danger at Nad Al Sheba golf course, and not from a horned viper or fox. The royals raced and trained their very expensive race horses at Nad Al Sheba, so he had to ensure his golf ball striking kept the little round white missiles away from the thoroughbreds jogging round the track inside the golf course. For that matter occasionally the track lights were on to allow a Sheik to go for a jog in some comfort, and not just any venerable local man of more than fifty years old, no, these were members of the Dubai ruling family. A Sheik would jog round the horse track alone some evenings and Eng. M. J. R. Tembo was aware the golf balls could do the Royal as much harm as his horses. Only once, many years before, he had been hit by a golf ball when a young Titus Tembo went back to play a lost ball with a six iron some 160 yards out from the green. He stayed one side but the drifting ball nevertheless caught him centre chest. He was felled immediately and his chest showed the bruising for the best part of a week. Impact with his head would surely have ended in death. Who would have guessed the gentleman's game was so dangerous. In the case of Titus Tembo, the experience had nearly killed him from his own laughter at his beloved Baba falling like a tree cut down in the forest and squealing like a pig in pain.

As time moved on, Eng. M. J. R. Tembo found himself working for a wealthy Egyptian family, three of the brothers had their fingers in many a business pie. The middle brother was a billionaire investing funds in a new massive United Arab Emirates cement plant, aiming to complete the project in a world record time. It seemed like the perfect timing for such an investment during the boom of building modern Dubai. One of the world's richest Arabs picked out Eng. M. J. R. Tembo for interview because Tembo knew the United Arab Emirates well, and just as importantly, he was known and well respected in their business circles having over the years picked up a number of the United Arab Emirates most prestigious business awards. The Egyptian cronies of the rich man warned Eng. M. J. R. Tembo to be prepared for a ten-minute grilling and no longer. The big boss had little time to waste and made his mind up very quickly in a job interview if he wanted you on his team or not. Eng. M. J. R. Tembo was different to those fellow countrymen around the big boss. Eng. M. J. R. Tembo was relaxed, confident, both intrapreneurial and entrepreneurial as and when needed. The cronies of the Big Boss were horrified, as to them it seemed Eng. M. J. R. Tembo was challenging in his conversation during the age the interview discussions seem to take. So, Eng. M. J. R. Tembo could make his own judgement. Did he want to join this group? Both Big men got their wish as Eng. M. J. R. Tembo enjoyed and thrived in the entrepreneurial company culture established by the Big Boss. He loved the wheeling and dealing as he was trusted, empowered with some big decisions if time was of the essence. They could not afford to miss the opportunity to get the massive cement plant on line in record time to ensure they maximized profitable sales during the peak of the Dubai building boom.

Eng. M. J. R. Tembo was content until the Big Boss did a deal on ownership with a French multi-national cement group. It was hard to imagine, but the Big Boss made himself even richer! This new windfall allowed him to fulfil his sporting dream and own an English premium league football team. His beloved Baba was forgotten about and left to his own devices in the French dominated company. For an English-speaking Eng. M. J. R. Tembo, his own entrepreneurial style failed to impress in the risk adverse, centralised decision-making culture of the French business school mind set. Titus Tembo understood why his beloved

Baba put into practice his camp fire advice! He recalled clearly all these years later, his beloved Baba preaching to him around the camp fire, '*Make sure you do something you have a passion for, you will enjoy what you are doing, it will never feel like work, you'll be good at it and you will be successful; do not follow the money as the money in the end will follow you.*' Eng. M. J. R. Tembo stepped away from his French masters but convinced them of his usefulness in consulting for the French Cement Group.

In the end it all turned out for the best as it always seemed to do for Eng. M. J. R. Tembo in life. His beloved Baba found his true calling as an industrial ecologist entrepreneur. Eng. M. J. R. Tembo started his niche by recycling hazardous industrial waste, business that helped save the environment while making very well-deserved good money. All his experience from the many industries he had worked in over the years came into play. His first small fortune came with some luck during his consulting period. Once again for his beloved Baba, hard work had turned into good luck. Eng. M. J. R. Tembo had been approached some time ago at a conference in Dubai when he posed a question on industrial ecology, and proceeded to lecture the presenter on the unsatisfactory answer. As luck would have it one more time, it turned out that Eng. M. J. R. Tembo had been noticed and had impressed with his lecture. Some Japanese oil executives realised before the end of his speech that Eng. M. J. R. Tembo knew how to help safely dispose of the oily sludge to be cleaned from some of their off shore island oil tanks. What the Japanese experts did not understand is that this waste had a very useable high energy content and could be pumped cheaply using a traditional concrete pump. With a simple concrete mixer set up homogenising the hazardous waste, Eng. M. J. R. Tembo showed how the French cement company, his ex-employer and now the client he consulted for, could utilise this alternative fuel that he would source for them. The Industrial Ecology solution involved charging the waste producer for taking their waste and recycling the same. In addition, it involved charging the cement company for providing a good quality alternative fuel. Once again it seemed the harder Eng. M. J. R. Tembo worked and the more innovative he was, the luckier he became!

What Eng. M. J. R. Tembo told his son was that the most pleasing thing about the project was not the excellent profits made, but the environmental benefit of using a waste to replace a fossil fuel that would have needed to be dug up in South Africa, railed to the

Richards Bay coal port in Zululand, then shipped halfway round the world to the Middle East, off loaded at the Northern Emirates port and then transported by road to the waiting cement plant. He would also avoid the traditional disposal effort of inefficiently burning of this waste and land-filling the toxic ash left over. Because of Eng. M. J. R. Tembo's hard work, and his innovative thinking, all that would happen now was like a magic trick; the alternative fuel would replace the dirty coal, the toxic ash would be turned into cement, then concrete and eventually the hazardous waste would be used safely in building a home for someone. It was a win-win outcome for all concerned - including mother-nature.

Eng. M. J. R. Tembo was making good money and helping save the environment but could not convince the dark suited men at the local banks to take the risk of lending him the further funds at reasonable rates that he envisaged would provide the waste treatment plant his business so desperately needed to ensure sustainability. There were however, visionary people out there without dark suits, who like himself were not great fans of the banks. And these entrepreneurial people were willing to take the risks for a good environmental cause if it gave a reasonable return on the cash they held. Eng. M. J. R. Tembo ploughed his first small fortune made out of waste oil, right back into the Industrial Ecology business and got an Indian engineering family to build the basis of a waste treatment facility to be paid back out of the projected business profits during the next three years. Yes, Eng. M. J. R. Tembo paid over the odds for the equipment and works, but then the investor took a high risk and delivered his treatment plant only slightly late. This lateness was anyway as expected in this part of the world. Without other investors on board, Eng. M. J. R. Tembo also kept control over his company and could run his business in a fair way, his way. All parties were satisfied except the dark suited bankers who in the end were never made aware of the deal.

Forgetting the important lessons his beloved Baba had shared with him. Titus Tembo blindly decided to follow the money and not his passion. He decided to leave Nairobi for Dubai where clearly his fortune awaited him - or not as the case turned out to be. When Titus Tembo knocked on the door of Eng. M. J. R. Tembo, he expected his beloved Baba to give him a role to play and this would lead to a share in the family industrial ecology business. Okay, Titus Tembo had no experience of such an enterprise, no related knowledge, no understanding of the business, the environment or the culture but what the hell, he was a willing and quick learner; after all what could go wrong? he asked himself.

CHAPTER TWO

A trip back in time

Before Titus Tembo started his first business of Hi-five pottery he dabbled with wildlife filming and kept the wolf from the door in the form of the occasional commission or royalty payments. It was an exciting time in more ways than one as the young Titus Tembo honed his practical photography and movie making skills in the real world. There were some close shaves with a variety of creatures and situations. And he came to understand the term flight or fight. On one occasion Titus Tembo was to film a world famous Kenyan long-distance runner on the white soda lakes in Magadi, on the floor of the Great Rift Valley.

After discussions with his regular lady driver Titus Tembo hired for these types of trips, they decided to set out when it would be cooler. They saw the sun plop down below the Ngong Hills before their vehicle dropped 1,200 meters to the Rift Valley floor. Mrs. Njeri was the taxi lady Eng. M. J. R. Tembo always took to-and-from the airport when in Nairobi and she had known Titus Tembo son of Eng. M. J. R. Tembo for many years. She was a lady that embraced her African heritage. It also helped that she sat most of the day, and this contributed to her idea of a conventional, broad, attractive African woman. She liked her staple food of ugali cornmeal, her favourite Kikuyu meal was mashed peas and potato mix, beans she'd eat with anything anytime but normally again with corn, and second best was pilau spiced rice. She prided herself on never leaving any 'Nyama Choma' on her plate whether the meat was fried or roasted.

She never touched beer, which was not the case with a lot of Kenyan drivers. Maybe her one weakness was snacking all day. She would stop frequently for a cob of roasted maize. There would be an inspection to ensure the corn had been picked when it was mature, so its dry starch would be perfect for roasting over the hot charcoal embers. Her first choice was a cob that some kernels had popped like popcorn mixed with blackened crunchy crisp. Mrs. Njeri also carried some chilli lime salt garnish just in case of emergencies when the street vendors failed to supply her favourite dressing. Another street food that would do her when cobs were not in season was Samosas. She always took the meat pastry wrap and when Titus Tembo was with her, he would take the vegetable version with a squeeze of lime juice. All this would be washed down with chai. Kenyan coffee may be world famous but like most Kenyans Mrs. Njeri took tea brewed dark, mixed with plenty of whole fat milk, sweetened with heaped tablespoons of white sugar. On a warm day both of them would take a Stoney Tangawizi ginger ale. Eng. M. J. R. Tembo used to make this ginger beer at home when they were in countries where it was not regularly sold. When not eating street food, Mrs. Njeri ate French fry's masala or ugali plus chapati flat bread with everything, and occasionally added sukumawiki kale, or fried cabbage. All the typical Kenyan foods were on her menu of choice and she ate in great healthy quantities, and maybe that is why the car leaned toward the driver's side a little.

Titus Tembo was being driven down the Nairobi Magadi road by his trusted driver Mrs. Njeri after dark so that they avoided the heat of the day. The joke in Magadi is that there were warmer places in Kenya but they were so hot they burnt off the map. Titus Tembo in reality had little understanding of the heat of the Emirates; when Eng. M. J. R. Tembo warned him if he came to Dubai, it should not be in their summer time. Titus Tembo thought of the Magadi climate and was foolishly unconcerned about the temperatures of a Dubai summer! It was a laborious journey to Magadi as the tarmac road was narrow and pot holed, there were no street lights and the surroundings were pitch dark. The view of this sky is, however, something everyone should add to their bucket list. Because of the close proximity to the equator, it means if you stay up long enough you will see both the Southern and Northern constellations in one night's sky. Mrs. Njeri had the car lights on full beam and they both caught from time to time the reflection from the sparkling eyes of the dwarf antelopes that were scampering away from the roadside. These dik-diks are common here along the road sides after the sun goes down, maybe they felt safer at night and they certainly enjoyed this area of dry African savannah. They were often in pairs, and even on a few occasions we saw a third young one with their parents. Even with them being so common here, Titus Tembo and his driver were still lucky to spot these tiny creatures. If one thinks the female is the larger of the mates, yet she is just 40 centimetres at the shoulder and maximum 70 centimetres long. Not much of a meal at around 5 Kilograms for any of the big carnivores. Maybe that is why they live for nearly 10 years in the wild. Coming round a sharp bend the headlights reflected what seemed like the eyes of a big owl in one of the larger than average acacia trees

They slowed down more or less automatically to check on the owl and Titus Tembo instructed Mrs. Njeri to pull the car closer to the tree. His beloved Baba had taught Titus Tembo to call it a 'ningojee' tree. As a kid Titus Tembo would always be saying 'wait for me' when he got his clothes hooked on the acacia thorns. Thus, the Swahili name given by his beloved Baba for the acacia tree. Close by a female dik-dik gave a wheezing and whistling "zik-zik" alarm call.   It sounded as if one of them had stood on a dog's chewy toy!   Right enough, when they both looked up into the tree a female leopard was crunching on the bones of what they assumed was the male partner of the dik-dik giving off the chewy toy call. This was in itself a mesmerising sight as the Magadi visitors stared up into the branches of the 'ningojee' tree, a sight made even more impressive by the stars filling the Kenyan sky.

Titus spoke to Mrs. Njeri, 'Surely nothing on the rest of this trip could be more exciting than the leopard experience?' Later that evening the bored glances from the two of them was their signal of enough wildlife thank you. The bat eared foxes did not really register with either of them and at this latish hour – they were more interested in arriving sooner rather than later at the nearby town of Magadi.   Thinking to himself Titus Tembo debated whether they should get a move on as these creatures were after all a fairly common sight throughout this dry region and are mainly active at night. The bat eared foxes like the areas where it's been extensively grazed and are highly social, so they saw a few too many of those fantastic foxes to be of interest. The foxes loved that area as before electrification, Magadi Soda Company used wood as its main source of energy. This saw the area deforested and no reforestation efforts were made so erosion has further degraded the soil, affecting the growth of grasses on which Maasai livestock thrived.

They were due to stay two evenings in the Magadi Soda social club but on finding it full, arrangements were made for them to stay in a mine guest house next to the General Manager's place. The history of the club itself was interesting as initially it was for whites only. It eventually became a club for managers and their families and at that time they had a line painted down the middle of the bar area to keep the races apart. There was a second Magadi club where Titus Tembo expected it may have been a little bit livelier. Here in the now fully integrated managers club without the painted line, the service still appeared to be modelled on the colonial past. It very much reminded Titus Tembo of the Muthaiga Country Club a few kilometres outside Nairobi city centre. The Muthaiga club had been established in 1913 long before Kenya became a colony in 1920. Mining started in Magadi in 1911 so Titus Tembo surmised the club was formed around the same time as the Muthaiga club but with less of a reputation of being 'the Moulin Rouge of Africa'. Titus Tembo could not visualize the elite of Magadi drinking champagne of an evening, dancing through the night and taking pink gin for breakfast. Maybe down the road in the second less salubrious of Magadi Soda clubs, there were wilder scenes, possibly Tusker, the favourite local beer, would be drunk in large quantities, cards played and the drunks could wake up to find themselves with someone else's spouse come dawn!

Certainly, here the expectations of Titus Tembo for the kitchen were not as high as the one in the Muthaiga club but fortunately for them, here in Magadi you did not have to dress for dinner. Also, unlike the Muthaiga club, his female companion would be allowed in the bar. Even today the only lady who had been allowed in that Muthaiga bar during regular opening times was the aristocratic Danish author Karen Blixen who wrote her memoir of seventeen years in Kenya back in 1937. How wrong could he have been about the food, as on this evening it was a Swahili theme night. That was peasant style food, food of the people, possibly the stuffy old Muthaiga club lot will not dish up of an evening for dinner. There's something comforting and alluring about the coastal specialties. Simple fresh ingredients are teamed with spices traded for centuries along the palm-fringed East African coast. They served bread as a side dish that you never knew you needed until that first bite. The main course must have been the best curry in town and they turned the stodgy plantain with sweet coconut sauce and cardamom into a piece of heaven.

The Magadi Soda General Manager had sent a driver to pick them up earlier to take them to the club in his company car for dinner and maybe they should have listened to the regulars who advised them not to walk the short distance from the club back to their guest house. Titus Tembo thought they were just being polite offering them a lift back that very short distance. They could see the light of the guest house a few hundred meters off but they had to walk along an unlit dirt track with the only light coming from the stars as the moon was as yet just a sliver. They had one hand-held torch between them and its weak beam picked up two reflecting eyes. This was the trigger for Mrs. Njeri to jump behind Titus Tembo and plead for him to protect her. Her body shape ensured she was as much on show as Titus Tembo who was standing in front. In fact, Titus Tembo would have preferred that Mrs. Njeri leapt forward with whatever her tribe carried as a weapon and saved the day. The noise of fear coming from Mrs. Njeri in the end won them the battle of wits with whatever wild creature stood before them and it darted away rather quickly.

They arrived back to an empty but well-lit comfortable residence. Titus Tembo requested Mrs. Njeri to ensure the car was secure for the night as advised by the driver who had picked them up earlier that evening. He had told Titus Tembo that a stray Vervet Monkey or a Baboon at first light could do a lot of damage if your vehicle was not secure. The car was only a few steps away from the back door and the area had a security light switched on. As such Mrs. Njeri did not give it a second thought and bravely stepped out and closed the door behind her.   It was a very short time lapse before two very loud screams galvanised Titus Tembo into action. What he saw was Mrs. Njeri screaming hysterically while pinned against the wall by her fear and an old male hyena making a terrifying call while frozen next to the car. Both the human and wild creature recovered quickly and departed the scene. Mrs. Njeri delegated the car checking to Titus Tembo as she locked herself in her bedroom with her windows securely bolted. And so, to bed and sweet dreams!

When planning the itinerary, Titus Tembo had expected their Olympic runner to be with them on the last day, while on day one he would scout out the locations with his trusted driver Mrs. Njeri, and set up for the arrival of the gold medallist. When Titus Tembo awoke early the next morning, he was greeted by the sight of the crusty white soda ash lakes sitting under half a meter of storm water. This was in one of the hottest and unlikeliest places on earth to be flooded. So, Titus Tembo never got to meet the great man, let alone film him running. This change of plan may have also pleased Mrs. Njeri, as, after her experience of the nightlife, she was keen to return to Nairobi and civilization, sooner rather than later.

Mrs. Njeri liked wildlife as much as anyone and often took her clients to the Nairobi National Park, she enjoyed as much as anybody else watching the dangerous hippos and the evil looking killer crocodiles on the Southern boundary next to the small town of Athi River. Occasionally she'd be lucky to come close enough for her clients to photograph a black rhino and everyone knows how dangerous those great grey monsters can be at times. Her car could easily manage the well-maintained gravel roads in the park and Mrs. Njeri had become a safari ranger of sorts.   The park had its dangerous animals and that is why the Northern and Western sides of the Nairobi National Park are fenced. These fences were there to keep wildlife out of Nairobi's residential areas, and off the Nairobi-Mombasa Highway. There are lions and cheetah, and despite all this Mrs. Njeri can proudly say she has sat at the picnic sites eating with her clients. The park was too small to sustain an elephant population but on the edge of the park, Mrs. Njeri took the occasional client to the David Sheldrick Wildlife Trust and there she had come into contact with elephant orphans. She had even fed Rothschild's giraffes by hand at the African Fund for Endangered Wildlife Giraffe Centre in the lovely wooded Nairobi suburb of Karen. All that track record with wildlife, but she had to admit she'd been shaken up a little by those eyes of some unknown creature on the night walk and even more by that hyena encounter. Mrs. Njeri was knowledgeable enough to understand that those creatures favoured attacking women, children and infirm men. It seemed she may have been on the menu as those hyenas did not differentiate between a well build traditional lady and a stick model as she liked to think of shall we say the more modern ladies, she drove these days.

The house servant at the guest house was instructed to set out breakfast so the lady and gentleman visitors could enjoy the view of the lake - if not its smell that morning. That strong aroma that many visitors found unpleasant but the locals never really noticed. The wind carried the scent of the unique stink of the soda lake, a smell like prawns that were no longer fresh enough to eat. The badly named 'house boy' was in fact a very old man named Joss. Yes, he told them, he knew of the old male hyena that lived around the village. He informed them that some people even left food out for the old fellow, just as he learnt that some Mzungus leave food out for badgers and foxes in their own countries. Joss did not participate in the feeding of the old male hyena as he did not want to encourage the jackals, bat-eared foxes, or other small carnivores and then possibly snakes that would relocate from their hang out around the rubbish dump on the out skirts of the town. There was also that menacing large baboon troop that needed no further encouragement to enter the town in the daylight hours.

Over a dark strong muddy coffee and fresh tropical fruit for breakfast, Titus Tembo considered the day ahead. His golf clubs were in the car next to the camera gear and in the end, there was now plenty of time to try out one of the most unusual golf courses anyone could dream up. But before that there was an omelette to polish off and a few cups to enjoy of the Kahawa Chungu, the best Kenyan coffee made the traditional way. Titus Tembo was ready for golf and popped into the bedroom to change into his golf shoes when Mrs. Njeri did whatever ladies find to do, getting ready in her bathroom. There were only a half set of clubs in the bag but having embraced her African heritage again over breakfast, Titus Tembo was concerned that carrying his bag may prove a little too much for Mrs. Njeri.

He was day dreaming of the golf ahead when he first noticed a giant of a baboon sitting at their breakfast table finishing off a large mug of chai that Mrs. Njeri had left for her return when she'd finished in the bathroom. This was a male and probably the alpha male of this particular troop which seemed to be surrounding the property. He certainly looked as if he would dominate a rival and Titus Tembo was not too keen to confront him. This guy appeared to be bigger and very much stronger than Titus Tembo. It was difficult to imagine what this animal could do if disturbed and understand how he may react to humans. He was inclined to leave sleeping dogs lie. Mrs. Njeri on the other hand wanted her chai left alone and became very brave, maybe seeing the close proximity to the house and the day light as her guardians. The alpha male showed complete indifference to the demonstration Mrs. Njeri put on to scare him off her chai. When Titus Tembo stepped out into the sun shine the picture changed and the alpha male raced off making some strange noises. The small primates joined in the calls and appeared to be playing hide and seek with Titus Tembo and ignoring Mrs. Njeri. They were there to check out the refuse bins before they were emptied and a potential meal taken away. The gardener arrived and made short work on moving the large troop out of the gardens before they caused to much damage.

Before the exodus, Titus Tembo took the opportunity for some action shots, he zoomed onto the faces of the individual members of the troop and avoided just focusing on their activities, he was looking for photographs that would tell a story, his shutter speed was set between 1/250 and 1/15 a second and he opted for continuous drive as he panned the troop with the background blurred. He would do the editing later, as now there was time for a round of nine holes and he accepted as Mrs. Njeri, after yet another encounter with the wildlife of Magadi, was in no state to leave the house or even leave the house door open, let alone carry his golf bag around in the wilderness of the Magadi golf course.

The putting surfaces could not be called greens as they were in fact browns made from mixing a small quantity of old oil with sand and rolling them out. There were a few blades of grass to be seen on the fairways only after the heavy rains. Goats were trimming the fairways and there was no rough to be concerned about if you hooked your shot. No, if you wandered off left or right, that ball was a lost cause. The highlight of the round for Titus Tembo was when a young Maasai man recovered one of his better drives; bringing the golf ball back to him at a much quicker pace than Titus Tembo could walk to it to play his next shot. He was a fearsome looking warrior but in reality, a very friendly chap trying to help Titus Tembo out by bringing back what he clearly needed, in the eyes of the Maasai man anyway, to fire off again at whatever the Mzungu was hunting! Titus Tembo relaxed as with his gold medallist runner missing, there was enough time for him to practice golf and better still enjoy another good meal at the mine club. His photography could wait for another time to capture the scenery, hot springs of boiling geysers, the pink waters, large flocks of dancing flamingos, the salt encrusted shores, the Maasai Manyattas and the warriors with their Roman like red togas.

Lunch was prepared for the managers taking a break from their mine duties. The plain food offerings consisted of white rice, beef stew and green peas along with the essential bread chapattis. No one was happier to indulge than Mrs. Njeri, who had not had the best of times with the local wild life, and thankfully she thought lunch marked their departure to civilization. Titus Tembo left the beef on one side and took additional peas. He focused and had the pleasure of talking to 'One Dan' about the mine, its surrounds and the local wilderness. Mnr. Dan Botha was one of the new white Afrikaners hailing from outside Bloemfontein in the Orange Free State. One side of his family could trace their African roots back to before the British arrived in the Cape of Good Hope in 1822. The other part of the family came on his mother's side, arriving from just off Carnaby Street, London, England, during the swinging sixties. His Ouma did not actually arrive emphasizing modernity, fun loving hedonism, or thankfully wearing a Mary Quant fashionable miniskirt, but nevertheless her best efforts at conforming would not fit in with the conservative *white only* practices of that time. She is the one who named Mnr. Dan Botha, 'One Dan' as she said five kids is enough, let Mnr. Dan Botha be the last one and so the name 'One Dan' stuck even with his Afrikaans side of the family.

There was a brief one-sided lecture on the factory from 'One Dan'. "Trona in the lake is a sodium carbonate compound which is processed into soda ash, it's what you may think of as a little bit like baking powder. The Magadi Soda Company is not producing all this for cooking, in the main it's exported to make glass, but can be used for chemicals, soap, paper and water treatment. Of course, there are also the salt fields but they are mainly there to provide work to the Maasai. These large Trona deposits are millions of years old, the lake was fairly shallow and evaporated rapidly and repeatedly, creating a climate that changed back and forth between humid and arid, trapping the once abundant life which is unique today in this environment. The mud on the bottom, the sodium, alkaline and bicarbonate were transported to the lake by runoff water coming from the now extinct volcanoes all around the Magadi town. The processing side sounded simple enough, a series of washing, filtering, and centrifuging, in order to remove the impurities. Finally, a large rotary drier similar to those at a cement plant gave the Magadi complex its industrial look and feel. The rotary kiln with heat from a fire of diesel drove off unwanted gases, turned the Trona into sodium carbonate and dried the mineral ready for transport by rail or road for export."

'One Dan' was a mining software engineer assisting the local team with mapping the lake and delivering a dredging plan to recover the Trona in the most effective way and reduce the refinery processing costs. South Africa was at that time seen as one of the leading mining nations anywhere worldwide. It was the same for the small Canadian railway team at Magadi who were working on improving the logistics of the railway line built in 1915. It was in a state that desperately needed their world leading expertise to get the product from the Rift Valley floor and down to the port at Mombasa. Obtaining the water from the river at the foot of the West side escarpment of the Rift Valley, dredging the Trona, pumping it, then refining the slurry and the other engineering magic was left to an old Australian and his Kenyan boss. The Aussie and the much younger Afrikaner got on like a house on fire. They were both making the most of getting out into the wilderness together most weekends if their work commitments allowed.

The lunch at the Magadi club led Titus Tembo to agree with 'One Dan' for them to go on a weekend photographic expedition at the end of the month when the rains would be easing off and day-time temperatures would be dropping; a perfect time to explore Lake Magadi and the Nguruman escarpment. Titus Tembo was excited about the prospect of taking photographs of bush camping, the hot springs, the indigenous forest, and particularly the epic wild life. Mrs. Njeri was most content that Titus Tembo, son of Eng. M. J. R. Tembo would need a 4 x 4 and not her and her trusted taxi for the upcoming off- the- beaten- track adventure.

Very early on the last Friday morning of that month saw Titus Tembo driving an old Defender Land Rover with a young, very enthusiastic mzungu school boy spouting off non-stop next to him in the passenger seat. Did my father tell you about when I was bitten by a dog and he drove from the bush in record time for my rabies injections? Or the time he caught me going to bed in my school clothes, or when I caught my pet snake or, and so it went on broadcasting. Well at least they had something in common even if it was just wearing school clothes to bed thought Titus Tembo. This kid tagging along was part of the price Titus Tembo had to pay for the use of the Defender and the loan of all the related camping gear. Bryn Darms was part of the package as his father lent him to Titus Tembo with the kit over the weekend. It seemed a cheap price to pay at the start, looking after Bryn Darms while his father flew on safari business to the Maasai Mara. Bryn Darms knew of Magadi town as he played football for an adult team that visited when the weather was dry and cooler one Saturday afternoon that season. He clearly had made a hit that day, he stood out not as the only kid on the field, but also as the only mzungu who most people could remember playing soccer in Magadi. Some of the local kids around recognized him and waved enthusiastically at the Defender crawling by.

First stop for Titus Tembo and Bryn Darms was an early picnic lunch, more like brunch-time, at the hot springs a little distance past Magadi town. For some time, they felt completely alone and at peace, apart from the running commentary of young Bryn Darms, as they soaked in the healing waters of the hot springs. In the distance, like an old Hollywood Western, two red cloaked figures approached in an unclear shimmering mirage. The two Maasai boys walked up to them with big smiles and spoke enough English to pronounce the word 'coooke' which Titus Tembo took as a request for a Coca Cola. Accordingly, two old fashioned glass coke bottles were removed from the cooler bag, the metal tops flipped open and the Maasai youngsters gulped the content down before falling to the ground in shock, making some interesting noises and holding their heads as they appeared to be in great pain. Titus Tembo did not think before handing over the chilled coke that these boys would not have experienced such cold ever before and possibly considered it witchcraft! The boys soon recovered and were on their way to where Titus Tembo could not imagine, or from whence they came.

Ten-year-old Bryn Darms assured Titus Tembo he was very capable of driving the Defender while Titus Tembo leaned out of the car window taking photographs. Next stop was 'Jim's Elbow' to film the miracles displayed by the flamingos as the easing of the seasonal rains brought millions of them from lake Natron across the border in Tanzania. Nearly three quarters of the world's lesser flamingos headed for the hyper-saline Great Rift Valley lakes in Kenya to feast on the water algae organisms. It seems like nothing goes to waste in nature as the blue-green algae called cyanobacteria was a poisonous plant producing a chemical that in most animals could fatally damage cells, the nervous system and the liver. The lesser flamingos, as if they had super-powers, consume enormous amounts of these algae with no ill effects other than the fact that it turned their white chick's plumage pink over some three years. It was a spectacular sight just seeing the magic of them feeding on poison, many of the tall birds were plunging their heads in the hazardous liquid that would strip the skin off a human body. They were twisting their heads upside down and using their upper beaks like a shovel.

The flamboyance of the birds followed the example set by Jesus as they were running on water but this was no biblical miracle. They had webbed feet and ran to gain speed before lifting up into the sky. To the side of the lake the birds were drinking fresh water, even at near boiling point, from the springs and geysers. Others who had been crowded out from the fresh hot waters, drank the salty water and drained it out via their nasal cavities. The tripod was set up and the video was directed at both the males and females participating in their elaborate group dances. As for most Africans, dancing came naturally to these birds, they had several moves which started with a 'head-flag' as the birds called loudly while they extended their heads and waved them back and forth. Filming from the one spot proved easy as the dancers seemed to be trapped by the invisible walls of a dance hall. Some of them must have been all danced - out, as the tired ones seemed to be asleep standing on one leg.

Titus Tembo could have not asked for a more spectacular start to this weekend's photographic journey and it was gratifying for him to know the soda ash dredging was in an area that was not impacting on the delicate balance that produced these unique fragile ecosystems. Or had the activity of man changed the area forever and become its new norm?

As they headed back toward the township, there was no need for Titus Tembo to ask to slow

down to change drivers. Suddenly Bryn Darms skidded the defender to a halt, and to Titus

Tembo's surprise, leapt from the driver's seat through the open window, rushing off for no

apparent reason. Bryn's young eyes had spotted the bold black and white Ostrich with his

two light brown female companions just before it registered with Titus Tembo. Titus Tembo

laughed loudly but still managed to snap away with his SLR camera on auto mode as Bryn

Darms joined in the sheet shaking mzungu dancing of the big black and white bird, too

interested in his girl friends to notice the small human company joining in the dancing.

Bryn Darms made a lot of noise moving his mouth more or less nonstop. Noise

suddenly turned into words for Titus Tembo as he heard the boy driver explain why there

were strips of plastic rubbish to be seen in the construction of the Inkajijik, the Maasai word

for house. Before he went on to that subject, he said 'By the way do you realize we white folk

use some 3,000 different words in total all our lives while these people living in these primitive

conditions use maybe ten times more words than us? My dad says it's because they see the

world in much more detail than us and therefore need more and different descriptive words

than us whites. Titus Tembo was not sure what to believe, and filed that bit of interesting

information away in the back of his memory so that one day he could read up and check on

that Bryn Darms claim. Bryn did not miss a beat, the loaf-shaped building is traditionally made

of mud, sticks, grass, cow dung and cow's urine. As was his way, he rambled off into the facts

that women are responsible for making the houses as well as supplying water, collecting fire

wood, milking cattle and cooking for the family. At the remark that they are nomadic, Titus

Tembo brought the subject back to the plastic rubbish but Bryn Darms had more to say on

the Maasai subject he'd started. In common with the wildlife with which they co-exist, they

need a lot of land, they are semi-nomadic, herding their cattle and goats to sustain the land.

They were the original eco warriors until the mzungu came and stole the most fertile land.

Yes, yes, all well and good Titus Tembo thought to himself but what about the plastic rubbish?

The Maasai people may appear backward but they live comfortably, for example they use

blow up mattresses and mosquito nets on their beds. The mud floors are both cool in the hot

weather and warm to the feel once it gets cold. The authorities want them to be educated,

so the mothers select half of the boys who should go to school and their Inkajijik remains close to the local schools. The other half of the family's boys continue to be semi-nomadic along with the majority of the livestock. The result is they do not have enough cow dung around the place to complete their Inkajijik. The adaptable Maasai had turned to the next most suitable material, plastic rubbish discarded by modern living that best stands up to the rain.

Titus Tembo had his own experience of the impact of the modern world of education on the Maasai very soon after the Bryn Darms' lecture. He thought it best to stock up with some charcoal for the cooking at camp. At the side of the road a young Maasai boy looked as if he had finished his schooling for the day. The school boy not only understood English, he spoke clearly in response to Titus Tembo's request for charcoal. He explained very clearly indeed the charcoal price he was willing to sell at to Titus Tembo. This was double the going rate and he defended the high price by explaining the economics of bringing the charcoal to market in Magadi. The reality was that this particular charcoal was likely made locally, and delivery should make the costs and therefore the market price, higher in the capital Nairobi than it was here! Titus Tembo accepted defeat and handed over the money at the higher price to only be asked for more as there was a refundable deposit charge for the plastic sack holding the charcoal! 'Maybe it is education rather than power that corrupts', Titus Tembo mumbled to himself as he loaded the sack into the back of the 4 x 4. Ironically the charcoal and its plastic bag remained untouched for the camping trip and returned home to Nairobi for future use.

CHAPTER THREE

Bush camping

Titus Tembo arrived at the agreed venue of One Dan's place on time to find their South African weekend ranger next door at what he learnt soon enough was the household of his Australian colleague. The garden was unusually green in comparison to that of One Dan's. The South African had little time and little interest in gardening. His desert retreat showed what planned neglect in Magadi Town could achieve in a very short space of time. Even at the end of a very unusually productive rainy season, the few trees in bloom shaded an area of dusty and stony lunar like landscape. He was happy with his environmentally friendly landscaped garden fitting in with its surrounds. As he was at work most of the daylight hours, he felt the grounds were suitable to keep away the likes of the local troop of baboons. While they appeared so human-like and quite comical, they are potentially dangerous wild creatures. Where there was one baboon you could be sure there would be up to fifty nearby. In Magadi town they had become familiar with human homes and their vehicles. One Dan new them of old and had seen these apes set up camp in the most unusual places as long as they had water and shelter. These creatures could pose a threat and cause much damage if left to their own devices and not controlled when in a human habitat. They are omnivorous, so their menu consisted of most fruits, roots and basically all things grown by humans, they saw humans as a source of food and sometimes took an interest in other objects. In that case they would attack if you had something they wanted. He was thinking, and not for the first time, that this lady when on her own in the oasis environment, had created what may even be seen as encroachment on part of the troop's territory. It was time to warn his neighbour before it was too late that the large adult males may put on a very brave display to keep the Australian lady away when protecting the troop enjoying her garden plants. If a baboon grabbed food from her garden, she should not try and retrieve the plant as the baboons will aggressively defend their loot.

One Dan was not surprised that in the contrasting neighbouring garden, the lady of the house seemed somewhat concerned. Maybe a baboon had mock charged or she may have mistakenly strolled out in her garden through a group unknowingly. The main thing is that she looked unhurt – fortunately, as one bite from a baboon can even break bones. He asked for the gardener with the intention of telling him to dissuade the troop, but if they were close and vocalizing a threat, then he should back off slowly, not run, not show his teeth, or stare them down, which would possibly provoke them. As a male he should protect the woman as the baboons may target her. He needed to be worried as George the old gardener was on his bed at this early hour resting in recovery mode. It turned out not to be because of the baboon troop. It was after his last meeting in the kitchen with a wild creature; twice in one day coming face to face with snakes had proven too exhausting for the poor man. The first encounter was with a large, unknown species of snake that had been chopped up into many pieces. This first disturbing incident took place as George was adding leaves to the compost heap the Australian lady had insisted on George establishing. One Dan forgot about the baboon troop as he came closer to the house next door. He could see his neighbours had created an attractive place of shelter and a food source for snakes. A welcoming canopy of leaves and garden cuttings in which to hide with the food scraps attracting rodents that are on the favourite food menu of most snakes. All in all, a snake paradise, a place of protection and comfort that a snake could enjoy with impunity.

The Australian lady clearly had green fingers. Unlike the surrounding desert, the houses of the mine managers had no shortage of piped water and this particular property was the only one in the small town of Magadi to boast a lawn and a border of many flowering plants. There was a wood pile ready for the Braai or the BBQ as the lady called it; that would also work very well as a safe place for snakes to hang out. On the patio there was clean and accessible water in the form of a shallow water fountain that any creature like a baboon or snake would need and appreciate in this dry desert region. The Australian lady was not a fan of trusting George with a mechanical lawn cutter or weed eater. No chance that a snake would be accidentally killed then when cutting back the lawn! The lady of the house disliked harmful chemicals in the garden, and that was the reason for going organic, using that compost heap to manufacture food for the plants. Little did she know she was helping her garden to be snake- friendly, not as she intended in just doing her bit for the environment.

There were no harsh fertilizers or herbicides used that would harm snakes or eliminate their food source.

Mid-morning on that fateful day, as she recalled for One Dan, she came eye to eye with a snake that put her off her morning blue mountain coffee. That snake may still be around but the creeper growing on the white painted wooden trellis work on the patio was no more. She closed herself away safely in the kitchen while George, under duress, chopped down the patio creeper. He made a lot of noise to ensure the serpent heard him and would move off. Like most people George did not realize snakes don't have ears, which makes them deaf. It did not matter if George sung 'Nkosi Sikelel' iAfrika' at the top of his voice; that kind of noise would not scare any snake away, it wouldn't hear any singing. It is actually the vibration of the noise that frightens the snake. He would have been better off dancing rather than singing, so sending vibrations through the ground, that way he could scare the snake into slithering away.

Possibly the snake that her cat caught was the one that moved from the patio? The tom cat took the wriggling reptile to his madam in the kitchen as a gift and put his paw behind the head of the small snake to stop it escaping. It was the last straw for the Australian lady who, soon after she recovered her wits, called her husband back from his work duties. Her scream scared the cat, freed the snake and brought George running. Man, and serpent met on the kitchen door step and George with his spade triumphed against the serpent for the second time that day. No wonder the poor man was lying in his bed recovering. This lady of the house wanted her perceived nest of snakes destroyed by the men before any weekend camp was approved by her to go ahead.

One Dan knew he could make short work of clearing up the snake problem. It was the second garden creature challenge he had had to deal with for this lady during the week. Many of the local residents of Magadi town who had small vegetable plots at their houses were capable of keeping the baboons at bay, but not their other nemesis that should have been on a farm far from their town. They thanked One Dan for sorting out the Maasai bull that had arrived in the town one evening uninvited. Earlier in the week he responded to the Australian neighbour's calls of despair to restrain a giant Maasai bull destroying and devouring her garden. One Dan and her husband walked the fierce looking traditional Maasai bull (in reality just a timid domesticated creature), around the back of the house, locked it in their garage for a day and a night with no food but sufficient water until they found the owners. Enclosed in its dark prison, the ever-hungry bull proceeded to eat the garage's chip wood dividing wall to satisfy its hunger. It had been let out by One Dan, then led away by the Maasai owners who heard of their prize bull's plight. One Dan explained through the translator who spoke English and Maa; 'Your bull is like a lion and the lady's flowers are like her cattle. So just understand the consequences like good Maasai.' What One Dan may not have appreciated is that the Maasai believed God created cattle specially for them and that they are the sole custodians of all the cattle on earth. This bond has led them into a nomadic way of life, following patterns of rainfall over vast distances. The Maasai measure wealth by the number of cattle and children one has. Planting and gardening were seen as unimportant to them, worthless labour, meaningless efforts, unlike the importance of herding cattle. To compare their bull to a lion was a great and puzzling concern to these Maasai, as the lion was their sworn enemy.

The day after his discussion with the Maasai, the bull was found dead a good one kilometre inside the Magadi town border. One Dan was the main suspect, thanked by the people of Magadi town and at odds with the Maasai elders. Even the Magadi Soda Company General Manager of the mine had remarked on the subject to One Dan in the club the previous day, during their lunch time get together. The Maasai bull owners were further upset as the mine company General Manager, who was one of their own tribe and should understand their needs, had stopped them from slaughtering and eating the meat from the possibly poisoned bull that was on Magadi Soda property. During the evening they somehow dragged the massive beast more than one Kilometre across the Magadi Soda town limits, so they could take charge of the corpse and the dividing up of the meat. That more or less ended the problem with the bull. One Dan just had to come back the next evening for the '*nyama choma*' as the Maasai elders wished to thank him for using his 4 x 4 and tow rope to pull their dead bull out of the Magadi town limits under the cover of darkness.

The snake difficulty was something slightly more straight- forward. One Dan walked around and immediately saw a highly snake friendly environment. 'Ma'am you do not have the means to stop snakes entering your garden. You need to eliminate the use of that compost heap right away. Get rid of the likes of that wood pile where these buggers, excuse my French Ma'am, hide when at rest. The cats are a good thing and will keep the rodents at bay and kill the occasional small snake. Ensure you keep your garden tidy and cut back on your plants including the flowers.' He joked, but it did not go down too well with the lady when he hinted that it's a shame the Maasai bull had departed as it was a good deterrent to snakes with the vibrations it made on walking around the garden, and chopping back of all the greenery. 'As a final resort you can keep the majority of the snakes in the vicinity away from your property by using ammonia as a deterrent. Snakes hate the smell and won't come near it. Soak rags in ammonia and place them in unsealed plastic bags. Leave the plastic bags where you usually see the snakes, and they won't come back. If you ever come across a snake again, keep your distance, use the garden hose to spray water on it and, trust me, most snakes will slither away.   If they do get in the house then open the door before you burn some rubber. Because of the smoke and smell, you will see them slither away through the open door.'

The lady of the house felt very confident that the men could leave her in charge, that she had been given very good advice to instruct George in solving any future snake intruder issues and prepare them for the visits of the baboon troop if needed. 'Farewell ma'am, we are off bush camping for the weekend,' One Dan waved, and gave a big smile. Bryn Darms was full on, talking about his pet snake and how to make one's garden snake friendly. He was going to put into practice what his English teacher would say was killing two birds with one stone. But in his case, it was attracting snakes to his snake friendly garden as One Dan had shown him this morning. It was way past lunch time and they been too busy to think about food until now. Titus Tembo broke open the package of Mandazi, Mini Beignets made with grated coconut spiced with cardamom, nutmeg and fried fluffy light. It must have been a favourite of Bryn Darms, who completely clammed up and forgot all about the snakes and his killing the two birds with that one stone.

The three 4 x 4 vehicles left in close convoy towards the west, away from the mine processing plant where the two tall chimney stacks were puffing white smoke into the clear blue sky. One Dan led the way and many kilometres of dust eating road later, he spoke to the Maasai guards in their make shift hut at the turn off heading to their intended camping area. No money exchanged hands, as unlike tourists down from the city for the weekend, the Magadi Soda people were given free access. The tsetse flies with their sleeping sickness kept the area clear of the nomadic Maasai cattle, and therefore to a certain extent the Maasai people, apart from a handful of hunters. This was true African bush-veldt or what people in East Africa referred to as savannah. Whatever the name they called the land scape, this is where One Dan expected they could possibly come across any of the big five.

The first clear objective One Dan had in mind was to locate a suitable camping area for the weekend. From past experience he was very aware that the site selection could make or break the success of the photographic safari. In his mind's eye he was first choosing the size of the spot, then where to locate the fire away from their gear and in a position that ensured the smoke did not disturb them. The site needed to be level as he did not want their Tusker beer sliding off their table, or for that matter sleeping with his legs higher than his head. With the day sure to be hot and dry, they would prefer some shade from which the tents could benefit in the afternoon. Privacy and noise were not an issue that needed consideration out here in the middle of nowhere. The Ewaso Ng'iro River was of no concern to them as it held no crocodiles and was some distance off. Sensible planning ahead by One Dan ensured they had brought sufficient clean water to sustain their good health, and independence from any other water source over the weekend.

After approximately a thirty-minute drive South Eastwards, an initial glance from his vehicle gave him a good impression that they'd found their weekend home. This was the site for them, and he slowed to a halt to check there were no ants there to bother them, the ground was clear of rocks, that it felt right, a site found and not have to be created. This place was perfect for them and even better was the fact that before them it appeared an elephant, which was rare for this area, and the giant gentle creature had spent the night here relaxing. If it was good enough for an elephant, then it was certainly good enough for One Dan and his companions. There were no signs of lions or leopards, just the smell of elephant urine which was no surprise as these guys could pass up to 13 gallons per day. They actually can recognise their kin from signature urine but its odour along with the large dung balls was hardly detectable by the noses of the human campers and they did not find the smell offensive. One Dan suspected they were very lucky indeed just to see and smell the traces of an elephant, as surely it was not a common occurrence for elephants to visit this area - well not since the days of those colonial settlers' hunting safaris when they shot the poor creatures for their tusks or just for sport. He kept to himself the thought that thanks be to God no such sporting events were allowed in Kenya these days. The elephant's earlier presence with its sixth sense for a safe location, confirmed for One Dan that this was a most suitable area for their camp site.

He decided to keep Bryn Darms with him to set up the camp site. The respite from the talkative young white Kenyan was also appreciated by the other two travellers. Titus Tembo headed out with his Aussie bush guide on a mini-safari before sun set. Young Bryn Darms was kept busy and quiet, well out of hearing range anyway, collecting firewood. One Dan expected that no doubt young Bryn Darms would most likely be having a conversation with himself. He kept a careful watch as the boy was searching for firewood just in sight, he was pleased to see the boy was sensibly not wandering off too far away from the camp, possibly following the lessons he'd learnt about the dangers in the bush. Fire was the next objective. He wanted to ensure they had a fire burning strongly in about an hour's time, a means of cooking, fending off unwanted night carnivores like the hyenas common in this area, along with the occasional lion; he hoped just a little that the smoke would help dissuade the insects from enjoying the flesh and blood of the campers. The bonus side of the camp fire for an experienced man like One Dan was its calming and relaxing effect. When one's eyes followed the sparks towards the sky and your attention moved to the stars, heard the crackling sounds, its ability to get nearly anyone to talk or was it down to the Tusker beers that often got consumed at the camp fires he attended! Hopefully, he thought, the warmth, light or smoke may also have the opposite effect on young Bryn Darms and shut him up a little to give the others a chance to tell a tale or two.

The last one of his three objectives, but not the least of the three chores needing his attention was the erection of the two tents. Positioning of the sleeping quarters was important as erection these days was just a shake of the modern tents and they were up with just a few pegs to push into the ground to secure them in the windless site. Pegs would give some confidence to the sleepers that no hyena, leopard or lion would sneak in during the dark hours and drag them away for a snack. Thus, his final advice as they slipped into their sleeping bags would be, 'Empty bottles in your tents at the ready guys as there will be no leaving your quarters after dark for whatever reason'.

One Dan was just a little concerned that it might be dark soon and neither vehicle could be heard approaching the camp. He called to Bryn Darms to come close to the fire with the last of the wood he'd collected. He was about to bring their camp fire to life and wanted the boy safely in the camp before it got dark. Titus Tembo had led the two 4 x 4 vehicles as what he had in mind was to make the best background scenes for photographs. He naively assumed the Aussie would recall the way home to the camp site. Both inexperienced bushmen ignored the warning signs given off by grass as high as an elephant's eye. On he drove, irrespective of the tall healthy-looking grasses and soon Titus Tembo got into soggy ground and made the fatal mistake of slowing the Defender right down instead of keeping going. At least between the two of them they had one 4 x 4 on dry land and moving. Their consultation resulted in Titus Tembo staying with the Defender while the second 4 x 4 headed back to camp for help from the experienced One Dan and the rescue equipment in his vehicle. It should take less than fifteen minutes' drive to reach the camp from where they were and they must have more than an hour of daylight left, so all was well under control thought Titus Tembo.

Fifty minutes later Titus Tembo was now anxious and seriously envisaged sleeping alone in the Defender for that night. He had water, a torch and a whistle but no food, while his tummy rumbled away, sending his brain the message he was in need of feeding. The mosquitoes were inside the Defender and making relaxing impossible. His would-be Aussie rescuer had taken a wrong turn near their camp site, and he headed away from One Dan and his help, until he discovered the sun was going down in the wrong place. Titus Tembo made a strategic decision to head for the camp site on foot, in the hope of something to eat, a beer maybe, and most importantly a comfortable safe night in his sleeping bag under canvas. His plastic beach flip-flop footwear was not the best of bush walking gear, they were caked in layers of sticky mud, under this weight the thong between his toes occasionally pulled out, there were little thorns everywhere on the ground that regularly had to be removed from the flip-flops by hand before they did him some permanent damage. It was a real struggle physically, very slow going and when he looked around him, Titus Tembo saw the sun starting to glow orange in the sky, a sure sign that made him feel there may not be much daylight left. The shapes of a herd of wildebeest were all around and he also wondered whether with all the abundant food on four legs, would the carnivores have considered him worth bothering about. Those creatures would be setting out for their evening meals about now. He accepted that if he was on the menu, his whistle would not be of much help as a deterrent if they took a liking to him. Many of the trees were acacia of the thorn type and most difficult to ascend in a hurry without causing many scratches and the resulting dripping blood. Their limited height could leave him within easy reach of a large lion that was in need of a good meal.

His thoughts started to grow into a script for one of those Hollywood action movies. Alternatively, there were much easier to climb and safer fever trees within running distance. The mud caked flip-flops might of course hinder Titus Tembo if he needed to sprint and out run a big cat. If Titus Tembo made it to the branches of safety, then he had his water to keep him awake plus the swarms of mosquitoes would stop Titus dropping off to sleep in his chosen tree and falling into the mouth of that hungry lion or it's like! The whistle would at last come into its own, as Titus Tembo, trapped in the branches of a tall fever tree, could blow into his whistle to signal for help in the darkness, albeit a piercing tune. Nevertheless, a clear call of save our souls could be made. It's really a shame, thought Titus Tembo, that he hadn't carried his camera from the 4 x 4 along with the other essentials to take shots looking down from his perch while a hungry pride of lions circled below him. Just as Titus Tembo felt his nerves getting the better of him, both the camp and at the same time the Aussie driving into the camp site, came into focus. Really, Titus Tembo had walked as straight as the crow flies but it was very hard to believe that whatever the route his Aussie rescuer followed to camp, it had taken as long to drive back as Titus Tembo did to walk there in those mud-encased flip-flops!

'Gentlemen' One Dan grinned with much relief at both of them, it was good to have them back and in one piece. He expected them to later recount their great adventure when stories would be shared around the camp fire as the sun finally sank out of sight just a few minutes after they returned home. Titus Tembo relaxed in the memory of the camp fire chats with his beloved Baba. And there was no happier a man than an Aussie with a cold beer next to a camp fire. All was well in their world as One Dan served up the good grub of pre-prepared Kenyan beef stew with its rich gravy, carrots, beans and onions out of the three-legged black cast iron potjies pot he'd brought from the Free State. He passed around the chapattis warmed and blackened on the embers of the fire. The secret of keeping Bryn Darms silent clearly was food, and the fact that he was tired must have helped a little; the young fellow's head was nearly falling into his metal stew bowl as he was nodding off.

During the night, all the campers except One Dan slept soundly; he heard the roaring call of a male lion in the distance and lay there for some time enjoying the bush night sounds.

Then he was disturbed, and at one time he banged the side of the tent to scare off whatever was sniffing around the foot of their canvas residence. As dawn lightened, he was first awake and out of his tent. After a long relaxing release of urine stored in his bladder overnight, and a splash of cool water over his head, in their great outdoor bathroom, he stoked the fire for the making of strong coffee. He was looking forward to making brown African millet porridge which, itself like the muddy coffee, was also almost drinkable. Watery yes, but yet the ragi meal was more nutritious, with more flavour than the rice porridge or Scottish oats equivalent; it just needed a little extra sugar as it is not naturally sweet.

One Dan wanted a quick getaway for his own reasons. He needed to leave his three companions to their own devices come lunch time so he could head for Magadi town and the Maasai celebration which he made possible with the contribution of his 4 x 4 and towing of the beast, even if he did not slaughter the bull, he was to enjoy its meat later that day. More importantly, right now was thinking about the game viewing as the bigger predatory animals were on the move. They should be easier to spot at this time of day in the open as they began to head to wherever they selected to sleep away the heat-of-the-day. Animals stick to their own schedules, and even if you're not a morning person, One Dan felt it's always good to motivate yourself to wake up early for a game drive and anyway he thought it's always best to get an early start in life whatever your schedule. Currently the likes of the blue wildebeest and zebras would be more relaxed and ready to pose for photographs after being on their guard since darkness fell the previous day. Thirdly, the sky was currently a clear blue and you could see all the way to Tanzania. It was getting to the end of the rainy season so there was always the danger of clouds rolling in later, and a storm forming with heavy rain falling on this side of the escarpment.

One Dan smiled to himself to see the youngest member of the party switch into top gear as soon as he pulled back the tent flaps. Clearly Bryn Darms was as excited as him to be in the bush, and appreciative of the opportunities. The enthusiasm of the young always impressed him, and it was no different for Bryn Darms as he guessed this must be a regular event for a son of a safari company owner. Titus Tembo was attuned to the morning bird calls and the smell of fresh coffee. He took a bush shower and insisted his young travelling partner did the same despite the boy's half-hearted resistance to having bottles of relatively cool water poured over his head and down his back. They both stood there naked as the day they were born. Each of them vied for the best position next to the warming comfort of the camp fire as they rubbed themselves down with the fluffy beach towels Bryn's parents had provided as essential camping gear.

They all felt good and ready, now clean, warm and well fed, the men at least drowned any further morning lethargy away with the strong black muddy coffee left in the pot. Bryn Darms needed no such boost as his engine was up and running in top gear, ready to take on the world once more. Before they headed out it was essential that they put everything away, particularly any food, into secure odour free containers, then make the tents safe from any troop of monkeys or baboons that would come looking for a change from their regular diet. They burnt the small amount of rubbish they had generated so far and did the same with the scraps of food left over from breakfast and put out the fire to ensure the safety of the surrounding environment when they were not in attendance. One Dan also made sure to pile lots of sand over the toilet remains left by all the humans who had done their business that morning.

Once again, the three 4 x 4vehicles drove out together in one line as there was little dust generated by the front vehicle and it laid down a safe track for Titus Tembo and the Aussie to follow in. Their journey took them south and the escarpment lay to their right. The camp site location seemed quite distinct, and all were confident of finding the site on their return. However, had they gone a little further and faster than was good for them? They got caught up in the joy of motoring along with the herds of giant eland and giraffe keeping pace with the vehicles. Bryn Darms was at the wheel while Titus Tembo did what he had come to do in the first place, both film and take photographs. Hindsight is a bit like a six sense, sometimes it is a good thing and at other times it makes no difference! One Dan had to leave a little earlier than he had planned as he estimated they were already in Tanzania and he had a long trek back to Magadi town with just about sufficient time to make the Maasai festivities.

The two remaining 4 x 4 vehicles moved through the savannah habitat and rediscovered the Magadi type arid and semi-arid habitat albeit south of the Kenyan border. They were once again coming across small Maasai villages. Most distinctive on the eye and therefore in Titus Tembo's camera lens were the new scenes sparked by the change in flora. The grey scrubland may be more alive with the good rains, but it was still barren, trees were sparse and flowers were a rare sight like those of the aloe or desert rose. A rare solitary baobab tree had survived somehow in this location. The change in indigenous plants corresponded with a change in the fauna Titus Tembo was viewing. It may have been interesting to some people, yet the likes of guinea fowl and the occasional antelope in the distance browsing, was not getting Titus Tembo excited, for all they could make out, one of these wild creatures could have just been a goat.

Titus Tembo decided to turn back north for the picturesque sights of the funny looking herds of playful gnu, the warthog moving around on their knees and the possibility of one of the big five making an appearance later in the day. Bryn Darms was disappointed they were to leave so quickly as he found this place fascinating. He explained to Titus Tembo that if they stayed until dusk, they may possibly see the peculiar aardvark feeding in this landscape of termite hills. The boy went on unconvincingly about the big five, that they are just here for the tourists, in fact in the old days the settlers were very keen on shooting the big five; he added that those were admittedly in the days there was still hunting in Kenya. Those five are old news, there is much more here he thought while taking a break from his commentator role; we passed a pair of black-backed jackal that no one took any notice of and he'd seen not so far away the den of a family of bat-eared foxes. And these grown-ups wanted to photograph stupid gnus; how disappointing. His father had told him these connochaetes are the same as cattle, sheep and goats. Grown-ups can be strange, he thought to himself, at times they are just like the stupid hyena and he did not want to end up like the baobab tree because of some stupid adult. He would just go along with them for now but he would always be on his guard with regards grown-ups as Bryn Darms knew the story behind the upside-down tree and at times those grown-up equivalents, the hyenas.

As the story goes, when God created the earth, the animals came to him and asked if they could be participants in the remaining portion of the creation. Since God was nearly done, he advised them that the only thing remaining was to create the trees. The animals were excited because they could participate in this work. They asked God to let them plant the seeds for the trees. God reluctantly agreed. He then started giving out seed, one particular seed to one particular group of animals. Another group of seeds to another group, and on and on until He got to the last seeds and the last animals. It was the seeds for the baobab trees that remained and the only animal left were the hyenas. Now everyone knows how stupid the hyena is, he observed. Well, when they went out, they planted all of the baobab seeds upside down. Stupid animals. That is why the roots look like they are growing up in the air and the leaves are buried out of sight in the ground.

Titus Tembo was leading them north, with the escarpment on his left, he expected it should be easy enough to find the camp site, after all what could go wrong? The clouds rolled in, the sky became dark and the sun was blotted out, the forked lightening sounded angry and the escarpment looked spectacular in the flashes. They just had to stop to film this. Time past, the sun departed, so all that was left for them to do was to follow their washed away tracks back to camp in the moon light. There was in fact no moon as the clouds kept rolling westwards. At least the rain had stopped and the ground was quickly drying out. Try as they might, they were not sure what direction to best take if they were to find their camp site before dawn. They had some food, enough water, they were dry and safe, so they both switched off their engines for the night. In the peaceful evening, the two disturbances were that of the buzzing of the blood sucking female mosquito and the fact that the inside of the 4 x 4s were so warm. The hot vehicle engines were acting like storage heaters. It did not seem to bother Bryn Darms as he switched stations from broadcasting a talk show to snoring like an old fat dog that has over-eaten.

The Aussie was just too hot in either of the vehicles to nod off to sleep; he took his bed roll and bravely laid it down some distance off under an acacia tree. Was he brave, was he plain stupid, or did he know something that his travelling companions were not aware of? Or did he give off some nasty odour that kept the carnivores at a safe distance that evening? As the sun came up the Bryn Darms broadcasting station started up, where are we? And what is for breakfast, 'Oh My Goodness, look at that striped hyena staring after our friend walking back to his car!' They turned out to be not such poor bushmen after all as the pair of them in the dark had got their 4 x 4s within walking distance of their camp but they'd just lost out to the jet-black night. The Aussie had slept well despite the attentions of the occasional buzzing female mosquito. In their last conversation, all three had agreed to pack up immediately so as to head for the Magadi Soda town where the Nairobi visitors would take a refreshing swim before ordering a big cooked breakfast. The Aussie looked forward to a warm bath, a very chilled Tusker and one of his wife's thick ham sandwiches with lots of horse radish.

And so, the safari would come to an end with tales over breakfast from a new friend. One Dan, who joined his by now clean Nairobi bound fellow campers. They were likely more refreshed and certainly smelt better than One Dan who joined them at the table straight from a night of Maasai celebration. One Dan was the worse for wear possibly because the meat may have been a little suspect, or maybe he had drunk a little too much of the local Maasai beer! The previous day the timing of his return was perfect. During the late afternoon his hosts were waking from a siesta-like lull in their manyatta just past the Magadi town golf course. Titus Tembo wondered if One Dan had met his Maasai golfing friend. It seems that One Dan had arrived as the Maasai were drowsily digesting the late morning consumption of blood and milk before the evening meat feast. One Dan had taken a harmless looking traditional beer that he knew nothing about other than it had been fermented in the roots of an aloe as there were no fruits of a sausage tree in that area, that would normally be used. So, the question hung in the air, bad meat or a bad beer?

On leaving the club, Titus Tembo was given a warning to be careful on that Magadi Nairobi Road as with that heavy rain the previous night, there could be impassable flooded sections of the road in some parts. There would have been no rush normally, he might have stayed one extra night to let the flood waters recede, but he felt it his duty to get young Bryn Darms back home in readiness for his return to school on Monday morning. The boy wanted to get back to share tales with his father and attend drama practice for the up-coming school play in which he had a big part. At the first area of floods, Bryn Darms switched channels to broadcast his navigator speak. The youngster advised Titus Tembo wisely to go around the shallow waters on the road by taking the hillside to the left through the acacia forest. This was less of a risk than the roadway as you never knew what the rain waters had carried on to the road, dangers that you could not see in the muddy flood water. It was easy enough to zig-zag through the thorn trees and no one would notice the additional scratches down the side of the old war horse. With the first flood waters successfully detoured, the old Land Rover returned to the tarmac none the worse for wear.

The Defender got to a low point on a long stretch of unusually flat road. There they were faced with a short line of saloon cars on either side of the rushing waters of a mini river with no dry bridge in sight. This was adult decision time and Bryn Darms switched to silent mode as he brooded the fate of that baobab tree they saw yesterday in the desert landscape. The discussion involved Titus Tembo asking what the drivers were waiting for and them telling Titus what they had seen during the time they had been there. The flood waters appeared passable for the old Defender but clearly not safe for the lines of town cars on either side of the storm waters. The interested observers had noticed water levels were, if anything rising slowly and had not fallen at any time during the morning. For the line of salons and the people It could be a long wait until it was completely safe to cross once more. The trapped people, keen to get to Nairobi, hoped Titus Tembo would ferry a few of them across. For Titus Tembo the more people who wanted to join this one time crossing the better as they'd add weight. He pushed the Defender in low gear with its nose slightly into the on-rushing torrent rather than follow the roadway at ninety degrees to the current. Everyone breathed a sigh of relief as the Defender did what it was born to do. The back wheels hit the dry section of tarmac and a big cheer went up from all his passengers and the small crowds left stranded on either side of the flood waters. As part of his good Samaritan act on crossing the river, not exactly per the biblical stories of the parting of the dead sea, but still a miracle of sorts and a good deed for the handful of travellers who joined him and Bryn Darms, he turned his friend's Defender into a free cockroach taxi for the onward trip to the Nairobi outskirts. There his ferry passengers could pick up a matatu or more traditional cockroach taxi than his Defender. Bryn Darms returned himself to broadcast in Swahili while enjoying chewing on the sticks of sugar cane one of his fellow passengers issued for free.

A safari is never over until it's over, and that does not mean just dropping off the interesting kid that tagged along. It was partly over when leaving behind the Defender and camping kit with a big thank you, a good bottle of scotch for its owner and red roses bought at the side of the road in Nairobi for the lady of the house. In fact, sometimes it's not even over when you lie down in your own bed! The influenza type symptoms hit Titus Tembo that very night, so uncomfortable, so hot and then cold at times, and when the sun comes up, the neatly made bed and the crisply pressed white cotton sheets have not only been in a war, but it appears the dampness could only be as a result of someone trying to put out a fire. You feel as if someone else is driving your car. You step out of the badly parked car, ignore the boy wanting to direct you into one of many spaces available. No, you do not need your car washed or guarded, you need a helping hand up the pathway to the doctor's surgery but people look at you and distance themselves as if avoiding the plague because you look so sick, and with some sickness that could possibly infect them! Then you arrive and how dare there be a line of sick people to see the doctor before you, the man who is at death's door. One hour later and the doctor does nothing but send you across the road with a note for a blood test. Maybe you'll be dead before the results are back? But no, fifteen minutes later you are in that long line to see the doctor once more. I'm not dead yet so maybe it's possible I'll be well again by the time I get to the front of the line? But no, Titus Tembo had spent the best part of the morning learning from the doctor on duty, that it was malaria. The suffering was so great that Titus Tembo felt close to heaven's door. Two tablets a day and a few days in bed and Titus Tembo's Magadi wildlife photograph safari was over apart from the editing. In East Africa malaria today is no big deal and Titus Tembo was back on earth, soon eking out a living in the big city. Back from the bush that had no internet or phone connections. He was back to the reality of the modern world with his inbox of emails and voice messages calling for his attention.

CHAPTER FOUR

Beloved Baba, the safety net

At the time Eng. M. J. R. Tembo was busy establishing his place in the United Arab Emirates, his one and only son Titus Tembo was starting up his first business in East Africa. Eng. M. J. R. Tembo had given his mtoto his blessing with respect to him running his own business, but warned Titus Tembo against marrying Nancy Wawira. Their or rather, Titus Tembo's attraction to Nancy Wawira was stronger than gun powder. No way would Titus Tembo allow Eng. M. J. R. Tembo to ruin their happiness and cause him to lose his one and only love, Nancy Wawira. So, they married in haste, and of course everyone should know what happens when doing things in haste. Wife number one, Nancy Wawira, was clearly wrongly named by her parents. Wawira means hard working. She was certainly hard working in keeping hold of her money. Any money Titus Tembo held became family money. The latter, Nancy Wawira trained to the standard of an Olympic Gold Medallist at spending. She specialized in many events, be it hair, nails, make-up, clothes, shoes, hand bags; in summary money was spent on all the little things in life that she felt were essential for her existence.

The pair had met through mutual friends who told Nancy Wawira how Titus Tembo was promoting 'would be' models through free, professional style photography shoots. Titus Tembo had a preference for making short movies of life in general around the capital, helping highlight the needs of the slum dwellers in Nairobi, and occasional safari work as the latter made money to subsidise the former. At the time Kenya had no approved drone law. Some police in and around the slums of Nairobi interpreted this as a ban on using drones for movie making. Subsequently, Titus Tembo was forced to give some small 'hongo' to cover the cost for the police to drink water on a hot day or tea on a cool morning, or whatever excuse was in fashion that day before the drone was allowed to take to the sky! The free girlie photography sessions were maybe less artistically and certainly less morally rewarding, but involved no outgoing payments. Nancy Wawira posed for Titus Tembo and he snapped in more ways than one!

With no plans for children at their young age, both of them enjoyed life as middle-class people do these days in Nairobi. They worked hard and possibly at times played even harder. There are many evening entertainment venues, lovely restaurants, and generally lots of ideas on how to spend both your precious free time and any hard-earned money. Karaoke was a particular appeal to Titus Tembo at that time and the more he drank, the better he thought he performed. This feeling was strengthened by the ladies of one particular favourite club of Titus Tembo, Crazy Mics. There, the ladies would encourage Titus Tembo to sing, they would sit on his lap and spend his money at the bar. In the end Nancy Wawira refused to watch her husband make a fool of himself at Crazy Mics. Not to put too fine a point on it, Titus Tembo thought, without the advice of his beloved Baba, he did not even need alcohol to make really bad decisions at times. Just a couple of years into his first marriage, Titus Tembo was in a state of financial limbo that caused great stress to his marriage. Money shortages were not totally to blame for the strains, as Titus Tembo still occasionally visited Crazy Mics place, drank too much and that sometimes resulted in Titus Tembo continuing a part time career of model photography with the ladies from the bar or their friends he was recommended too.

At one point in time Hi-five Pottery of Nairobi seemed a wonderful business idea for Titus Tembo and his new wife to set up in Kenya. Being their first business, they did not think they would need a great deal of money for capital investment. The plan was to contract out the manufacturing part of the business that needed expensive equipment like a kiln. Their fancy goods would satisfy local demand of the growing middle class and delighted tourists would surely snap up the well-designed ethnic quality ceramics. One of their good friends was, they thought at the time, a very gifted young designer. Titus Tembo was the technical expert, having spent some time working in the English Stoke-on-Trent potteries before supposedly heading for University in the United Kingdom. Titus Tembo liked the old fashioned pottery industry so much it curtailed the advancement of his proposed academic studying. Titus Tembo returned to Kenya without a full time British University education. His academic path took a bit longer than a traditional degree as he went the route of distance learning provided by the British Open University, a bit like his beloved Baba who also did distance learning but in his case at the University of South Africa Business School in Pretoria, where he graduated with a Master's in Business Leadership. In fact, an equivalent of an MBA with distinction. Titus Tembo's studies were combined with the pursuit of his love of photography part-time, and eventually the business of Hi-five Pottery of Nairobi. Titus Tembo had much to think about, in fact just another example of 'Matatanisho', and his degree studies were not at the top of his to-do list.

Photography was, and it seemed had always been, Titus Tembo's number one passion, but at this time the money was expected to come from his main job - the Hi-Five Pottery business. The marketing side of the business offered Titus Tembo the opportunity to take some fantastic photographs of the new pottery in places like Giraffe Manor in Nairobi and Hemmingway's in Watamu on the exotic northern coast of Kenya. In Watamu the relatively newly married couple enjoyed the beach life for a week courtesy of Hi-five Pottery of Nairobi. That was the life, white sand, sunshine, blue sky, turquoise clear salt waters, warm weather, casual summer clothes, a pretty lady on Titus Tembo's arm and freedom to use his camera and film equipment. The one disappointment in paradise was the bargain 4 x 4 vehicle pre-booked and paid for in advance. A small Duster saloon, nothing like the Defender they may have needed, was waiting for them when they arrived at the new railway station in Mombasa. The new train service took exactly 4 hours and 30 minutes from Nairobi to Mombasa, it was not crowded, it was clean, efficient and comfortable. This was a revolutionary change in the Kenyan public transport system. Prior to the Chinese involvement, the *lunatic express* that the British built around a hundred years ago, took 15 hours to complete the same journey and that was on a good day; given a little luck and a following wind some regular travellers may have added! Their Duster, Titus Tembo felt, was more like the *lunatic express* version than its replacement the new Madaraka Express SGR that they had just alighted from.

The Duster got them through the city of Mombasa with some challenges. Titus Tembo drove and was successful at dodging those auto rickshaws called tuk-tuks used as open-air taxis. These ant-like work horses filled most of the streets around the city, along with other polluting trucks, buses, minibuses, a hive of modern clean looking motor bikes, cars of various vintages and consequently in varying states of repair. The road traffic seemed to be able to carry everything and seemed to be able to go anywhere at very short notice without the use of any indicator. The wall of sound from the small-capacity two-cylinder diesel engine tuk-

tuk, and the pounding of the truck engines, tried to drown out the loud music coming from the gap formed by the rolled down car windows of the Duster. The car window positioning was set as a compromise between cooling off and being killed off by the fumes and noise from outside the Duster, and the feeble air-conditioning it provided. The final ingredient added into the chaotic road mix, like a secret herb to complete a fine evening meal, came in the form of matatus, privately-owned minibuses long past their reasonable working life, and interestingly decorated before being pressed into service as shared taxis. Many of the drivers had missed their calling as F1 winners and regularly demonstrated the formula one driving skills and lack of any signalling to warn other drivers or road side spectators of their intentions.

Eventually admitting defeat to the fumes and noise emitted from the tuk-tuks which were banned in Nairobi city centre, they rolled up the car windows to isolated the interior inhabitants of the car from the unpleasant sounds and fumes polluting the city highways. The air-conditioning machinery of the Duster worked overtime, drinking fuel as if it were a desert camel arriving from a long hot trek. Once out of the crowded city roads, the Congolese rumba tunes were again shared with the world as the front windows of the little car could be left wide open without threatening the driver and passenger's health. The air-conditioning mixed with the sea breezes coming through the open car windows. Appetites and thirsts were well taken care of from the road side vendors jostling with each other at both open windows when the opportunity came as the Duster was forced to slow to a walking pace for any reason.

More than three hours after departing the train station at Mombasa, the Duster arrived in the coastal holiday come fishing village of Watamu. The Duster and its two occupants were to stay one night in the exclusive and expensive Hemmingway's hotel. It meant for a whole day they had access to take photographs in this exclusive venue of the new and only range of Hi-Five pottery currently in production. Titus Tembo had carefully packed a full set of pottery before departing Nairobi; matching ceramic handmade contemporary cups, plates and bowls. Once checkout time came around the next afternoon, and after ensuring they had completed what was needed to do in terms of photography at Hemmingway's, Titus Tembo moved the Duster from its more expensive surroundings to the much cheaper hotel next door. There the Duster sat comfortably, looking more at home parked around cars of its own status. Titus Tembo and Nancy Wawira saved a small fortune that would have been paid out if they had stayed in Hemmingway's for the whole of that week. As a direct consequence of their move, they would enjoy the less formal atmosphere of the Ocean Sports complex, but would have to go further afield for their photographic sessions.

The Duster made it to *'Hell's Kitchen'* the next day. From the description provided on line to tourists, neither of them was sure of what to expect. Parts of the fifty-kilometre road trip could have been named *'The Road to Hell'* right enough. From Watamu to Malindi the road resembled a mirror image of the same highway the Duster had experienced on their way from Mombasa, less all that city traffic right enough. The obligatory police road blocks were in place and several times the driver and passenger had their documents cursorily checked out before being waved through after a few standard exchanges between the two up country visitors and the coastal cops.

The traffic built a little around Malindi where the main street gave an occasional glimmer of what it might have been in the glorious high days of Kenyan Coastal holiday fame. This is where tourists were rewarded with a beach stop-over after a dusty safari to Tsavo East National Park. Today the town seems to have been overrun by tuk-tuks and their competitor the boda bodas as they were known up country but here at the coast piki pikis, motor bike taxis to service the surrounding population of more than 200,000 people. These bikes at one time serviced just a handful of people on the Kenyan Ugandan border, thus the name boda bodas possibly grew from its use and remained today. With that minor success, they then multiplied like a virus, it seems the infection spread to every corner of Kenya. Even in the midst of all this humanity, Titus Tembo felt there was an air of coastal laidback culture, a case of 'we can always do it tomorrow' attitude. Titus Tembo very much liked the relaxed holiday feel of things in this town. The condition of the buildings in need of a coat of paint, and how people ambled along in no hurry, sent a clear message to visitors and tourists alike of 'just chill, people', or as the tourists understood, *'hakuna matata'*, no worries. It was different to the mainly tourist holiday feel of Watamu. The Duster pulled over as Titus Tembo and Nancy Wawira stopped for a drink in one of a handful of Italian coffee houses along the main strip. Here Titus Tembo got the feeling that in this town, everybody knew everybody else. It reinforced his positive feeling for the place, and he decided he might come back in the future to check out the location.

There was very little difference in the main road infrastructure on the northern side of the seaside town. There certainly was less manic traffic, and some road paint markings which were missing further south. These lines of paint, mark the road edges clearly and others in the centre of the road were there to guide a driver on where or where not it was safe to consider over taking. Titus Tembo appreciated the efforts of the painters to make things a bit safer, but also recognised that most of the other drivers ignored this guidance as they seemed to drive without a care in the world. It was an uneventful drive until the Duster reached the bridge over Sabaki river. This was the second longest river in Kenya and Titus Tembo remarked to Nancy Wawira, 'maybe that is why it has three names, Athi where your people come from and nearer the coast Galana, then the Sabaki river.' Here the local cops had set up an elaborate road block. It seemed to Titus Tembo the police needed to find something wrong with most travellers in order to extract Hongo. He thought to himself that this was wrong but he had some sympathy for the local cops as it was hot out there and they were not paid well. So, were they looking for a gift of cool water to ease their suffering of being out in the hot sun all day keeping people safe, or a little cash to help feed their families, or in some cases just plain greed? As they waited for the cops to finish their negotiations with the drivers in front, to pass the time Titus Tembo told the story his beloved Baba had shared with him some years ago around the camp fire when they were on a safari holiday in Tsavo East National Park. They were in a region famous as the home to pythons from the Sabaki river. 'It's a while back but close to here in Sabaki Village, a farm manager was attacked by a very long python. After a struggle of some hours the snake dragged the man up a tree. Some villagers saw the man in the tree with the snake and called the police who rescued the man.' The story goes that the man was saved as he bit the tail of the snake who also had a happy ending since he or she escaped police custody overnight. In-fact that dangerous snake may still be around this area as a python can live up to three decades. 'Maybe that is why dogs practice chasing their tails just in case they were taken by a python and applied the tail bite as a means of escape?'

He admitted to himself the story had been changed over time by his recollection but it still was an entertaining time-filler while the cops did their thing. When he occasionally told this tale, he felt happy and yet sad, 'Matatanisho' strikes again he pondered. Happy because it was a good memory of being on holiday in the bush with his beloved Baba but sad because the talk turned towards not wanting to be eaten by a snake, or crocodile or lion or anything for that matter that would not allow his beloved Baba to donate his organs for transplant, or leave his body for medical science. This was the first time there was any talk about his beloved Baba leaving this earth and this made a massive impact on that day and he'd never forget that part of the tale. He had never shared that part of his story with anyone as yet.

Driving a hired car and looking like tourists gave Titus Tembo and Nancy Wawira their *'get out of jail free'* card and they were just waved through the police road block but not before Titus Tembo of his own free will handed out a few bottles of clean cool drinking water. The return passage across the river bridge was somewhat different as the road block was now manned by armed men and ladies of the Kenya Defence Forces. There was no memory of his kindness in handing out water on this journey through the road block earlier that day. All Titus Tembo's camera equipment was unpacked, either in an effort to find terrorist weapons coming in from Somalia, hippy drugs from illegal coastal bush farms, or just as an opportunity to chat to a pretty lady while you kept her man busy. There was however no question of hongo from these disciplined military personnel.

In his research for this trip Titus Tembo had read that *'Hell's Kitchen'* was a popular local name for the Marafa depression. He was not so easily fooled by the claims made to market this attraction, unlike some of the naïve overseas tourists he did not expect they would find a scaled down version of the Grand Canyon. Rather than think of the American valley tourist attraction, Titus Tembo preferred to think of the Marafa depression being formed by the local Gods. Titus Tembo told Nancy Wawira the story about the local tribe who showed off their wealth to the poor bordering tribes by washing in milk as opposed to using water. Their Gods punished their pretentious and showy display by sending a storm to wash them and their wealth into the Sabaki River. Their Gods left behind the gorge coloured in their blood and milk as a warning to man on how the Gods would react to such bad behaviour. Titus Tembo hoped that Nancy Wawira may even cut back her spending on luxuries after such a tale but he doubted she would change her ways with regards spending the family money. His impression of Godly involvement was further enforced as the Duster must have upset their Gods somehow. The poor little car was also being punished as soon as they left the main tarmac highway on a road which surely had been modelled on a mini-version of the Grand

Canyon, but for what reason was the poor Duster being tortured Titus Tembo could not fathom.

The photographic shots of the ceramics in that environment did not work out as well as Titus Tembo and Nancy Wawira imagined. They were soon heading back but the Duster's suspension struggled even more on the return journey along the miniature impression of the Grand Canyon. One of the front lights was cracked, the bumper hanging a little, and it appeared that a minor body work remodelling had taken place. The vehicle was worse for wear in areas Titus Tembo dared not to crawl under the chassis of the car to inspect. Despite this their speed was much higher than the pedestrians marching along from nowhere to nowhere.

Titus Tembo took pity on an elderly couple suffering under the weight of a small shopping bag carried between them. Nancy Wawira urged him to continue on so they could enjoy the beach in Watamu before the sun set. Titus Tembu thought it kinder to stop and offered the old couple a lift to their home. Such a small offer was welcomed with great big smiling toothless mouths. They were returning from their weekly shopping at the local market somewhere in the distance. The old stooped grey headed man was a Lay Minister and spoke reasonable English; he insisted that Titus Tembo and Nancy Wawira come in for tea. Nancy Wawira for once was not to have her way. The Lay Minister sent his wife off to another mud-constructed hut to make two cups of tea. Their generosity was hard to imagine as they had so little, when Titus Tembo and Nancy Wawira had so much. The son of the old couple and their five grandchildren joined the party but with only Titus Tembo and Nancy Wawira drinking out of very shoddy earthenware cups.

The old man had a lot of wisdom to share with them. He spoke on how in the old days before global warming. 'People in this area grew so much that any person walking past was always welcome to share in their abundance of home-grown food. Today the rains often fail, come at the wrong time or too heavy, they could no longer be relied on and people had very little they could offer any visitor. God give us this earth and freedom of choice and sadly man is not looking after nature, but we do our best and he sees to our needs.' Titus Tembo thought as his beloved Baba before him, in such poverty, this family appeared to have nothing and yet clearly were grateful with what little they had. This is where Titus Tembo once again saw the teachings of his beloved Baba in practice. Titus Tembo walked back to the sad looking Duster and brought from its back seat his camera and all the china they had with them for the photographic promotion shots in Hell's Kitchen. All the family had fun posing with the finely designed modern china and Titus Tembo and Nancy Wawira had even more fun getting the photographs they so craved for to promote Hi-Five Pottery of Nairobi. Yes karma, he could hear his father speaking, 'Remember my Moto, the more you give out, the more that comes back to you.' Titus Tembo decided to leave the newly produced fine china set with the delighted family and Titus Tembo felt so happy to give a discreet financial donation to the Lay Minister and head of this happy family.

With the gifting of the pottery, there was no longer any product to photograph on this trip. Titus Tembo and Nancy Wawira planned to just spend the next three days exploring, but the chill factor at the coast soon got the better of their well-intentioned plan. In addition, the state of the poor Duster also forced a change of plan to a much slower pace! On day one of their three-day exploration, the Duster was driven to its limits looking for elusive forest elephants in Arabuko Sokoke Forest Reserve. Sadly, for all that car damage and the efforts of the Duster, between them they only saw an elephant shrew and that was on a short guided walk near the main entrance gate to the forest. Titus Tembo by now thought the Duster looked relieved, if a car could look relieved then this one certainly did, maybe it appreciated a welcomed rest when Titus Tembo and Nancy Wawira explored the Gedi ruins on foot?

The two humans had a discussion as Titus Tembo by then needed a rest as much as the Duster, which he suspected was ready to give up on them. He took into consideration that soon they and the Duster faced a journey back to the railway station in Mombasa. They agreed that Malindi town tour with Vasco da Gama point, its Museum, the Portuguese Chapel and its other splendid offerings would wait for the next Coastal Safari and Titus Tembo promised himself there would be one. Nevertheless, they headed for Malindi town for an Italian dinner that Nancy Wawira had set her heart on. She compromised a little by allowing her husband to quickly call at the 'Home for Hope' he'd heard about over drinks at Ocean Sports. Here the kids grouped together to sing for their unexpected visitors. They were of all ages and there must have been around forty of them being cared for by a saint of a lady, her grown up daughter, clearly following in mama's kindly footsteps, and a handful of what he assumed was paid help. The experience was a repeat of the visit to the home of the Lay preacher as it moved Titus Tembo to tears of joy.

This interesting part of Kenya he had never visited with his beloved Baba for some unknown reason; it was an area that Titus Tembo would very much like to return to one day soon. As is his habit, Titus Tembo immediately started working on his return list of where to go, it included a longer visit to the wonderful *Home for Hope* in Malindi town, added to the list was what to see in far more depth second time around; the Marine National Parks of both Malindi and Watamu, Mida Creek Watamu, the monkey centre in Watamu, its turtle rehabilitation centre, Old Malindi town with its markets, the falcon centre, the de Gama Cross, Uhuru Gardens, the snake parks and the old fishing village at Mambrui and in the months of July through to August the migrating whales performing off Watamu bay and the bays of Malindi. Titus Tembo decided he would add more to the list as his research continued back in Nairobi. The Next few days were ones of pure relaxation of walking on turtle beach, swimming in the turquoise waters and enjoying Swahili foods.

It was a pleasant trip back along the coast road at a very leisurely pace. Pole-pole as their mood was one of no rush after a relaxing few days in Watamu. Slowly slowly indeed as the Duster was in no state to rush anything. The poor car looked and sounded a little different from the one they had collected before the punishment she took off-roading when visiting 'Hell's kitchen' and searching the Arabuko Sokoke Forest for the elusive forest elephants. Fortunately, police manning the many road blocks on the way must have had orders to check documentation only on that day. Certainly, for Titus Tembo and Nancy Wawira the only thing road worthy at that time was their documentation. In between the police road blocks there were other stops to top up on tropical fruits that would fly back with their new temporary owners to Nairobi.

The Duster hit the hubbub of minibus taxis and people well before reaching the city limits of Mombasa. The relaxing effect of the last few days would soon evaporate, but as for now Titus Tembo amused himself people watching. Most of the matatus had an aptly named conductor hanging out of each vehicle guiding the human traffic. A potential passenger would signal to the conductor using fingers, hands and facial expressions which seemed to work, as drivers responded so quickly to these messages. There was no time for indicators and often the rear-view mirror was completely ignored.

A lot of hooting and honking took place which did not seem related to anything specific. Further entertainment could be obtained from the cheerful messages and art work adorning the battered and bruised vehicles of mass destruction. On entering the train station, people seemed to change, more serious faces were put on in readiness for life in Nairobi.

Titus Tembo wondered how the car hire people would react, and if the Duster would ever be the same again? A simple picture can tell a story of a thousand words and the face of the car hire representative who met them in the Mombasa railway station was very sad and shocked. No tears were shed but certainly it required a phone call back to the office for further advice before she would accept the Duster back into her custody. More money had to be handed over with the car keys and an unconvincing promise of a refund if the damage was not as bad to repair as it appeared at first glance. As predicted by Titus Tembo at the time, no news about any refund came as the weeks past; Titus Tembo did not feel too bad about the charges, as he expected it was more or less a break-even affair for all parties concerned. He did, however, ask for forgiveness and pray that the little Duster made a full recovery.

The coastal break had delivered potentially new advertisement material for the marketing efforts to come. There were to be no worries on the marketing side of things as, like most Kenyan people, Nancy Wawira talks as if she is the best sales person on the planet. Having been exposed in Stoke-on-Trent to those wonderful old English world leaders in pottery, Titus Tembo knew it all, or so he believed. At the start of the Hi-five journey, Titus Tembo was on a high, he had found the girl of his dreams and had just obtained a British Open University degree in commerce after seven years part time study. The cream on top was that Titus Tembo had lots of time for his beloved photography. The dowry money Eng. M. J. R. Tembo provided was just currency that anyway was losing value nearly every day. The happy couple needed to turn the currency into something real, into hard assets. After all, Titus Tembo argued mentally within himself, what does currency really mean? Yes, he thought – it means many things to different people. In church we called it 'offerings', for schools it was called a 'fee', for the marriage it's called 'dowry' and that soon changes to 'alimony' when divorcing, when we owe someone it is called 'debt', then if we pay government it's called 'tax', in court it is called a 'fine', when the government pay us it's called a 'pension', when banks lend you currency it becomes a 'loan', when we offer it for a service it is called a 'tip', even kidnappers give it a different name called a 'ransom', in Kenya politicians take it as a 'bribe'. So, what do I call it if I give it to my wife, Chai, Vivwanda or Baksheesh? In fact, Nancy

Wawira called it 'assistance' and Titus Tembo posed the questioned 'what possibly could go wrong'?

And as it stood, the Kenyan banks were prepared to match the family investments. Nancy Wawira spent the Hi-Five annual marketing budget in the first two months of start-up. This of course included the coastal trip and the repairs to the hired Duster which were unexpected when she put the marketing budget together. Both Titus Tembo and Nancy Wawira were having great fun in this business with the money provided by Eng. M. J. R. Tembo. This considerable sum was handed over to the newly married couple instead of the traditional cattle dowry that normally is paid to parents of the bride. Eng. M. J. R. Tembo was an old fashioned man in many ways, but when it came to business, he was a man with modern ideas. He was not concerned with being popular with his new extended family. Cattle were not his idea of wealth. Providing for the young couple was most important to his beloved Baba, no matter what he thought of the woman his son had picked as a first wife. As far as his beloved Baba was concerned, he explained that a good start in life for the happy couple was much preferred to making the Kikuyu in-laws set up for life.

Yes, what possibly could go wrong? Along came China with its influence both economical and therefore politically in East Africa. China lent its money and expertise for infrastructure projects; its traders and their cheap goods followed like the migration in the Masai Mara when the rains came. The Hi-Five company looked profitable on paper at first, but in the end the cash flow killed it off. Hi-Five were left with no working capital, a mountain of debt in terms of a warehouse of ceramic domestic ware worth a good sum on paper. But from this highly valued stock, only a handful of goods would sell to tourists. The rest of the Hi-Five products could not compete with the low prices set by the Chinese traders. Those were the prices their fellow country people felt comfortable with.

Titus Tembo's Kikuyu wife Nancy Wawira was from one of the most populous tribe in Kenya. They had ruled the roost in Kenya since independence up to today. And so was the case of their marriage and business which both ended as quickly as they started. Nancy Wawira bought Titus Tembo out of the Hi-Five business for a Shilling and Titus Tembo left a poorer man in money terms, no longer married and yet Titus Tembo did admit, clearly he must have learnt something from his ordeal so why should he feel sorry? After all what did his beloved Baba always say in times like those, 'we will all be dead one day whatever befalls us.'

Soon after Titus Tembo arrived in the United Arab Emirates, it dawned on him that Eng. M. J. R. Tembo saw no reason to make it easy for his mtoto to become a rich man. My beloved Baba believed in a person making mistakes in order to learn and eventually prosper in life. He was, however, regarded by me as my safety net. Looking back, I appreciate very much that my beloved Baba guided me to be my own self-made man doing something in life that I have a passion for and therefore would enjoy.

Wife number two in the form of a very pretty exotic Egyptian lady named Hehet Salah, joined Titus Tembo with the germ of an idea to invest in her country. Only later did Titus Tembo come to know she was named after the goddess of things immeasurable and the famous premium league football connection was just maybe a distant relation. The population of Egypt was growing and there was insufficient new housing stock to meet the needs of the nation. Titus Tembo understood the opportunity as it was a mirror image of East Africa. The local banks were in the mood to lend money and saw fit to finance the real estate dreams of Titus Tembo and Hehet Salah. Indeed, Titus Tembo asked himself the question, once again, 'what possibly could go wrong?

Hehet Salah was clearly a modern Muslim woman in her thinking as she'd left her family home and was working for a multinational company in the United Arab Emirates. Titus Tembo and Hehet Salah dated like a normal Kenyan or any other western couple. For Titus Tembo he was not aware of what marriage meant in Egypt and how very important it was to their society and family structure. Titus Tembo had faced the traditions of a Nairobi wedding already and surely the Egyptian equivalent could not match the demands of such an event.

Little did Titus Tembo know at the time that marriage remained the centre of contemporary Egyptian social life. After Titus Tembo's experience with Hehet Salah, he would realize too late that marriage remains the primary focal point in the lives of both women and men in that culture, only followed by the birth of a child. Being a Christian Titus Tembo had to convert, if only on paper, and have his certificate ready when he visited the offices in Cairo to arrange the formalities of the wedding. Titus Tembo was still a Christian and knew very little of his traditional tribal Gods or even his tribe, was he British or Kenyan? 'Matatanisho.' In his heart he was a Christian but had no choice but to convert if he was to marry Hehet Salah where the rights of both women and men are defined by Islamic law. Even the division of labour is covered by gender, and possibly and fortunately for Titus Tembo by culture, that in practice he could renegotiate with his modern wife. Or so he assumed, which is not a good thing to do, especially when dealing with different culture.

The first part of the custom and practice that went out of the window was down to finance, as his beloved Baba ended up paying for the engagement ceremony of Katb el kitab, paying for the signing of the wedding contract which at the time, Titus Tembo did not even know was taking place. The naive groom to be, sat with Hehet Salah in some ministry building in the two dilapidated chairs made available before Titus Tembo entered another room, while the future bride stayed outside and Titus Tembo signed with one of her male relatives; to whom his beloved Baba had to hand over hongo, which was referred to as baksheesh in this part of Africa.

His beloved Baba was prepared when it came to paying for the wedding ceremony, the party with lots of people, whom Titus Tembo did not know, and possibly Hehet Salah also did not know. Another payment was for the shabka that the Kenyan side of the family understood was for the engagement ring. The fact was the payments were traditionally down to the groom, but in Egypt, as with Titus Tembo after his first divorce, no youth could afford such expenses. Congratulations, the thought came to him more than once during this expensive time, yes congratulations and thank you to the bank of my beloved Baba. Without you none of this would be financially possible. Hehet Salah took for granted that her future father-in-law would pay, and spared no expense in getting her gown made in Dubai. Everything else came from her homeland. The fancy hotel located near the newly opened International Airport were hands off most things, and just provided the infrastructure that excluded basically anything other than the room and staff. There was no mama to represent Titus Tembo, so he had to sit through the pain of selecting everything from the place settings, covers for the chairs, the glasses, cutlery, table linen, and on and on it went and up and up the bill went until Titus Tembo stopped the idea of hiring the best and most expensive disk jockey in the country. It seemed to Titus Tembo that this was going to be a wedding party to compete with one the current dictator would put on for his sons - no expense spared.

On the big day, the wedding music could be heard across the first two floors of the five-star hotel as the guests waited to be served. There was entertainment as the bride was led down the stairs inside the hotel by her father, holding her hand as the wedding guests cheered in the background. Once that was over, Titus Tembo recalled being serenaded by the sounds of music from the band his beloved Baba hired, and he walked slowly with Hehet Salah to best show off the lady of the hour. Titus Tembo and Hehet Salah were surrounded by wedding guests, decked out in stunning attire. All the people there appeared to be very happy and were singing and clapping despite not one drop of alcohol being poured. Unlike Titus Tembo, Hehet Salah loved being the centre of attention, she gave a great big smile as mobile phones flashed their cameras before the official camera man took up his role.

Around the couple were entertainers who were traditional Egyptian folk dancers. The men wore long colourful skirts decorated with lights which came on when they spun endlessly until their skirts got wider and wider to their full width; by that time the dancers were exhausted and had no choice but to stop. Titus Tembo joined in with the guests clapping along, and once in a while got up to dance with Hehet Salah. This went on well into the night but his beloved Baba wanted to leave just before the clock turned to the next day. At the close of events for his family, it was an unpleasant situation for Titus Tembo to experience on his wedding night, that his beloved Baba, even after all the money that he had spent, the relatives of Hehet Salah were insisting he paid baksheesh to the serving staff. Just as with the previous Kikuyu in-laws, his beloved Baba drew a line in the sand and left the small baksheesh payments to the parents of the bride who'd had a free ride until then.

The payments from the groom's family did not end there. As part of the wedding traditions, it was necessary for Mahr to be paid by the groom as per the requirements of Sharia law. This had been interpreted by the family of Hehet Salah, on the insistence of her father, for Titus Tembo to buy a property in Egypt and hand over gold jewellery as part of the protection for his daughter in case of divorce. Titus Tembo's beloved Baba was unwilling for any further involvement and on her side, the father was not going to hand over furniture, appliances, crockery, bedding and various household items since the Kenyan side of the family had not negotiated this well! Hehet Salah said nothing and traditionally it was not a woman's place to do so, that there was no show at the wedding of the Gehaz from her father to enhance the bride's status within her new Kenyan marital family, who were not aware of such a tradition. She was very happy that Titus Tembo's Baba was taking them on holiday the following day and therefore again paying for what she regarded as the honeymoon on the Red Sea.

Buying a new property to satisfy her father was easy as Titus Tembo and Hehet Salah had already committed their business future to property purchases and management in Egypt. Titus Tembo thought to himself once again, what possibly could go wrong? It was a money printing business until the Arab Spring and a weakening currency brought Titus Tembo back to earth with a bump once again. Wife number two fled and all the equity in the business was lost as the property prices fell along with the currency value. Eng. M. J. R. Tembo bailed his mtoto out of the second failed business and again it turned out to be not such an expensive divorce. Nothing chanced, nothing gained as Titus Tembo realized he had lost nothing, after all, 'we will all be dead one day, whatever befalls us.'

CHAPTER FIVE

Kahawa Chungu

Titus Tembo, or as he had referred to himself since early childhood TT, was enjoying very much life on The Palm under the roof of Eng. M. J. R. Tembo, his beloved Baba; for that matter he was delighting in the Dubai life style in general that was so different from his experiences in Kenya and the rest of Africa. Every morning TT gazed out on the sparkling turquoise waters of the Gulf. Once again TT found himself sat next to his beloved Baba, they relaxed together close to the temperature-controlled infinity pool under the shade of the palm trees. It was heading towards summer so the outdoor fans were switched on. There was a breeze with a gentle stream of misty water wafting in the direction of the eight-seater breakfast table. Trixie, the Filipino live-in-maid of his beloved Baba, prepared and cleared away the breakfast. It was a joy to roll out of bed each day during the infancy of the morning knowing Trixie would have everything ship-shape in his bedroom before TT came back for his late morning shower. There is a party somewhere in Dubai every night so TT was never in a rush to start the day too early. Most days TT headed for the beach just beyond the swimming pool. He saw nothing wrong and he felt comfortable that his beloved Baba approved this life style of luxury and the fact that he was subsidising his mtoto for this short time of contemplation about his future.

Before his swim, TT sat in his T shirt, swimming shorts with water proof jandals on his feet that were tucked out of sight under the breakfast table. This eight-seater magnificent solid African hard wood table was decked with silver cutlery from Sheffield, Wedgwood fine bone china from Stoke-on-Trent, Egyptian cotton, white linen and an out of place blackened tall brass kettle, God only knows from where? Eng. M. J. R. Tembo looked cool despite being dressed very conservatively in a traditional Safari Suit as if a board meeting was just about to be brought to order in the Nairobi business district. Eng. M. J. R. Tembo insisted TT said grace before he allowed him to devour the fresh tropical fruit and nut bowl prepared and set before him by Trixie. This treat was accompanied by Kahawa Chungu, the Kenyan bitter coffee that he was introduced to in Ghana as a child by his beloved Baba. Back then he never drank it other than for an occasional sip, but he liked the whole ceremony surrounding the grown-up treat. As an adult TT took it the traditional way out of miniature cups, albeit English fine bone china, they were still Arabic style cups. This is the way he took Kahawa Chungu for many years, ever since he joined an elderly Swahili man drinking early one morning on the Kenyan coast. Those Kenyan men of Arab descent reminded him of how the locals dressed in the United Arab Emirates, head to foot in white and never a coffee stain to show.

Most Kenyans preferred tea to coffee but even the hardened tea drinker would succumb to Kahawa Chungu. TT had shown Trixie how to prepare his favourite morning drink properly the Kenyan way. The beverage is typically brewed over a charcoal stove in a tall brass kettle very much like the ones available in the United Arab Emirates. It derived its bitterness through the inclusion of ginger, cardamom, cinnamon and some other secret spices. TT always bought the best coffee available, every time he would select Arabica beans. TT checked that it would be coffee from its birthplace, East African coffee of course. Like its people the coffee beans were so different from the ones grown and processed in the Americas, Asia and even the rest of Africa. Just like French wine, East African coffee was different, as farmers owned and operated small plots, or as in the case of the French, wine differed from field to field and he believed it was the same for coffee.

TT presented Trixie with the recipe; two to three cups of cold water, seeds from one or two cardamom pods, three tablespoons of freshly ground coffee beans, a quarter teaspoon of ground cardamom plus a quarter teaspoon of ground ginger, finally TT's secret herbs brought from the markets in Mombasa which Trixie could use until it ran out, or TT bought more in Kenya. TT and Eng. M. J. R. Tembo both liked the water and cardamom seeds brought to the boil together, then kept on a low boil for exactly ten minutes, no longer, no shorter. At that stage and only at that stage, add the ground coffee. After simmering for five minutes or even longer, add ground cardamom, ginger and if desired when available, the secret spice from Mombasa. Pour through a strainer into a coffeepot and serve hot. TT in fact liked his coffee unstrained with the muddy substance at the bottom of his cup. Thus, the tall blacked pot for making their favourite coffee, sat on the breakfast table among the other finery.

Kahawa Chungu is frequently touted as an aphrodisiac by Kenyan coastal tribes as it helps with blood circulation and alertness. TT bought into this idea as no matter what time he got to bed, Kahawa Chungu triggered his bodily systems to fully function once more come the morning. The real physical stress would come later in the early afternoon at the local professional gymnasium. There, TT would also take the opportunity for practising his camera work and occasional video takes.

Luckily for TT, Eng. M. J. R. Tembo would often be working from home past mid-morning during most weekdays. On weekends TT was up much later due to the need for him to recover from his exploits in the clubs. He was not much of a dancer, so he spent his time drinking lots of water since he had decided to give up booze, coughing in his attempt to smoke shisha, the Middle East hookah pipe, enjoying long meaningless conversations and staying up far too late until club closing times in the early hours of the next day. TT gave up alcohol for good even before he decided to come to the Emirates to join his beloved Baba who he knew, had never touched the stuff. His beloved Baba called it poison for the mind and the body. TT decided to give alcohol up one morning in Nairobi when he looked back at how he had behaved so badly in Crazy Mics once too often. The hookah pipe bad habit soon followed on his not to do list. Within a week he started to feel much better from the lack of smoke entering his lungs.

Both Friday and Saturday being the Middle East weekend, Eng. M. J. R. Tembo would be in the desert very early. This was the time to catch the best light for his photographic shoots in the sandy-wilderness. It was in fact a deliberate action and change of habit from Eng. M. J. R. Tembo on the arrival of TT in the United Arab Emirates, to be at home at least until midmorning during the weekdays. They often shared points of discussion together with respect to the photographs each had taken the day before. Eng. M. J. R. Tembo knew TT of old and expected late morning would provide a suitable opportunity to share TT's latest business thinking. On those occasions after one cup of strong muddy coffee, TT shared his ideas with his beloved Baba. Often TT gained more insight, but was just as pleased if it was simply to hear the encouragement his beloved Baba gave every new business idea put forward. Eng. M. J. R. Tembo was a great believer in positive reinforcement and never criticised an entrepreneurial idea in what he referred to as the 'brain storming' stage of the business thinking process.

As yet TT had not shared with Eng. M. J. R. Tembo why he was so keenly leaning towards investing in a new venture - yet another United Arab Emirates gymnasium or rather a fitness centre as TT liked to emphasize. TT felt the title 'Fitness Centre' already differentiated their ideas from that of yet another Dubai gymnasium. Photography and video feedback of the personal trainers in action with their clients would play a key role in developing the business turnover. The focus was to be motivating individuals as part of a group and specifically families to move towards repeated class-based fitness. Mums would enjoy music, lights and dance, making fitness fun while their kids took part in self-defence activities like karate or active sports like mini-soccer. All this fun had a serious side as fun was mixed with recommended life style changes, not just diets, changes for the best chance of sustainable fitness for life and maximising the business income streams. What similar businesses in this field did was membership focused in order to avoid cash flow pressures. They then missed the opportunity to maximise short term individual client expenditure that improved the business bottom line longer term. TT had a good feeling towards this *'Fitness Centre'* concept. Not only that, of late he felt he was starting to have a passion for fitness and believed in what they wanted to achieve in making people healthier. They were committed enough to complete an on-line diploma from a British University.

The *'they'* in this plan was TT along with the new love of his life, a Russian fitness model. Mila Nadia held the United Kingdom fitness model title for the current year. His new love lived with two other Russian ladies of what he thought was a dubious profession. He kept his opinion of the two women to himself, as after all they had come up with the cash to float the business. TT had learnt the lessons of his two failed businesses. Cash was King and cash float was the master of killing a profitable start-up. The start of this week being a Sunday in this part of the world, saw the Lords Day of rest being used by Mila Nadia and TT setting out to establish their business for the four shareholders. His target was the cheapest possible business license. The free-zone company meant there was no local partner to be paid a sponsorship fee. All the documents were standard issue by the free zone authority, both in English so they could understand its content plus the Arabic legally approved language, and so no big legal fees to pay. Even the power of attorney for managing the business was a standard document and again it was low cost. Mila Nadia and TT's names and passport details were filled in on a standard form along with the current date, the notary rubber stamped it for another small fee. The business was set up in one day on that first Sunday and the name *'Fitness for Life'* and its Arabic equivalent name was approved quickly by the economic department for Dubai and thus it covered the United Arab Emirates. This pleased them no end, as the new owners they had dreams for expanding the business first throughout the United Arab Emirates and then franchise of the business model in the Middle East.

All was going smoothly, yet they were still on a tight deadline as both their visit visas were soon to expire. These tourist visas needed to be replaced by investor visas pretty sharply. This involved security clearance, and here the free zone authorities had no sway. In the end if TT was honest with himself, he was not so unhappy to learn that his new Russian love would need to have the support of a husband, and be accepted on her husband's visa. Mila Nadia and TT excused themselves to rethink and remake their plan. In the One and Only exclusive beach hotel, over a healthy lunch, TT made his unhealthy rushed proposal to his soon to be third wife. If he had only spoken to Eng. M. J. R. Tembo first, it would have saved them a whole lot of grief further down the road.

Money talks it seems, and they were accepted to be married in the wonderful Russian Orthodox Church in Sharjah on Tuesday of the same week. Eng. M. J. R. Tembo was swept up in the excitement of being best man and wedding photographer for the special day. One of Mila Nadia's Russian professional lady friends gave the bride away and the other acted as bridesmaid for the event. The Church must be the best kept secret in the United Arab Emirates. Its architecture put in the shade that of the great mosque in its capital city Abu Dhabi! Clearly the secret was working so well that they had very few people attending mass and contributing to the church fund. The result was their money bought Mila Nadia and TT this marriage of convenience, and its lovely ceremony in record time. Not one of the five of them attending the wedding understood a word of the service that appeared to be in Bosnian or possibly Greek, or some other similar language as far as the tiny congregation could tell! The conservative lady attending the minister made it clear from her repeated tut, tut, that the bride and her lady friends were not dressed suitably. It soon became evident there was no way the ladies would be welcomed back or ever be allowed to step inside this church again once the powers that be in the church secured all the payments for this wedding.

In their excitement and relief, bride plus groom rushed to their car as soon as the minister indicated they could seal the wedding with a peck. There was no issue with further payment as the money was grabbed with both hands in advance by the tut- tut lady, before they were allowed anywhere near the minister. And so, they found themselves signing the wedding documents on the bonnet of their car in what they thought was the church car park. A car parking lot in where they now found themselves and their cars locked in! Subsequently they read the sign on the car lot barrier, made the phone call and like many people before them paid the price for the freedom of their cars. Due to the unexpected events of this day, the business plan cash flow projections for visas was short of the mark by a hundred percent, this was the cost of their wedding, including the high cost of parking. It crossed the mind of TT, and he hoped he was wrong this time, that this trend would not continue like it did for the Hi-Five Pottery business, it seemed at first glance however to be a repeat of the Watamu marketing budget over spend. Eng. M. J. R. Tembo provided the celebratory lunch, paying for all five to enjoy 'nyama ya mbuzi', goat cooked the African way at the South African owned Meat Factory restaurant situated next to the waters of the gulf.

Over lunch all admired the wedding photographs taken by Eng. M. J. R. Tembo using TT's A7Riii high resolution camera. TT knew his beloved Baba had a gift for photography. Many years ago, even before TT was thought of, Eng. M. J. R. Tembo had started out with a simple Single-Lens Reflex Russian camera that was designed with mainly manual settings. This simple camera made Eng. M. J. R. Tembo learn the basics of photography very well indeed. This is how he became so gifted at his art, and he followed the same learning process for TT, presenting him with a manual Single-Lens Reflex camera at an early age. His beloved Baba's fine dedication to his love of photography is what started TT's passion for the art of picture taking.

All the three Russian ladies fussed over the magnificent pictures of the church building, the close ups of people inside the church, the exchange of rings, the traditional attire of the priest shown in black and white, and so it went on with Eng. M. J.R. Tembo being christened that day by the three Russian ladies as *'Africa's best photographer.'* TT therefore, as the son of Eng. M. J. R. Tembo, inherited and accepted the title of *'Africa's second-best photographer'*. And there we have it, the *'HOW'* and the *'WHY'* that saw TT become known as *'Africa's Second-Best Photographer'*. Of course, the story has a long way to run just yet.

With not much money or time to spare, this ensured the new partners were motivated to be back at work early the very next day after the wedding ceremony. As a result, Eng. M. J. R. Tembo was at least spared the cost of another honeymoon. The free zone rules allowed Mila Nadia and TT to recruit cheap and pretty Asian ladies for the front of the house and cheap and sometimes hardworking Asian labour for keeping the fitness centre clean and presentable. No need for Mila Nadia and TT to worry over accommodation, medical cover, visas, etc. for their staff, as again the free zone authorities took care of all the headaches. They subsequently forgot the small matter of health insurance for themselves.

And with no taxes to pay, so far so good as they only utilised a minor part of the investment cash to date. They had secured a simple warehouse provided by the free-zone authorities. By signing four cheques made out over the year, the rent was covered for the one-year period of the licence. These cheques were needed by the end of the week to close the deal, finalize the business licence and secure the all-important investor visas. The warehouse had never been used as a gymnasium before but had dual changing rooms and bathrooms, which TT named the WCs, or water closets, and which his business Russian partner failed to understand as TT first referred to them in the British Pub way of 'Without Charge'. Client lockers were an easy fix on the cheap. Luckily the air-conditioning was just perfect. There was only need for a further minor investment and a quick fix to improve the lighting. Ikea provided the off the peg equivalent of hardware for setting up a healthy drinks and snack bar. The parking lot seemed very suitable without the need for any further modifications. A large sign board *FITNESS FOR LIFE* was ordered to go up by that weekend. They were nearly in business. There was just the small matter of equipment, clients and opening a bank account.

The new bank account issue, proved a challenge TT did not expect as they had a wad of cash from their Russian investors to get things started. The first thing TT discovered about banking that differed from Kenya; not many of the big banks like HSBC were interested in small business accounts even if Eng. M. J. R. Tembo had a premium personal account of good standing with HSBC for many years. In the end they used the Wasta provided by their two Russian investment partners and they then had to face up to the next hurdle, a wad of cash in hand.

The Russian ladies' Lebanese friend Byblos, waltzed them into the manager's office of what they were led to believe was a Jordanian Bank. Arabic coffee in small cups was offered along with dates. Much of the conversation took place in Arabic between the two charming men. The first man they knew as Mr. Byblos and the second man they assumed was the branch manager. Niceties over, these gentlemen switched to English for the benefit of Mila

Nadia and TT. 'Mr. Byblos, please just email a copy of the new business licence once it is issued, that will be sufficient for now, no need to see their visas as this would come with time, a few simple Arabic forms to sign, no matter understanding them as they are just formalities.' Cash we'll have to give you details of how you generated this cash so you can sign it off. Yes, all is in good order, just make out these counter cheques for security and we'll issue you credit cards in three days to the limit set out on the cheques signed today. Welcome to our bank and please drop by for an Arabic coffee any time I can be of assistance.' And, so what yesterday seemed the impossible, come Wednesday was done painlessly over a strong Arabic coffee and dates. Clearly, they both agreed it is more important the 'who' you know rather than 'what' you know to get certain things completed in good time in this part of the world.

The nicety of a cheque book secured the lease on the warehouse and gave them the tool to secure all the reconditioned gymnasium equipment they needed to impress their future clientele. The three big Pakistanis assisted by their equally fierce looking driver, lugged the equipment from the back of the open truck into the air-conditioned warehouse. They then sat on the floor and dished out rice and water as if it was their last supper. The Ikea delivery had none of the drama displayed by the Pakistanis hired by the gymnasium equipment seller. The Ikea delivery arrived in the agreed time slot after they phoned ahead to confirm the location. The team of two Filipinos unpacked the food bar and its accessories very efficiently and put everything together effortlessly. As soon as the food bar was in position, they moved on to their next delivery taking the waste packaging with them. By then the Pakistanis had completed their meal and were ready to depart. The last piece of the jigsaw for the day was the signboard and its erection.

The first phone call came one hour after they were due to deliver the signboard. 'Yes boss, we are not far away, just wait ten minutes.' What sounded like an Indian had reassured TT it would happen today. One hour later a little Indian man arrived with an even smaller assistant. The sign board was just as ordered, correct size, right materials, good eye-catching colours but with a slight variation in meaning as it said *'FITNESS FOR WIFE'*. TT at that point did not realise how aptly named the sign board would become! Their weekend was spoilt by the attempts to get the correctly worded sign board in place in good time. The *'FITNESS FOR LIFE'* signboard was eventually fixed the next day at the correct angle despite the two little

Indian men struggling to fix it without any form of level gauge and just one step-ladder between the two of them.

The beginning of the week came soon enough and the cleaners did their best, huffing and puffing to clean up the warehouse after the installation of the lockers and the minor work on the lighting. Subsequently TT had to call back the painters to retouch the paint around the warehouse from the work men as they managed to damage and dirty the newly painted areas during their efforts. After the painting on the ceilings and walls was put right, the cleaners had to be recalled by TT to scrape and clean the paint spots from the warehouse floor. Labour may have been cheap but getting things right first time was only a vague concept not dissimilar to his own African continent. TT realised for the first time in Dubai, efficiency may not be the reality he had expected in this part of the world. All was set for an effective opening with the pretty front of house girls more than capable of organising the health bar from purchases made at the local Carrefour super market.

CHAPTER SIX

Wisdom of the ancients

Mila Nadia had the brains, and the good example of her near perfect body was the driving force behind that *'Fitness for Life'* business concept. TT was swept along in all the excitement Mila Nadia generated for their new venture. Titus Tembo saw his main roles as firstly putting together content, mostly photographs and videos starring Mila Nadia for their social media marketing blitz and secondly a most important role of keeping a close eye on the costs and cash flow. TT was the work horse who had compiled a whole lot of content for them to share about *'Fitness for Life'* on social media platforms. Everyone was singing the praises of social media for marketing, as this modern new marketing communication means was two-way. However, there were so many platforms on which to share the treasure trove of content; TT pondered where he should start?

Social media was not a subject TT expected to get advice on from old school business man Eng. M. J. R. Tembo. This was a part of the new business he would need to deal with himself. His beloved Baba had general management business experience, but that included traditional marketing, with little or no experience of social media. TT began his work by thinking about what sites their audience would probably use. It was a no brainer for TT using 'YouTube' for his video productions, but what was best suited to the case of *'Fitness for Life'* he was not sure of as yet. They were in the early days of the business start-up. At this stage TT had compiled plenty of content, but was scrambling to create posts at the last minute, which led to him being disappointed with some low-quality outputs. TT remained determined not to waste the impressive content of photographs and videos he had put together using Mila Nadia as his fitness model. He had even gone back just over a year ago, and up-graded what he could on the video and photographs he kept of her victory in the British Fitness Model championship. If he was totally honest, TT felt a little overwhelmed at the lack of organisation they had put in place. It was becoming obvious to TT, but not Mila Nadia, that they were repeating posts or in some important channels they lacked enough presence and focus.

Recalling some of his beloved Baba's teaching, TT recognised his '*Matatanisho*' was taking over due to the heavy work load and the subsequent stress he was under. He leaned back in his chair, the fans and the shade of the palms tempered the heat a little. Suddenly the stress lifted off his back. He smiled to himself for how easily you forget the simplest of lessons that you use every day. Work was started immediately by TT to put things right as he created a social media content calendar. This was a fancy modern name; TT was in fact dipping into the wisdom of the ancients that Eng. M. J. R. Tembo had shared with him when they sat round the camp fire in Northern Kenya. Again, putting it in modern fancy jargon, TT had a personality type based on the element of wood. Other people could fall into the categories of fire, metal, water or earth; TT definitely belonged to the element of wood. He understood this was his true nature and when he applied this knowledge, he time and again regained his sense of direction. Recognising and acting on his element led TT to live and behave in a way that supported his energy and reduced his '*Matatanisho*'. The Social Media Content Calendar was just like his daily, weekly and quarterly and specific 'To-Do' lists divided into urgent or important or other. Urgent tasks needed his immediate attention and were normally simple tasks requiring little thought and completed quickly. Important tasks waited to be thought about before being tackled. The so-called other tasks he did when he had time. This gave TT the confidence and feeling he was on top of things and once more in control.

No way did TT fit into the fire, metal, water or earth personality types. Eng. M. J. R. Tembo had drummed into TT that his wood element needed an overhaul of your 'To-Do' list regularly; for TT and his Social Media Content Calendar it meant creating a new list every day. Each time he completed something TT made sure to cross it off his list. And so, it was the case with his Social Media Content Calendar.

TT listed in his head his wood element characteristics as typically applying to himself. As soon as he finished one thing, he'd think, what next? Yes, he was always on the go and in fact restless at times and unhappy if he had nothing to keep him busy! His weakness, he accepted, was having very little patience with people who wallow in their emotions. He realised he got frustrated too easily with anxious people who nitpick about every tiny detail. His strength was that of being a lifelong student and always looking for ways to improve himself. The latest impact of this was his Diploma in Fitness obtained with distinction from a United Kingdom distance learning University based in Dubai. His need for action plans and lists for himself in all he did was more or less a daily event at the closing and/or opening of each day. TT mistakenly expected the same from anyone he depended on for a successful outcome. Here he felt uncomfortable with the attitude of his wife and business partner. Mila Nadia really was a more 'what will be will be' type of person and on failing to cross off items on her 'To-Do' list successfully, she would be inclined more towards Eng. M. J. R. Tembo's school of thought that TT had in error shared with her, and she used as an excuse for falling short, *'we will all be dead one day, whatever befalls us'.*

TT did not rate highly such a thing as common sense. It was not needed but would follow naturally if one was logical. What TT believed in was - stay organised and you get things done, and never put something off until tomorrow what can be done today. Eng. M. J. R. Tembo instilled in TT that tomorrow never comes! TT accepted his way. His style, you could say, sometimes led him to failure as was the case in business as well as in life, which was also the case with his first two marriages. TT appreciated at times that his 'Matatanisho' led him down the wrong paths. He looked back on his successes and realised most of all, his weakness was one of the things that helped him so much in life, his desire to get going. Indeed, he recognised that his frustration in not making quick enough progress could lead him at times to make impulsive decisions. On those occasions his safety net Eng. M. J. R. Tembo often came to the rescue, thank God for his beloved Baba.

TT appreciated the rainy and dry periods, his experience at home made him dismiss the European idea of four seasons when it comes to Africa; Spring, Summer, Autumn and Winter were non-events on his continent. Rather renewal, growth and the future were brought by the rains. The alternative was the land drying out and certain death for crops if the rains failed. It was TT's stance in life to get going as the rains may fail next time around. Get active, stay fit, eat healthy, just love life and make the most of your opportunities.

After this reflection, TT was to see to it that they could avoid some basic mistakes that had happened recently. Together Mila Nadia and TT would create goals and update their strategies for meeting their goals, then track the progress the business was making towards success. Today was getting better as a start was being made, a 'To-Do" list for each social media channel they would target. By the time the sun was going down and one or two *'mbu'* started to feed on the blood from his bare legs, TT had formulated a plan for posts in advance, complete with hashtags, links, images and the best content taken from the mountain of photographs and video compiled on Mila Nadia as his star.

Weeks flew by, TT was getting busier and busier with people having fun with his posts. Their content appeared to be encouraging interaction and Mila Nadia was also enjoying this aspect. TT was naturally pleased that there would be no need to consider spending on regular advertising. People were apparently enjoying the content he put out. They were sharing fitness articles, grabbing people's attention with video content. TT was so pleased that he was good at putting together content where Mila Nadia came across as conveying her personality and passion to potential clients, commenting on the impact of good life style changes, posting healthy recipes, including links to relevant book reviews. All this was positive, in fact only one in ten of the 'Fitness for Life' posts were direct promotional posts or so TT thought all was going swimmingly.

The visual content stood out as this was TT's forte and Mila Nadia was a star. These videos on the social media platforms were a wow factor, getting great reactions. There was no requirement to spend time dealing with problems as none were ever encountered, no one was upset, argumentative or said anything negative about Mila Nadia or *'Fitness for Life'*. In fact, there was little integration of the latter as Mila Nadia was standing out alone as the star. The local papers started to feature her on their Friday issues. Friday was the big deal in this part of the world, just like Sunday newspapers in Europe. Mila Nadia had followers in numbers comparable with the best-known people on the Dubai scene. She had become an influencer in a big way.

The brand of *'Fitness for Life'*, or rather 'Mila Nadia' as their brand, was building quicker than they could have ever dreamt of when compiling the business plan. *'Fitness for Life'* followers - or rather Mila Nadia's followers were increasing and customers came to *'Fitness for Life'* as a result. TT was so busy and excited he failed to see they were no longer finding customers who were interested, loyal and engaged in *'Fitness for Life'*. Yes, they did repost content, yes, they liked the posts and customers were bringing cash to the business. TT was so caught up in their success he failed to understand the brand was becoming Mila Nadia and not as planned, *'Fitness for Life'*. Their social media community had been built around Mila Nadia not *'Fitness for Life'*. Online people got value from learning something new about Mila Nadia; they laughed at and with Mila Nadia, she was the big attraction and the success of the social media marketing campaign. The social media Gold Mine was Mila Nadia and '*Fitness for Life*' benefited greatly from clients she brought to the business.

Mums came as they hoped to somehow have a good body and the perceived glamour Mila Nadia enjoyed. They brought their kids along as, in some cases, without bringing their kids, they would have been stuck at home looking after them. Dads came along at weekends and evenings after work as they were set the example by the rest of their family. Single men came just in the hope of talking to Mila Nadia. Families were the core of the business plan and 'Fitness for Life' geared their offerings to families. The business welcomed the loyal Mila Nadia fan base, while the fickle single guys moved on to greener pastures on a regular basis. Of course, these youngish guys were easily replaced with the stream of people on the '*Fitness for Life*' waiting list.

The costs crept up as more staff were required to cater for the higher number of clients. A specialist was added to assist TT, as the work load related to social media had become more time-consuming. Additional hours were being put in by the whole team, be it cleaning the warehouse, servicing reception or just dealing with the natural consequences of the higher numbers of clients. Regular monthly income masked the running away of fixed costs. The bottom line was healthy and no one bothered to push the concept of higher annual membership numbers as those few clients interested, seemed to be just looking to save money long term by asking about annual membership.

The '*Fitness for Life*' star Mila Nadia was on the verge of providing the business a further boost as she prepared to defend her title of Miss Fitness Model United Kingdom. These fitness modelling competitions all sound very laid back but TT knew differently after his experience in the United Kingdom at the Birmingham National Exhibition Centre the previous year. What he expected then was a degree of physique and muscularity, but typically similar to a bikini competition with a focus on modelling. Last year TT had looked forward to seeing Mila Nadia in a multiple of cute outfits, and her striking some poses beyond those typical for plain simple straight forward fitness competitions. Indeed, the success in the United Kingdom provided Mila Nadia with two sources of income, the first her personal training one-on-one with want-to-be fitness models, and both men and women with differing reasons to get into shape. Mila Nadia's second line of business had become a more lucrative source of income than her physically taxing personal training. Dollars came from her on-line selling of designer branded 'Mila Nadia' bikinis. It just required Mila Nadia to select from options on the manufacture's web site in China, ensure she had the right size for the measurements provided, then deliver it worldwide via Dubai to add her label, some small additions and her fancy packaging. Mila Nadia ensured her PayPal account was credited before posting on the goods at an eighty percent mark-up. Sometimes no money came and, on those occasions, Mila Nadia offered the fancy, unpaid for bikinis in a promotional deal. She hired another member of staff to deal with the rush of enquires as Mila Nadia needed to focus on her fitness in readiness for bringing her United Kingdom fitness modelling crown back to Dubai.

Looking back Mila Nadia felt very satisfied with how things had turned out for her. Thinking about his observations in the run up for the first competition, it left TT with the firm opinion that the rewards coming from the title as winner fell well short of the effort needed just to appear let alone win. He was not looking forward to a repeat experience this year as Mila Nadia defended her title! TT listed mentally what Mila Nadia would face and the consequences for TT. They, Mila Nadia, and TT would need, like last time around, to agree how long before the show the diet would start. This was a major factor in Mila Nadia winning first time around. How was her physique? How lean, what type of metabolism (endomorphic, mesomorphic, ectomorphic) was she? What body parts needed more attention? Studying this new subject first time around fitted nicely with TT's type of personality and organising for readiness saw TT in his element. Second time around defending this title and TT now had the benefit of an education and diploma in fitness behind him. The main lesson learnt by TT from the first-time victory was the keeping of those diet weeks to the exact requirement and no longer, as it could be hell for Mila Nadia and him as her nearest and dearest. Mila Nadia needed to lose around one to a maximum two Kilograms of body fat and yet maintain as much muscle mass as possible, not gain muscle. So, in Mila Nadia's state of fitness and condition, TT estimated this further weight loss would take just four to five weeks.

The diet design was to keep protein in a close range based on Mila Nadia's body weight. They would again keep the protein source to lean, ground turkey, lean ground beef, whole eggs but in the main just egg whites, low fat cheeses, fat free Greek style yogurt, skinless, boneless chicken breasts and finally fish. Luckily for TT he had quickly discovered last year that Mila Nadia liked fish more than any other protein source and this made things a little simpler for him. This food is an excellent means of accelerating fat loss as the white kind like tilapia contain little or no fat, with significantly lower amounts of calories and yet with an ample amount of protein.

For the first two weeks they were to start with a carbohydrate intake in a similar range to the protein target. That was the easy bit, eating brown rice, dark green vegetables, slow digesting fruits like apples and oranges, regular oatmeal and any other grain foods they could get, 'yum yum' he thought to himself. The first challenge for sweet toothed Mila Nadia was later in the day as the best and really the only time to include small quantities of sugar or refined carbohydrate was in the morning. TT saw the impact of this diet on her moods later in the day when she was not so pleasant to him if other people were not around to impress!

Healthy fats are always important but TT needed to limit Mila Nadia to a range of some twenty to thirty percent of fats in her daily calories. The lesson from the first-time round saw TT introducing Mila Nadia to the use of all-natural peanut butter, extra virgin olive oil, and macadamia nut oil. Cooking with the nut oil provided an easy way for Mila Nadia to get her fats and keep her from eating extra fatty food like olives, salmon or avocado. TT was keeping it simple in preparation and choice of food. Mila Nadia's whole routine was changed to accommodate eating every 2.5 hours during the waking day. That way Mila Nadia got around the hell of feeling hungry most of the time. TT also fitted in the meals around her pre-workouts and post-workouts. He, motivated Mila Nadia to make every workout like it was her last.

It was so demanding that TT and Mila Nadia neglected relationships, friends, clients, the business, and this was tough, certainly it also impacted badly on their own relationship. It was a monotonous, four-week journey to that stage in Birmingham in the United Kingdom. After the first ten days together, they assessed the gains made. Because Mila Nadia was endomorphic, TT had to drop the carbohydrates further and fingers crossed she maintained her hard-earned muscle. This did not help at all with Mila Nadia's mood swings and the relationship with TT. He tried to be patient but he really feared the consequences of the mood swings that the extreme strategies for dieting would bring in the days and hours running up to the competition.

When preparing for the contest, TT drafted a cardiovascular plan nearly as punishing as the diet, and added to it a strength training plan in order for Mila Nadia to achieve that crisp, contest winning condition. The clients at the warehouse all knew their heroine was on a mission to bring back the fitness model title from the United Kingdom to Dubai. They were all willing her on to victory. Everyone in the warehouse was so pleased if they saw her going through one of her two moderately intense 30-minute cardio sessions each week, or that one high intensity cardio session that lasted just 15 minutes. From his studies, TT expected the low-to-moderate intensity cardio to increase blood-flow, result in an uptake of nutrients, and accelerate metabolism. Why TT included the high intensity session was so as not to burn as many calories during that workout as the low-moderate session, but to burn those calories in the hours after leaving the warehouse and, ultimately to a much greater level. Just like the diet, TT adjusted this plan as Mila Nadia's physique continued to get leaner with her journey's end at Birmingham drawing nearer. As Mila Nadia's body type was endomorphic, TT saw no need to reduce the cardio. This was unlike himself as an endomorph who consume more carbohydrate during the diet and needed less cardio. At the opposite end of the scale, endomorphic types needed more cardio throughout the contest preparation stage.

The third part of the contest preparation is the strength training. This was not a matter of gaining muscle mass as after all this was a fitness model competition, not a body building event. TT saw it as an opportunity over the four weeks for Mila Nadia to refine, shape and condition her body as he believed she'd worked hard enough up to this point. There was nothing new to be done, just more of the same without the mistake of over training. TT intended to keep it simple and within the limits of Mila Nadia's abilities. The plan was based on a power/hypertrophy training of two power days, first upper body then lower body. The approach was conservative, with weights using barbells and low repetitions, to ensure there was no injury. Mila Nadia would help the business by training in the warehouse three times a week over the next four weeks.

TT repeated the practices that won them the title one year ago. Mila Nadia was asked by TT to pose in a bikini until she was thoroughly used to it; TT felt this aspect was just as important as the diet, strength training and cardio work outs. To pose you needed as the champion, dramatic music, and a routine that showed you were the champion here to collect the trophy one more time. Last year their preparation was one of consistently practicing posing on multiple nights in private. This time round Mila Nadia did it with loud music in the warehouse seven nights a week before admiring clients. This built the confidence needed for being onstage and winning back the title. The second benefit was for the business as clients enjoyed the entertainment provided by their champion.

Mila Nadia was like a film star by trade, she presented well and it's one of the reasons she was champion. There were no excuses for getting the fundamentals wrong. TT had to be her coach along with the mirror, TT's video camera and the clients in the warehouse. Four weeks were adequate to hone those pose sequences in timing to the chosen music. TT was the choreographer and Mila Nadia just practised non-stop until it became second nature. TT felt Mila Nadia was ready as ready as she could be, she was lean and conditioned close to perfection. They had prepared in plenty of time to complete their plan on diet, cardio and weightlifting. No need to be concerned about a sun tan as Dubai weather had naturally taken care of the skin colour. They had been honest with each other and had kept things simple, not tried anything unfamiliar.

TT had not had to diet or train but he had gone through a hard time dealing with Mila Nadia's moods. He had adjusted the diet, dropping carbohydrates, he realised it was not enough, and added those two low or no-carbohydrate days at the end of the four weeks, and this was hell for both of them. The fear was how things would be in Birmingham between them as they restricted her water intake and sodium manipulation for final shaping. Some of the gurus recommended this approach, but TT believed it to be bogus advice. Nevertheless, it had worked first time around so, Mila Nadia over ruled TT and insisted that for victory, they took the risk of the health issues this final tactic came with.

Their plan was to avoid too much time in the cold of a United Kingdom autumn. At Terminal Three in Dubai, Mila Nadia felt tired and very hungry but she admired herself in the lady's bathroom's full-length mirror. Mila Nadia was not concerned who else was in the competition, she focused on herself, she looked good, she was the best she could be, she was on her own in this competition and was better than anyone else who would come to the stage. She was competing against herself, let the judges decide the rest. It would have been good to have a professional trainer and nutritionist. She made-do with Titus Tembo for now and next year just maybe she'd get a sponsor to pay for professional people. TT was good at camera work but she felt he did not have the same passion when it came to fitness. If she posed this question to TT, he would have to agree.

The Emirates flight landed after eight hours in the air and typically they were greeted by grey English skies and a damp cool day. For some reason they were questioned by a friendly enough official after passing the passport checking desk. He was charming in fact, and put Mila Nadia in a seemingly good mood that consequently relaxed TT. The slight delay worked out well for them as their baggage with the stage angel wings were all there on the rotating carousel as they joined the rest of the passengers waiting for their belongings. Thirty minutes later a single-decker passenger bus pulled up outside the terminal building. They took their luggage on board as they alighted for their two-minute journey to the National Exhibition Centre in Trinity Park. TT today just wanted Mila Nadia to register and scan the set-up of the stage, see the changing rooms and greet some of the judges in advance of tomorrow. Mila Nadia was ready to sleep and forget about her thirst, she was glad to slip into the back of the taxi that would take them to the Four-Star Crowne Plaza. She needed to eat something. Then if she had a soft bed and a dark room, she could close her eyes and hold off taking too much water.

Mila Nadia was not feeling happy carrying her own bag the short distance from the taxi to the hotel entrance. Check in was not as efficient or as friendly as Dubai. And to cap it all they had to take their own bags to their room which stunk of stale smoke. Mila Nadia's mood was changing for the worse and she blamed TT for all these things, her hunger, the grey sky, the smell coming from this smoky room and she snapped at him. Mila Nadia lay in her single bed, waiting for the last meal of the day and a welcome good night's sleep before the late morning show kicked off the next day. The early hours of the morning saw Mila Nadia complain of terrible leg cramps. She had very little sleep, her left calf was so painful, she limped around the bed to the bathroom to start on her make-up. She was in no state mentally or physically to take to the stage. TT bore the brunt of her anger when he suggested they wait a little before deciding whether to withdraw or not from the contest.

By the time they landed back in Dubai, the only reason Mila Nadia spoke to Titus Tembo, was for him to arrange a wheel chair for her to come off the plane and then for him to drive her to a hospital. They were soon turned away at the private hospital reception, as they had no medical insurance to cover the costs, and could not even register for Mila Nadia's much needed treatment.

Titus Tembo was to blame for everything according to Mila Nadia. She got her Russian partners to buy him out of the *'Fitness for Life'* business as quickly as they could. In reality he traded off some of his equity cheaply in a side agreement in order for him to retain his prized investor visa. Mila Nadia instructed her lawyer friend over divorce proceedings. TT was more than happy that his beloved Baba welcomed him home with no comments or difficult questions.

CHAPTER SEVEN

Happiness Is a decision

Several weeks had slowly passed for TT since returning to the United Arab Emirates from the United Kingdom and the Birmingham fitness model show fiasco. TT relaxed in the knowledge that he still had an investor's visa for Dubai which was so important to him at this time. His bank account would not be frozen, he could use his credit cards, keep his Emirates Identification Document which allowed him to access many government services, own a car locally, hold a local sim card, sign a lease agreement for housing, go in and out of the country freely; so basically, he could continue with life here in the Emirates as his three-year visa still had some time to run. There was a tidy sum of money sitting in his bank account from the sale of his shares in *'Fitness for Life'* A tidy sum of money would be sufficient to take care of his needs short term, but would not cover an emergency case that might come along. He did not worry as his beloved Baba was still there as a safety net.

'Fitness for Life' TT regarded as his first truly successful business venture to-date in that he came out of it with a substantial return on his investment. That investment was very little in monetary terms, but he put in ideas, and some considerable efforts that were for sure valuable. The relationship with Mila Nadia was no more but he accepted that. He really did not see this break-up as being down to his bad behaviour and he would soon be moving on with his life. TT decided there and then he'd not ever again marry, with the one exception, only to a very wise woman, nearly as wise as his beloved Baba, he clarified to himself. TT, was ready to get on with his next business venture. The only cloud on TT's horizon was the poor health of his beloved Baba. He had brought up the subject of being a donor once again, which was not significant in itself, as they discussed this subject on several occasions over the last decade. As his beloved Baba made clear, when he passed, he did not what anyone stopping his donor wishes, and the other issue of the disposal of his body as he expected his Titus to ensure his wishes were fulfilled no matter what. The discussion of organ donations was

definitely significant, and worrying when one added the fact that Eng. M. J. R. Tembo had recently been in and out of hospital several times for tests. Currently he was under-going cancer treatment. His beloved Baba was so lucky to be in Dubai and get the illness attended to here rather than struggle back home. There was just the one private comprehensive cancer hospital in Nairobi and it was the only one in the whole of East Africa. No doubt it would be a five-star experience, but the people with political influence would be first in line for any required treatment. The care and patient support would no doubt be as good as money could buy and yes, these days Eng. M. J. R. Tembo could afford it. However, Eng. M. J. R. Tembo had never in his life ever been involved with any politician, political party or politics, full stop. Dubai was the place he needed to be for his treatment to give him the best chance of living a long life. TT was so glad he could be in Dubai, to be there to support his beloved Baba. The tables had turned, his beloved Baba needed TT for the first time in his life. TT prayed that His beloved Baba would firstly recover, then retire, returning home to Kenya, possibly to his village, where ever that was, and there enjoy his old age with his tribes' people around him.

'*Matatanisho*' once more crept in as TT debated with himself. But in the end, he felt that taking a bank loan at this time was the right thing to do to start a new business venture. He'd not use the cash he had sitting in his account at this stage as debt was relatively cheap and easy to obtain. Was it not the case that even the President of the United States took a loan for his business? Why should money stop TT getting what he wanted to allow him to follow his dreams in photography? After all, he asked himself not for the first time, what possibly could go wrong? Why should TT worry about things that may never happen? He expected to turn the loan into making him money and if it did not work out, he'd benefit from learning from his mistakes. Eng. M. J. R. Tembo had drummed into TT that not all debt was bad, in fact if debt made you money it was good debt! 'Thanks, mzee,' TT thought 'I am taking to heart a little bit of wisdom you invested in me at our camp fire talks in the African bush. As you told me time and again, in life do something you have a passion for, that you enjoy, that as a result you are good at, that will not seem like work, success will come and the rewards will follow.' His beloved Baba's advice was to chase the money as the basis for a career, a profession, work, income or whatever label you wish to put on how you'll spend the biggest part of your productive life. At last, after all these years TT felt he would be following his passion and not being led by a woman he had a passion for.

Eng. M. J. R. Tembo had also told his mtoto not to count his chickens before they hatched. What possibly could go wrong he asked himself one more time, just see how wealthy the President of the United States became on borrowed money! TT, was not going to spend precious hours fearing or celebrating the inevitable; 'what will be will be.' He was going to use his time wisely, cherishing the precious time he had left with his beloved Baba and making the most he could out of the rest of his life. He felt happy that he was doing the right things and no longer following the money. To be happy was a decision made; TT felt good about where his life was going.

He spoke aloud to himself, 'photography helped me to see a world I couldn't have imagined with my own eyes. That is my true passion, not manufacturing, not real estate, not fitness and health and to be completely honest with myself, not making money. Part of that passion is to look for opportunities to be creative and to take photographs in places I would have never dreamt of venturing if I'd not taken up photography. I never go anywhere without my camera. If my camera is not with me then I am not going. Around thirty years of practicing photography from when I was a toddler, and today still always learning on every shoot. I love the fact that it's a skill that you only get better and better at as you practise. But then comes along 'Matatanisho' as many times I genuinely go on adventures just to take videos, those times I don't do so much photography, these days I lean more towards videos than still photography. But then do I become Africa's second-best photographer as my beloved Baba christened me or follow my heart and become Africa's second-best Film maker, or maybe do both?

That bank loan helped TT buy all the top-quality tools for his art to be further developed into a business. Since his shopping spree, the tools and equipment took up most of the living space in his large bedroom on the Palm. It was 35 centigrade in the shade, far too warm to venture out to have fun with all his new kit taking photographs and making movies in the desert. TT sat in his bedroom and he gazed at the mountain of equipment strewn around his room and wondered how Trixie would work her magic when it came to tidying his room. Two drones, a Diji drone phantom 4 Pro cost $1,500, it was the big one for professional work and the Mavic Air 2 drone cost $1,000 and was smaller for travel work. An A7Riii high resolution camera along with an A9 camera with 20 frame per second for photographing sports and the wildlife of Kenya and maybe other African countries in the future. Lenses from 17mm to 200mm, with the 70 to 200 mm 2.8 being the most expensive Sony G master lens, it was top of the range with an asking price of $2,000. This one would be ideal for sports, wildlife and weddings. It was the one lens every photographer wants and it's the first time, other than hiring short term, TT would be using such a prize of his own. The other lenses included a 50mm 1.4, 35mm 1.4, 17mm to 28m 2.8 and 28mm to 75mm 2.8 coming to a further $6,000. TT added a GoPro 7 action camera to fix to an off-road bike or himself for close up or action shots. With the Sony Handycam camcorder full HD, TT's camera budget crept above $7,000.

Filters were another essential item to add to the total price tag. TT took lots of scenery shots and used neutral density filters for this to slow his shutter speed down, this made the sky and water look blurred, flowing naturally. TT did not know how best to describe this, but it was a signature effect of his. If ever asked about them, he would recommend the neutral density filter as a tool for almost every photographer's camera bag. But in his experience, they were something that many people taking photographs found mysterious, and just did not understand how to make the most of them. The different manufacturers added to 'Matatanisho' by giving different names to the filters. During one of his regular meditation sessions, it came to him that these filters were just like sun glasses for his camera lens but they did not change the colours unlike sun glasses, they just neutralised bright light, let less light through the lens. With less light coming in he could slow the shutter for a given aperture setting. But the secret was to use them with a tripod to avoid movement blurring the photograph. The filters were useful to emphasise movement. He'd used them for taking shots of waterfalls, traffic, seascapes, rivers, clouds, smoke, streams and even moving people but of course no portraits.

The lighting equipment cost a further $1,600 and this included the money for the Godox 600 pro flash. TT knew this was a sound investment in his future, in his opinion the best money he had ever invested in a business. It was easy to obtain a bank loan today so he did not want to put this off until tomorrow and risk his future. 'Okay, life and business decisions are not that straight forward.' he had learnt the hard way and a little bit of 'Matatanisho' once again crept into his thinking. Maybe buying the best golf clubs available every season does not make you the best golfer who ever lived? Possibly using last season's clubs and investing in lessons would prove more rewarding to most amateur weekend golfers!

It was a good point he made to himself but golf is a completely different situation and lessons in camera work were not for TT. He would not benefit further unlike the weekend golfer. For TT was already a master of his art though maybe not the equivalent of Tiger Woods in the golf world admittedly. However, TT's passion was photography and it was not just a pastime but a real passion.

TT smiled and felt good about the decision to invest in his art. Wow, TT had the latest and best equipment any photographer needed. All was good in his business world except that he would need to be patient, as enough income would come to pay off the loan from his future photography business. The credit cards on reaching their maximum limit were no longer on his side, so he needed to earn some income. Short term he decided to use those social media experiences in health and fitness to get clients and work at his photography and film business as the loan payments came due.

One morning TT went to his beloved Baba's recovery room, no one dared call it the sick room; this previously had been the main guest bedroom and it was selected for the recovery room since it was on the ground floor to make life easier for everyone concerned. Trixie cosseted Eng. M. J. R. Tembo, and the maid's quarters were very close to the guest bedroom. Trixie was an angel, god sent, very much appreciated by TT and Eng. M. J. R. Tembo. She was at the beck and call of Eng. M. J. R. Tembo 24/7. However, of late it had become TT's habit to be last to see his beloved Baba drop off at night and first to see his beloved Baba each day. Once the new sun drove away the darkness of the night, the Kahawa Chungu was made ready by Trixie and prepared in the way that TT had instructed her. Each morning it had become his habit to take the traditionally made coffee to his beloved Baba and they would greet the new day together.

TT had a sudden shock and dropped the tray with the blackened brass kettle along with the rest of its contents. Two fine white china cups lay smashed on the ceramic floor tiles and the brown sugar was spread around them while a dark liquid poured out of the brass kettle. The priceless fine Persian rug on the floor next to his beloved Baba's bed, sucked up the liquid mess. TT noticed none of this as he found his beloved Baba dead in his bed. He was at rest with his eyes open and a peaceful look on his grey face and a woollen scarf pulled over his bald head. The shock of his beloved Baba's sudden death was bad enough, but the trauma that followed in getting through all the legal and administration tasks would test TT to his very limits.

Surely no one else could be better prepared than Eng. M. J. R. Tembo; he was expecting his death to come soon. He had prepared a flash-drive to guide his mtoto in the early days following his death and provided the key to his safe with cash for both TT and some for Trixie. All the documents needed were there, like his last Will and testament, the house registration, vehicle documents, bank details, all his financial cards, his investment portfolio file, passport, birth certificate, his wedding certificate, the death certificate of his mama, her out of date passport from many years ago, insurance papers, statements, receipts, warranties, cheque books, his business ownership papers, his collection of business cards, his membership cards; you could safely say it was every document that needed to be there and more. This was all arranged in order to make things easier for TT in these few days when he would be in shock. The brown envelope he had put out every night and taken back early every morning for the last three weeks, today it lay next to his body. It was addressed simply, Titus Tembo, Heir to Eng. M. J. R. Tembo. On his death bed Eng. M. J. R. Tembo knew little of what TT had done recently and his plan to fulfil his dreams of being a professional photographer. He had hoped and prayed that TT would eventually find and follow his passion. He did not expect him to pick up the reins of his eco business.

His beloved Baba had spoken on the eve of his death, 'You are good with people, you like to tell a story or two, travel is in your blood, you will be dead one day soon enough, so do not leave things until tomorrow that you can do today.' Those last words were not like playing a musical instrument to a goat. Eng. M. J. R. Tembo expected his Mtoto to mull this over, and possibly come up with a plan that would bring him satisfaction and happiness when he, Eng. M. J. R. Tembo was no longer there to advise and support TT. And these last words from his beloved Baba convinced TT he was on the right track as with the vision of putting his camera to work at home in Africa. After glancing through the pile of documents left for him by his beloved Baba, TT eventually turned to investigate what was on the flash-drive.

With the death of his beloved Baba, it dawned on TT that there was no extended family he was aware of, he never knew the village of his father in northern Kenya or that of his mother in South Wales. He could not recall ever visiting either his mother's or his beloved Baba's villages. Possibly he was there as a child but those memories were not accessible. TT faced the prospect of being alone for the first time in his life. He was not sure how he felt about being truly alone? TT was a little anxious, how would he handle the death of his beloved Baba? Once all the practical arrangements had been completed, would his beloved Baba always be with him in spirit? First things first. TT was to check the safe and that flash-drive. His mind was wandering once again, after taking care of the matters related to the death of his beloved Baba, and to add to his anxiousness, TT would need to clear all his debts. All this to do in the United Arab Emirates before he'd be able to travel and to take photographs or make movies in his beloved Africa; but rest assured Africa, TT expected he would be there once the formalities were all done! But it could not be just yet. TT had no idea what practical challenges were to be served up with the death of Eng. M. J. R. Tembo in Dubai. Little did he know at that time that the flash-drive and the contents of the safe would be such a great help.

How would Titus Tembo go about reporting the sudden death of his beloved Baba? TT's common sense won out when he called the police on 999. He had simply informed them, and before long the police were filling out an initial death report and they arranged the removal of the body of Eng. M. J. R. Tembo, first to the government morgue before it was even cold. The death certificate declaration was stamped by the police and they issued TT a no objection certificate; why? thought TT. In fact, TT in certain circumstances required a further no objection certificate to release the body for embalming at the mortuary. TT considered what his Baba wanted for his body but just in case, if he would need to convey the body home, what documents did he need? There was also the question to consider, where exactly was home for his beloved Baba's body to be put to rest or good use? Titus Tembo still did not have the death certificate! It was the case that TT had to produce the police no objection certificate to get the official death certificate. With this certificate in hand TT headed for Jumeirah 2, turning off Al Wasl Road, to 15 Street, he parked outside Villa 5 where the Kenyan flag fluttered in the strong warm sea breeze. It was a very relaxed location unlike Government buildings of this nature in Nairobi where TT had experienced armed police questioning him on his approach for any matter in hand like a simple passport renewal. Just inside the gate he was greeted by a group of Kenyan ladies sitting on the grass, all chatting in the Luo language as if sharing the tales of their Lake Victoria village. Directly ahead, some fancy Kenyan Government cars were parked in the shade next to an expensive looking three-story villa. A well-dressed chauffeur, polished what TT assumed was the Consular General's car. The previous Consular General was a man Eng. M. J. R. Tembo knew as his friend.   TT was introduced to this gentleman at his beloved Baba's Jumeirah Palm Villa on one balmy evening not so long ago. TT immediately recognised the same black HSE Range Rover that just a few months ago parked in Eng. M. J. R. Tembo's driveway. However, today TT was no longer well placed to use the name of the new Consular General for any special assistance he may need.

Just to his right a short flight of steps led straight into a disorganized room with a few uncomfortable seats fixed against the wall either side of the entrance door. To the left another door led to a waiting room. The two civil servants dealing with enquiries sat comfortably some distance away at their desks protected by a counter that several people crowded around. Well only one civil servant was actually on duty, as the second desk was deserted despite the crowd of citizens needing assistance. TT joined the kundi and eventually the civil servant exchanged some typical Kenyan pleasantries with him before a hand shake, and sent him off to the main villa to see the assistant Consulate General.

Everything seemed clear cut on the death of an expatriate with regards further formalities. Deceased expatriates may be cremated or buried in the United Arab Emirates or their bodies may be sent to their home countries on showing the requisite documents. No mention was made of the arrangements in the case of organ donations or for that matter any wishes of the deceased. For his beloved Baba to be flown back to Kenya, TT needed the death certificate translated into Arabic and duly attested in the courts. He also needed yet another no objection certificate, this time from the embassy, which is based in Abu Dhabi. The Kenyan embassy would cancel the passport of Eng. M. J. R. Tembo and register the death in Nairobi.

The fact was, that just like any Kenyan's death in the United Arab Emirates, the concerned United Arab Emirates applicable authority had already sent a message to the Kenyan Embassy in order to confiscate the passport. Not only that, they had also sent messages to the local banks around the same time. All the bank accounts of Eng. M. J. R. Tembo deceased had been frozen. Sharia Law, the law of the land, was now being carried out, and no other law in the world would take precedence over it, in fact it was very straight forward; but without a Will, TT was informed he could be in real trouble that could take years to sort out.

TT decided there was no need to contact a lawyer for advice until he had gone through the flash-drive and the documents in the safe at least one more time. Eng. M. J. R. Tembo had left a mini-bible of advice for his son on that flash-drive and enough funds to assist him to live comfortably until his inheritance was released by the courts in Dubai. Not enough cash at this stage, however, to fund paying off the latest debt incurred by TT. The facts were that on his death bed Eng. M. J. R. Tembo was not aware of the loan TT had committed to for a new business venture. The advice provided was so comprehensive there was also a number for 'bereavement counselling', but fortunately for TT there was no response when he called. TT needed something for peace of mind and he turned to his regular transcendental meditation.

TT's strength came from him being part of the wood element, one of being a lifelong student in always looking for ways to improve himself. As such TT was destined to cross the path of Maharishi Mahesh Yogi at some time. Young as he was, TT loved the Beatles music first heard when his beloved Baba played them during the evenings when TT was still a child. TT particularly liked listening to the double White Album when he believed the Beatles were at their most creative. 'Dear Susan' would not come out to play with John Lennon when they were in India learning the gifts of transcendental meditation. She locked herself in her room until the time for food or learning came around. His other favourite album of his beloved Beatles music also came to mind, 'Whisper Words of Wisdom Let It Be Let It Be.' This was possible reference to the mantra practiced in what TT saw as the silent meditation of the 'Matatanisho' of his mind or for that matter anyone's mind, during transcendental meditation. His beloved Baba led TT to believe that up to today, Paul and family, along with Ringo and family, remain dedicated transcendental meditation practitioners. Eng. M. J. R. Tembo had told TT, he would know when he was ready for transcendental meditation and TT felt this was his time to take it further with some checking of his mantra and possibly some advance classes.

TT, had paid his $1,000, or rather his Baba had given him the money to pay and he had taken the very simple two-day meditation training course back in his homeland. He was given his mantra but wanted to check that all was okay with his meditation as he'd not been involved with group meditation - only his Baba these last few years. There was not much to the training he thought at the time. Just twenty minutes meditation alone or with others, first thing in the morning and the same repeated late afternoon. By god, at the time he thought he and his Baba had been ripped off- a $1,000 fee for what? As he drove away from his first transcendental meditation class, he left feeling a little strange or was it just a little different? He felt more relaxed, not angry at the crazy driving on the Kenyan roads. Next day TT realized, on driving away from the second day of training, this so simple technique was easy to apply. Just like many other meditation techniques he had tried, many of those cool people claimed they experience something unique during meditation, once again TT had no special experience on meditating. What transcendental meditation gave TT was results, he was released from his anxious feelings inside, it centred his thinking and suddenly he was not stressed by the challenges he faced. With the death of his beloved Baba, he needed reassurance and visited the centre of transcendental meditation in Dubai.

TT started to read the advice on the flash-drive his beloved Baba had left him for guidance. Eng. M. J. R. Tembo had written his last Will and Testament based on English and Welsh law which he saw as the most reliable legal system available to him. It had been translated into Arabic and notarized in the Dubai courts. It could go through the courts in the United Arab Emirates without TT being involved. As far as he was aware, TT as the only male relative was assured that Sharia law would serve him well. The plain fact was that probate would take up to six months for any United Arab Emirates asset, whatever documents were in place or not in place. All the United Arab Emirates assets of the deceased are frozen and only released on advice of the court. Eng. M. J. R. Tembo's biggest asset was his house on the Palm or maybe the value of his business. But there were also other assets, his bank account including investments, that bank account that TT had used via the ATM card provided by his beloved Baba, was no longer available, his car, off road jeep, his motor bike, his small fishing boat were all impounded. TT had nothing from his beloved Baba that he could as yet call his own, just the small car his beloved Baba had bought him and put in his name as owner plus a nice amount of cash that Eng. M. J. R. Tembo had included in the safe under Titus Tembo's name in a brown envelope just before he knew his own life was coming to an end. There was even a question mark over where TT would live. As for Trixie, Eng. M. J. R. Tembo left her a sealed envelope in the safe that TT handed to her. She seemed very happy and enquired would TT need her services any longer as she intended to return to the Philippines as soon as she could, to live off the small fortune in cash she was given by Eng. M. J. R. Tembo. She saw no need to work any longer in Dubai and could soon be with her two young girls. The only thing holding her back at this time was her visit to her twin sister based in the Northern Emirates; her name was also Trixie. They were identical twins so their father thought it easier they have the same first Christian name not to cause anyone embarrassment when they mixed up the two girls' identities.

TT did his twenty minutes meditation regularly twice a day as instructed by the transcendental meditation course tutor from Dubai. From the tutor he'd been advised to try to meditate in the same place at the same time each day. Furthermore, not to worry about the time and checking it was twenty minutes exactly. He understood that even on sleeping for a full eight hours he seemed to be refreshed further by this short twenty-minute morning meditation session. During the first week of practice following his visit to the centre in Dubai, one day TT dozed off for an hour while undertaking his morning meditation. Had he transcended, who knows? He was no longer stressed - after all he had his investor's visa; he did not have to leave within 30 days, unlike the case if he was on his beloved Baba's sponsorship. Indeed, he just had to survive on the cash he gained from the sale of his fitness for life business and the cash his beloved Baba left him whilst the probate was completed. His own cash as it stood was insufficient for the photography business which included paying off the loan he taken only recently. He assumed he would inherit the local assets to at least clear his debts in the United Arab Emirates and pay for his flight home with all his new photography gear to Nairobi and onward to the rest of Kenya, then the continent was his to explore with his new camera equipment. There was only one stipulation in the Will, that TT knew about in advance of its reading, he had been told by his beloved Baba, the need to find a good cause in Kenya and share his new found wealth in helping that good cause.

CHAPTER EIGHT

Long term memories

TT looked through the contents of the flash-drive. Eng. M. J. R. Tembo had made sure the first file on the list was a selfie video, albeit of short duration it was his beloved Baba speaking to him from beyond the grave. It was sad but yet pleasing, relaxing him and making him feel happy inside, close to his beloved Baba one last time, it was typical of his beloved Baba in life and now beyond the grave, via the wonder of a video on his MacBook Air.

'Titus, do not cry for me as I am in a good place; I want to see you smiling and I want to hear you laughing. My Mtoto please promise me that you will dedicate yourself to living and love life. I am your example that we will all be dead one day, whatever befalls us. Above all my Mtoto, be honest, and kind. Firstly, honest and kind to yourself. Be honest, work hard, give value for money and never put off for tomorrow what you can do today. Remember if your plane goes down, and you do not climb in that life boat first, how can you help save the rest of the people floundering in the seas! Be honest with yourself in all you do and generous of spirit. Remember my Mtoto, the more you give out, the more that comes back to you. Learn from your past but do not worry about it and the same for your future, prepare for your future but do not worry about a future that may never happen. Live with honesty and kindness in the present. You remember our ninety ten rule my Mtoto, learn to react correctly, and you'll never spoil a day in your whole life. Accept that ten percent of your life you cannot control, but remember ninety percent of events turn out the way you would like, as a result of how you react to the ten percent you cannot control. It is simple my Mtoto, you cannot control that Dubai traffic, you cannot avoid my death, you cannot change the weather, ensure you control your reactions to these things you cannot control.   Finally, please do not forget one of the most important lessons I taught you in life. Take it to heart in all your business dealings. Make sure you do something you have a passion for, you will enjoy what you are doing, it will never feel like work, you'll be good at it and you will be successful; do not follow the money as the

money in the end will follow you. Before I close this video let me remind you to check through the guidance documents I saved in order on this flash-drive. The papers in the safe are to be presented to my lawyer who will be in touch. The money I left use wisely. Please do with my body what you think is best. Remember my Moto I will always be here looking down proudly on all you do. Good bye, good luck and no need to worry. I love you my Mtoto'

His beloved Baba had provided a wad of cash to see TT through until probate was completed. He had his own bank account, so there was no need to hide this pile of notes under his mattress or buy a safe to hold it. Wherever he stored the money, he would have to be frugal in the way he spent it, and be sensible in managing all the money in-hand -assuming it would have to last him six months. Titus Tembo felt he could just about make it through the next six months without any other income. In fact, over the next few months he expected to earn some money through his photography and video work. In the case of injury or sickness his beloved Baba had paid for health insurance. Titus Tembo had a little car of recent vintage in good condition. TT had all that camera gear that would almost fill his car when he needed to move it, this he would need to do shortly, to relocate somewhere in the United Arab Emirates. What TT badly needed now was a plan of action, a 'To-Do' list, as the authorities had requested him to move out of the Palm Island house by the end of the month.

The second file on the flash-drive was related to a handful of people who could be of help. Well, Titus Tembo certainly needed help at that time. TT was on his own, days away from nowhere to live and he had yet to face up to what he would do as regards his beloved Baba's body and the funeral. With regards to where to live, one issue was the price to rent in Dubai was much too high for TT's budget. That was a concern, but what was the alternative? The first name was that of the Kenyan Consul General in Dubai, well, he was the man in charge up to three weeks ago. The name of the previous Consul General in Dubai he would not follow up with as TT decided he would not be of much use helping in Dubai from wherever he had relocated. Disappointed, TT reviewed who was up next. From the notes TT felt like the name of Mr. Robert Joramogi was God sent. He read that this was an old friend of his beloved Baba from his days in Cardiff University. Mr. Robert Joramogi lived in the Northern Emirates and it appeared he was a long-term resident and, wow he had married a mzungu who had been a friend of TT's mother. This fellow Kenyan may yet come to his rescue, thought TT.

On calling the mobile phone number provided on the flash-drive, TT was pleased to hear the friendly welcoming voice on the other end. 'Tell me' was the response on the phone, a cold statement to an English ear, but not in fact a cold statement to him, it is a throwback to a standard welcome used in Kenya. Robert Joramogi had been prepared for such a call from Eng. M. J. R. Tembo's son. There was a letter from his very old friend Eng. M. J. R. Tembo posted on the back of his front door that he saw every day these last two weeks or so. When he arrived, Titus Tembo would discover this fact for himself and very quickly the reason behind this unusual behaviour of pinning up such a letter in such a place.

Earlier that evening, after his twenty minutes meditation, TT headed north toward one of the seven Emirates which he'd never visited previously and as of now could not even pronounce the name, Ras al-Khaimah. It was a pleasant enough drive once he got through the tangle of rush hour traffic heading from Dubai to Sharjah. As soon as TT and his little silver car passed Mirdiff City Centre, another of the giant Dubai malls, he merged his car on to Tripoli Street with its three lanes of very light traffic. There was no rush as Mr. Robert Joramogi would provide Titus Tembo, son of Eng. M. J. R. Tembo with traditional Kenyan hospitality and a bed for that night at least. His beloved Baba had detailed that Mr. Robert Joramogi was divorced, and as such TT expected some advice from his beloved Baba's friend about living on his own.

TT hit some heavy traffic on the by-pass road and looked around to try and figure out exactly where he was; just over the Dubai boarder in Sharjah he guessed, as the speed limit was different? To the right of his silver Mini Cooper S, stood a magnificent piece of architecture. A Muslim place of prayer, an untypical Sunni mosque that looked like it could accommodate the majority of the male population from any one of the individual Seven Emirates! TT was not sure how it would measure up to the big mosque in Mecca but certainly it was a more modern building and he was pleasantly surprised with the colourful, attractive exterior.

With the moon and the sun in the sky at the same time, it was too tempting a picture to ignore. With time on his side to spare, TT pulled off onto a desert road, next to a red painted metal barrier running around a camel race track. From where TT parked up, the giant place of prayer was looking good, but behind him the roaring of the eight lanes of busy rush hour traffic detracted from the relaxed atmosphere.   TT put his camera down on the passenger seat; he decided for now to leave this photographic opportunity for another day when the time was a little more auspicious and he did not have to contend with the heavy traffic disturbing his thinking process. That was just the first stop as TT slowed down and pulled over once more to watch the red sun dip majestically below the tall sand dunes. In the dark TT was now just blindly following the directions spoken to him in an American accent by his latest iPhone.   The latter part of his journey now saw TT and the little silver car work its way towards its destination on an old road running parallel to a sparkling ocean. The street lights were dull but there was a full-moon, and it reflected off the waves breaking the ocean surface.

Another hour would pass as TT parked up near the beach. He leaned against his car and checked out the views around him. He put his camera on manual mode, dug his tripod out of the pile of equipment that littered the passenger seat of his car. He set his aperture as low as it could go. Then he set the shutter speed to 10 seconds although unlike the day shots the shutter speed was the last thing he worried about. Finally, TT set the camera at a low ISO of 1600 in order to further offset the digital noise. Night photography opened up a different world for him. The darkness for TT turned places that seemed rather pedestrian during the day into some stellar and exotic subjects at night.

Titus Tembo was enjoying the possibilities the outside venue offered his camera at this time of night. TT the artist, was taking more time than he would during the day, there was no one around and he did not have to worry about the light changing. His main challenge was getting the proper exposure and he avoided digital noise through the use of his tripod and a remote shutter release. On departing from Dubai, TT had no plan to take photographs in the dark that evening and so brought no flashlight with him. It was not a big problem however; he knew his camera so well he made changes to the settings without seeing everything. From his frequent times of shooting in the bush at night, TT decided once again to shoot in raw format. This allowed his camera to better capture the large dark portion of colours. The photographs of the modern pyramid type structures on their island location were well worth the one-hour or so delay in his estimated time of arrival at Mr. Robert Joramogi's place.

It was just after eight-thirty when TT pulled up in his little silver Mini Cooper S, at one of the Al Hamra Village security gates. In their earlier discussion over the phone, Mr. Robert Joramogi had prepared him for this encounter, and the fact the security men could appear difficult or could be helpful depending who was on duty. It was his lucky night as the African on duty was a Kenyan, and waved him through with a big grin once he heard TT was heading for Royal Breeze two, to visit Mr. Robert Joramogi. TT had lived on the world-famous Jumeriah Palm, and so had become accustomed to spectacular up market environments. Yet tonight TT once again was a little taken aback by the fact that several mini type sky scrapers stood and guarded a well laid out complex of gardens, and Villas, that TT would not think of as a typical village!

There was a place for TT to park his Mini Cooper S in front of Royal Breeze two, but he requested the Nigerian man on security duty to allow him to park under cover so he could protect his photographic equipment from the harsh sun come morning. Much to his relief, once again the mention of Mr. Robert Joramogi's name worked its magic. It was expensive equipment but unlike his own capital city in Kenya, he had no fear of anyone taking another person's property without permission in this part of the world. Was everyone so honest here because it was a Muslim country, or were, they so fearful they may get caught, go to court, spend some unpleasant time behind bars and forever lose their livelihood in the United Arab Emirates. Titus Tembo was not sure if the true answer really would ever be known, but it seemed the zero-tolerance policy towards criminals was working? Whatever the answer, rest assured you can feel very safe in the United Arab Emirates at all times.

TT took his suitcase from the small boot of the car and wandered to the lifts without warning his host he'd be with him in a matter of a few minutes. Thus, Mr. Robert Joramogi answered the door with a steam iron in one hand and a large grey cat stepped out into the hallway making itself heard. It seemed that his host was not really ready for TT even though he was arriving later than expected. In fact, Mr. Robert Joramogi seemed a bit puzzled at TT's arrival and looked further shocked at the suitcase he carried! Nevertheless, he soon recovered once he glanced at something behind the front door of the apartment. 'Welcome my friend, son of Eng. M. J. R. Tembo, do come through and let me take that suitcase from you. And Pat, not so much noise please, in you come boy' he advised Pat. TT had never owned a cat but he was immediately taking a liking to this talkative and friendly large grey tom.

Wow what would my old head teacher who also taught us English, Ms. Akinyi, say if she was here now? Ms. Akinyi was always well organized and planned ahead. Ms. Akinyi was named after being born early in the morning and lived up to her name, always up early and ready to face the day ahead. That Ms. Akinyi, who made us carry sticks to school so she could cane us if we were late. The same Ms. Akinyi who made us carry dry cow dung to school during the winter as fuel, just in case we needed a fire to keep us warm during break time. Yes Ms. Akinyi was always the one who was organized and well prepared. She marked the head of any unruly child with a white chalk cross. It's something you can do on African hair but while in Europe Titus Tembo's experiences were more of teachers throwing the chalk at the offender! The African system proved much more effective in controlling poorly behaved kids as the chalk mark had other benefits, to the teachers anyway, on marking the badly-behaved child for the day, and forcing them to shower before their parents saw the cross on them when returning home and caned their child. That dear Ms. Akinyi had a big impact not only on Titus Tembo's English but his good manners and his organizational skills which were all still evident today.

That lady was so busy teaching children that she never had time to produce her own brood. If she were here right now, I suspect her words would be, 'Well done Mr. Robert Joramogi, I like it very much, 'spic and span', neat, clean, well looked after and organized.' Looking at this place, Mr. Robert Joramogi must have a super maid, surmised Titus Tembo. But he pondered what it was with all the papers and notes stuck behind the entrance door? On first impressions very out of place with the rest of the apartment? Other questions came to mind. Why is Mr. Robert Joramogi carrying a steam iron and why is the ironing board out for use at this time of night along with the hangers, as well as a small pile of creased shirts in the lounge? Maybe Mr. Robert Joramogi had his super maid living in and she worked odd hours?

With a big smile and a strong handshake, Mr. Robert Joramogi was eventually welcoming Titus Tembo son of Eng. M. J. R. Tembo as at last it dawned on him who he was and he slowly realized Titus Tembo, son of Eng. M. J. R. Tembo was his house guest for the night, and he was just an hour or two later than the planned arrival time. 'Welcome my brother, son of Eng. M. J. R. Tembo, please excuse 'Manchester United.' he clearly likes you very much as he is not talkative like this with everyone. And do not worry, he is cleaner than clean can be as I washed him in honour of you coming and he only goes out of the apartment when I walk him. And walks for me are not so frequent these days. I gave him his full name 'Manchester United' as his previous owner, like me, is a big fan of the Red Devils. I call him Pat as it's simpler and it reminds me of that great Irish goal keeper Dunne. He played under Matt Busby you know, kept us ahead of Leeds United to win the Championship back in the sixties. I can vividly recall how Pat Dunne made the difference between us and the opposition in several games towards the middle of the season, when the muddy fields bogged down our great forward line. Dunne was the difference indeed; we can thank him time and again when we took the two points for a win. Pat, the cat that is, is getting on a bit but is still good company. He still plays a good game in goals when I test him out with a table tennis ball. I am not sure how I'd survive on my own without Pat to talk to?

That is enough talk from me for now, please come in and let me show you round my small place.' Pat followed behind them, he rushed forward occasionally and rubbed against TT's legs and made strange noises of contentment. Clearly, he enjoyed the company of Titus Tembo for some unknown reason! The feeling was mutual as TT immediately took a liking to Pat the cat. It was not such a small place and TT was led into a spacious bedroom with two single beds and its own bathroom leading off to the right. The bathroom housed twin sinks, a bidet, toilet, a power shower, a full-length mirror and plenty of built-in cupboard space to meet the demands of any woman. Mr. Robert Joramogi placed Titus Tembo's suitcase next to the double wardrobe, offered TT a set of white fluffy towels and a large white bathrobe plus perfectly fitting, matching white slippers for his exclusive use when he was staying with Mr. Robert Joramogi.

Mr. Robert Joramogi spoke at length as he left the bedroom as if he had pressing important matters to get off his chest, 'I just need to finish pressing my shirts and washing the dishes before preparing a late, light dinner for you and me. I do find all these domestic chores therapeutic and that with Pat around it keeps the loneliness at bay. One of these days I will permanently return to my village near the lake in Northern Kenya or to my other village home in the Valleys and be with my grandchildren in Wales. It's a decision I keep on putting off as I love this environment that I've experienced for the last eighteen years. It's a joy to relax in this ark of safety, isolated from some of the more unpleasant developments in Western society and modern Kenyan city life - like bad manners, disrespect of elders and disbelief in a greater being. Everything works so well here, in the village and everywhere else I go, I can honestly say the places are clean, well-organized, the locals are very helpful and friendly once you get to understand that old fashioned behaviour is the best way to get what you need. Even the weather here for me is an attraction when you consider God loves Wales so much, he (or she?) washes down the whole country most days. The sheep there looked to me like the cleanest in the world. No wonder there is not enough rain left over to make Northern Kenya green! Global warming means less predictable rains; during those dry times, the wealth of its people, their cattle, suffer and people go hungry. As a child I clearly remember the cows were healthy and fat, that we grew enough food to share with anybody who visited our village, but today it is not the case.

Here in those very hot and humid summer months it's a perfect time to do my duty of visiting my home villages, relatives, friends, and share the benefits I experienced in life with the less fortunate. Sadly, I admit that one day my old age, possibly poor health and failing short term memory will bring that decision of settling away from this village and the United Arab Emirates to the fore soon enough. The good thing is when I decide to permanently leave my Middle East home, I will remember everything about my two home villages be it the one in the United Arab Emirates or the one in the Welsh valleys. All my past from many years ago is a clear memory to me and then the homesickness will be for the United Arab Emirates and Wales rather than Wales and Kenya as it is today.'

There was a strange ringing sound and to the amazement of Titus Tembo, Mr. Robert Joramogi responded by answering his antique like clam shell mobile! Gosh, thought TT, the old chap does not even have a smart phone! It was just a call back from the local grocery store to see if they could change part of his order for the morning. 'Sorry for the interruption son of Eng. M. J. R. Tembo, but I prefer my groceries delivered as I no longer drive in the United Arab Emirates, and If I walk to the shop, by the time I arrive I forget what I needed. I write everything down and pin it behind the front door to remind me of what I must do and when. It is very strange that I recall the littlest details from many years ago but if I put my phone down and it can take me some time to find it again! Seems like my short-term memory is playing up just a little.'

So, no maid, TT thought Mr. Robert Joramogi is not paying to create time but using time to save money, or was he genuinely lonely and filling his days with domestic chores? On top of this, an ancient mobile and no car indicated to TT wrongly that Mr. Robert Joramogi was not a wealthy man. In fact, he was the opposite of a 'chizungu', acting like a poor man yet Mr. Robert Joramogi was indeed very well off with his pension from his long-term employers in the United Arab Emirates and his investments guarded against tax in an off shore account. He had been sensible with his money all these years, struggled a bit during the divorce but still managed to buy his property in the Emirates and build his small home on the plot of land he inherited in his Kenyan village. His ex-wife reaped the benefit of her investment in the early days of their marriage. She had a lovely home in the Swansea Valley near the grandkids, her very elderly mother, younger brother and other extended family members. In cultural family terms, Titus Tembo saw the Welsh lady appearing to be more of an African than the one she married!

Over a home-made dinner, Mr. Robert Joramogi seemed desperate to tell Titus Tembo how all these years he had felt guilty over his divorce. Instead of TT pouring out his heart-felt regrets as he had expected and getting advice from the more experienced man, it would be the other way around at least for this first evening together. Possibly the younger man may have to offer his support to the elder statesman.

Both Mr. Robert Joramogi and Eng. M. J. R. Tembo met their future wives when at University in Wales. Eng. M. J. R. Tembo moved back to Africa with his wife once he completed his postgraduate training at the South Wales Electricity Board. Mr. Robert Joramogi on the other hand took a different route. He stayed on in the United Kingdom after graduating in arts, got started on a career with British Airways, won the right to his British Passport and brought a boy and girl into the world before his itchy feet saw him make a radical change in his life. To everyone's amazement accept his own, Mr. Robert Joramogi left the United Kingdom for Dubai just as everything seemed so settled in his career and his home life. That was the whole point, settled at too young an age, no challenge, work his way up the organisation, pay off his mortgage and then retire on a small pension; he wanted much more than this.

He was happy with the way it turned out and regretted very little other than whether he had done his duty by his family. The kids turned out okay and his ex-wife had eventually forgiven him, but not forgotten that he left her with two kids to bring up alone. Robert Joramogi appeared happy about how it turned out and clearly was more concerned about his future than his past. The visit was not going according to plan as Titus Tembo used the advice of his beloved Baba to be kind to Mr. Robert Joramogi, who seemed in greater need for his empathy rather than the other way around!

All those years ago my beloved Baba's friend put himself first and left his family in the United Kingdom to pursue a more exciting career in the budding Dubai aviation industry. His ex-wife may have forgiven him after many years, but never forgot the predicament he left her in as she could not come out at that time and later would not live among the Arabs who she saw as untrustworthy. Mr. Robert Joramogi told Titus Tembo that both kids still loved and depended on their father despite them reaching their own adulthood and one of them having two children of his own. He insisted, despite what his ex-wife thought, that he had continued to do his duties as a father in supporting them as best he could from a distance for all these years. He even assisted his Disk Jockey daughter with her music career as best he could, despite his ignorance of modern Western Music.

Mr. Robert Joramogi explained to Titus Tembo that his father, Eng. M. J. R. Tembo understood him better than he understood himself. From when they first met in Cardiff at the University of Wales Institution of Science and Technology, that everyone in the know called UWIST, your father referred to my situation as my '*Matatanisho.*' It is a word that fails to translate fully into English but it's a cross I carry and I learnt to live with it. My ex-wife in Wales described it in her language as '*Hiraeth*'. She empathised at first as I was a Kenyan in a foreign land in so many ways. Yes, so strange a place, that is what it was and despite it, I lived a happy life, just different from many of my peers. For me I have come to understand it is more a feeling or sense of alienation and loss born of distance and estrangement wherever I am. Put simply by some people who do not understand let alone have experienced '*Matatanisho*' or '*Hiraeth*', as my itchy feet; they miss the point completely.

Now TT understood more fully why his beloved Baba had brought him to this man, as Mr. Robert Joramogi spoke about their inner feelings. It's a lack of clarity in what you want, a homesickness for a home to which you cannot or do not want to return, a home which maybe never was, a nostalgia, a yearning, a grief for the lost possibilities or places of your past or future, a confusion or restlessness, so hard to explain. TT, as Mr. Robert Joramogi did, would learn how to carry this cross and learn to live with it and remain happy.

They were destined to talk long into the night. Yes, I remember your mother Marian Davies, so well. A lovely innocent girl who loved your father so much, she left her family behind for the Zambian copper mines, her first overseas travel outside Wales, apart from the short honeymoon they took on the island of Crete. As students they had very little money when first married and as a result they honeymooned before they had the church service. They went to the Greek Islands, stayed in a very small hotel on the big island of Crete.

This one-star (if it could be classed as that good) hotel had a very friendly owner and he was accomplished at welcoming and making Welsh people feel at home for some unknown reason. Possibly he lived in Wales at some time. Mr. Robert Joramogi remembered Eng. M. J. R. Tembo writing to him to say they hardly slept for the week. And not for the reasons many would be thinking of for honeymooners; it was down to their mattress which was like a concrete block. Their room on the first floor was opposite the main road and there was only one main road going around the island, so lots of traffic noise late into the early hours. The soon to be Mr. and Mrs Tembo had a choice of cooling the room, as there was no air conditioning unit, with an open window or lying in a hot but quieter place of rest.

Another interesting fact your father wrote me about is that they went in late August when it is traditionally very hot and dry. They experienced many days of heavy rain and floods, as if it was an African rainy season. It was often the case that they were trapped in a small bar to shelter, as they were forced to leave the beach but could not make it as far as their hotel without an unpleasant soaking! From Zambia your father had a short stay in the Ghana Gold mines. It's a shame your mother got a form of hepatitis in Zambia, that she would never recover from and neither would he from her passing. Thank God he had you to look after and something to keep him going. What I know is that once your mother was gone, his letters to me were not so frequent. It's such a strange co-incidence that the start of our careers was in the same country and again at the end.

Mr. Robert Joramogi put a cup of camomile tea with honey on the bedside table set for a left hander as he recalled incorrectly that the son of Eng. M. J. R. Tembo was left-handed. Just to confirm, he asked a rhetorical question, 'You are left-handed, aren't you? I Hope you brought enough clothes to stay a few more evenings? If not, Al Hamra Mall is near the Village and you, son of Eng. M. J. R. Tembo, can buy some things to top up with, a few shirts, shorts and underwear perhaps? You, son of Eng. M. J. R. Tembo are most welcome to stay as long as you need. If, in the morning, you are up before me, as I suspect you may be these days, just go out for a walk to the beach, as I never lock the apartment door. Pat the cat may even get up to join you in your walk. We can have breakfast later at the Muse Waterfront.' With that TT was left to his own devices and thoughts about their 'Hiraeth', how to adapt and live with it happily. He sat up in bed for a few minutes to clear his head, then he slept until sun up at around 6.15 am.

Titus Tembo sleepily opened the blackout blinds and looked up into the sky to see the sun was still fighting its own waking battle just below the high mountain range in the east. He vaguely noted the long stretch of green fairway just beyond the second row of terraced villas. After a quick shower and the other morning bathroom essentials, one of the first things for him these days was the everyday closing of his eyes for transcendental meditation. Normally he would find the same peaceful spot each morning and do his usual twenty-minutes meditation. The comfortable bedroom chair next to the double wardrobe would serve his purpose until he found somewhere more permanent. His normal habit would be to take some exercise soon after the meditation session energised him. This morning an early walk on the beach with talkative Pat would suit his needs very nicely.

After his meditation, he headed for the kitchen; TT prepared himself a strong caffeine filled Starbucks lungo espresso from one of those modern machines. He picked up the clear glass insulated coffee cup in his right hand, drank in the aroma and took a big swig followed by a noise of satisfaction. That first coffee drink of the morning in recent years always signalled to TT's brain and body that we are in for another happy day. There was no sign of Pat the cat who was sleeping soundly under the covers on the feet of Robert Joramogi. But as soon as TT pushed the bedroom door of Mr. Robert Joramogi a little ajar, Pat came a running and talking in his cat language.

This particular drink on this particular morning was good, yes, but would always be second best to 'Kahawa Chungu' for TT, but okay it is what it is for now. On his way out through the unlocked apartment door he noticed a new sign had been hung during the previous evening. In large yellow capital letters was handwritten by a yellow highlight pen, BREAKFAST WITH ENG. M. J. R. TEMBO'S SON IN THE MUSE.

The apartment door always remained unlocked with no key in place. Other people did leave their apartments unlocked and Robert Joramogi had twice before walked confidently into the wrong apartment on the wrong floor, not because he forgot the number, but was not concentrating when getting out of the lift so early. Robert Joramogi saw little point of locking the door in such a safe Village location, really it was just like being home in his own Lake Victoria village area where there were no locks anyway! With no key in place, he was confident he'd not face the predicament of locking himself out! In fact, he did the opposite when he was still driving his car, until last year when he felt safer to go by taxi; always leaving the key in the ignition of his own car. His further lack of security precautions including him writing all his passwords down and pinning them to the back of the apartment door. Online he would try and use voice and face recognition to get around this problem, but his face cream caused a reflection that outwitted modern technology. His finger print helped him access his laptop computer, but anyway, as a backup he used the same sequence of numbers to access his latest MacBook Air, his old HP desktop computer, his PIN number for his ATM card, his credit cards PIN numbers, a shorter version for his phone password that only needed four digits, his airmiles account, his online banking access, his home safe, his combination cycle lock and so it went on.

His memory today was not like that of yesteryear. He clearly remembered from more than twenty years or so ago his good friend Eng. M. J. R. Tembo writing to him to say his mtoto Titus was bringing his handicap down to single figures despite him playing left-handed, and his father trying to teach him when Eng. M. J. R. Tembo was right-handed. He could even remember all the names of the guys of the football team in that photo he still proudly hung in the apartment hallway. They had gone on to play in the University Championship finals in London. He was at his best in the final, but still they managed to squeeze two goals past him and win the day two goals to one. That season from all those years ago, he recalls the names of the teams they played from the opening game, and the closing game, the scores of those games, the names of those who scored from their team and the name of the other player who along with himself was selected for every game of the season. He felt he had a very good memory indeed.

He recalled that fateful day more than forty years ago when he lost his two brothers and father. They were not part of the 200 people killed at the United States Embassy bombings in Nairobi. But they were more or less killed simultaneously on the road leading south from Lake Victoria to the capital City Nairobi. The bus was travelling too fast and the driver lost control. In those days there were not so many vehicles on the road, yet the accidents and deaths were as frequent as they are today. Did we not learn anything from this unnecessary carnage? So, taking the bigger picture into account, he worried very little over these small short-term memory lapses. He had never walked into the wrong apartment on purpose, just got off on the wrong floor one stop too early, possibly due to his poor eye sight when he pushed the wrong stop button in the lift. Whereas that young man from the floor below entered his apartment on a few occasions in error; and that clever young man had a very good memory!

CHAPTER NINE

Exploring present and past

From nine floors up or as marked on the lift bottoms the eighth floor of the Royal Breeze mini sky scraper TT approached the lift doors. On either side of the four lift doors there were large windows, one looking west over the beach, the other east over the golf course and lagoons. Titus Tembo as always had his camera at the ready. He quickly took shots on automatic mode from the eighth floor of the building. He took a series of quick photographs of the pool area, the beach, the strip of land jutting out into the sea, the village layout and distant mountains. He was not too careful with the pictures as he was stuck behind the dirty windows of the Royal Breeze tower. The photographs were just something to remind him of this Village for when he returned to Dubai and considered where he should live for the next six months or so. Pat the cat rubbed up against his legs, talking to TT in an apparent attempt possibly also to have his photograph taken. From the reception area TT and Pat walked past the empty security desk with its handwritten sign, mobile contact number for security guard 059 67839 bla - bla. He wondered if the guy was sleeping somewhere at the end of his shift or out walking on his rounds, checking on what? Seems that in a safe place like this, the security guy would not have much to do to keep him awake!

The layout of the reception area naturally led TT through the automatic glass doors, onto a covered shaded area. From the air-conditioned interior of the building, man and beast needed to brave the humid air and walk across a roundabout. Pat was okay with his paws on the tarmac this early in the morning as the sun was yet to start cooking the earth. The design of the exit layout from the tower slowed down any approaching traffic from the narrow currently deserted two-way lane mini-highway that skirted the Royal Breeze buildings' Tower One through to Tower Five. On the other side TT kicked off his jandals so he could feel the damp green grass on the soles of his feet like back in Africa. Pat the cat rolled around on his back to cool off on the wet grass. Here the difference for TT between the United Arab Emirates and Africa was that he could not smell the fresh rain on the earth, but there was an aroma of sorts. A slight smell of the recycled sewage water that came via the pop-up sprinklers automatically twice a day. He saw what he took to be a Filipino maid scooping up the dog droppings of her small liability on its morning walk. No need for that in Africa he fancied, as the dung beetles did the cleaning up from all the cows that would have enjoyed this green patch. Pat made himself bigger-looking and just stared the little dog down. In its turn the dog pretended he did not see the cat. Jandals back on, TT crossed the second stretch of empty road and Pat the cat followed close behind.

There were mums out pushing prams for those early rising babies who could wake the dead if not given their milk on time. In Africa you had a village to take care of every child as if it was a lion creche with the village population being part of one big pride, but here it's down to the mum or her maid; the male as in Africa, or for that matter in the lion pride, would not generally get involved with babies as he needed his energy for working. In Africa the man would of course be ready to dish out the disciplinary stuff as the child grew older. Well, he would in an African household or a lion pride anyway. Even his beloved Baba had taken a stick to him when he tried it on as a teenager. In looking back, he realised he was so lucky to have had that steadying moral influencer even if it was so painful at the time.

Still today, in Kenya, the stick was seen by many of the old school, as an essential tool for good parenting; it did its job for example by just possibly stopping an unwanted child being born from a school girl. After Mama caned you, your Baba was called in to reinforce the message at times, and if he failed to convince you of your bad ways, you would be taken to the police station for a good caning from the cops. You certainly learnt to be honest as sometimes you were just caned for running away from the cane even if you did nothing wrong!

The only traffic in the deserted ghost-town like village of Al Hamra in the very early morning were the unlucky, or was it the lucky, maids not living-in and having to cycle to start their domestic duties. He saw that most of the cars were still parked outside their villas waiting for their drivers to wake, prepare themselves and head off to take the kids to school or themselves to work or both these things in that order. All in all, he thought a pretty normal western type environment a lot different from the Palm Jumeirah in Dubai. Here he also saw people greeting each other with a wave or a good morning or even an occasional hand shake. People were walking at a slower speed here and many of them had a smile on their faces like in a real Village, like back in Africa. In Al Hamra Titus Tembo could see the easy companionship of the village had not been replaced by the anonymity of city life like Dubai. He did not expect to find this type of community life style in a city like Dubai or for that matter anywhere in the United Arab Emirates, this was more like the outskirts of Nairobi and TT felt more comfortable in this so-called village than his experiences on the luxury of the Palm Jumeriah!

On passing between two rows of Town Houses, TT entered a red brick pathway that led in both directions, possibly one he presumed heading for the sea and the other the golf club house? If it were a quiz question, Titus Tembo would have drawn a blank score! TT turned left and wandered a little to his right, as a result he was nearer to the golf course. A sharp male North of England voice called loudly and urgently from close behind, 'Ey Up mate' as a golf cart skidded to a halt with a dangerous sounding squeal. TT slowly turned and he stood above the seated driver. A chunky looking, sun tanned, long grey haired, shall we say slightly older gentleman, seemed in two minds whether to drive on to the next tee or chat to TT. Once he saw and heard Pat the cat, he seemed to make his mind up to stop and chat. The golfer looked as if he had just showered, as he was soaked through with the humidity. His clothes were rather loud even for a golfer and that was an understatement. To TT, as soon as he saw the golfer, he thought of that Old British DJ who hosted the 'Jim Will Fix It' shows he had watched as a kid! Not a good image, he realized and decided to keep that observation to himself

'Ey Up lad, sorry about the close encounter. Lovely cat you have there. It's been a long night on this well named midnight madness golfing challenge, played those front seven and back two holes many, many, many times under the floodlights and to finish we get this back nine completed as the sun gets up. It was cheap mind-you, and that is the most important factor of this whole affair every year. Luckily, we had the strong black Yorkshire tea and many a Bulmer ice cold cider to keep us going. I am already savouring in my mind that full English breakfast at the club house, with fried bread, mushrooms, blood pudding, baked beans, pork bacon, toast and marmalade, YUMMY. I pile it high as it's included as part of the midnight madness; what in the world could beat a free English breakfast.' TT realized why the gentleman looked a little stocky on first impressions.

'But Ey Up mate, what you doing on our golf course with that big grey cat?' He never introduced himself with his proper name but one of his playing partners apologised for the ignorant northerner everyone called 'a bit of Yorkshire'. Later TT understood how well he had been re-christened by his pals! It just happened at this fortunate time for TT, that this loud, larger than life, friendly character just had available for rent a large studio in the Marina building here in the Village. In seconds he got over the message to a potential client in Titus Tembo; fully furnished studio that he indicated was available for rent at a very competitive price apparently. The focus should have been on *apparently* as it depended on the view point one took, the landlord yes, the renter no! TT took the business card of 'a bit of Yorkshire' that simply stated DJ & gave his mobile and a Hotmail email address.

TT watched from a short distance away as 'a bit of Yorkshire' demonstrated a most unusual but effective golf swing. The ball sailed strongly towards a watery grave in the right-hand lagoon and then to none of his playing partners' surprise, turned around and proceeded its way to swing left and land nicely on top of the rough on the right-hand edge of the fairway! The ball set out on its path as if it was a boomerang but without the means of coming back to the thrower. 'Shot', he shouted at 'a bit of Yorkshire' and turned around to get back in time for breakfast with Pat running alongside him. He wondered if breakfast would only be with Robert Joramogi, or possibly Pat the cat would join them at a venue yet to be remember?

It was a good day for Robert Joramogi, he was dressed very smartly and only needed a jacket and tie to be ready for a church wedding. Little did TT know, but that was Robert Joramogi down to a tee, he'd change his clothing maybe four or five times in a day, and that daily count excluded his PJs. Once decked out in suitable clothes for going out, as now, then dressed in an attire for ironing, a different outfit for reading and afternoon tea and then again smartly turned out for dinner be it at home or out somewhere. Robert Joramogi cast an eye over TT, then agreed he was suitably dressed for the Tucana coffee shop venue he had in mind. It was situated next to the marina, but they would sit inside to benefit from the air conditioning, while still enjoying the view of the yachts from their table. He also insisted that they took Pat the cat and travel there by car, as he did not want to sweat either possibly on the way there but definitely when it warmed up, that is if they were to walk back. There was also the possibility to drive around and show the son of Eng. M. J. R. Tembo the village; Pat would also enjoy such a trip out.

These opportunities did not come along so frequently for Robert Joramogi in Al Hamra Village. This morning he had a friend, albeit a lot younger than him, he was Kenyan, and so it would be nice to chat together over breakfast. Friends to share a tea with, sharing their worries and hopes together, to chat over while putting the world to right. To discuss whether he should stay here, move back to Wales to be near his grandchildren or go back to his village in northern Kenya to be near his tribe. This was a friend from his country who he could help out for a while at least, share his experiences here and advise him if required.

It was a struggle for Robert Joramogi to slip in and out of the mini; just maybe, slip is possibly not such a good description TT thought to himself. 'Wow, what a lovely spot and not over crowded like it would be in Dubai. Lots of free parking along the Muse area. A British style pub, a traditional ice cream parlour, an American burger joint, Irish traditional fish and chips and, near here, it looks like a fancy restaurant with a terrace over-looking the marina with its fabulous boats. I love the wooden pier type structure boarding the eating places and the marina. All this surrounded by clear waters and brilliant views across the lagoon to an island and across the waters to the golf course; I see great photograph opportunities. It's my idea of a paradise and I dream that the tea or coffee and breakfast live up to the billing I'd given the whole muse location!' With such a speech, it became a joint decision to move outside and sit under the shade of a large square umbrella, sitting next to a strong fan to keep them feeling cool. TT studied the menu after his long speech of praise for the breakfast location.

They ordered a pot of herbal ginger tea to share and a healthy option of a veggie wrap each. Robert Joramogi seemed very well known and well-liked by the serving staff. He instructed them to set Titus Tembo's place for a left hander! 'Did I tell you about your father, Eng. M. J. R. Tembo understanding me from when we first met in Cardiff at UWIST, he referred to my situation as my 'Matatanisho'.' Here we go again thought TT. And yes, he was right, as at the breakfast table they went over all what Mr. Robert Joramogi forgot about from their conversation of the previous evening. He repeated his internal debate of where he might end up with the choice of his tribal village or the Welsh Valleys. Both now a bit alien as he had lived in the United Arab Emirates for these last 18 years.

Eventually it dawned on Robert Joramogi he was losing the interest of his guest, but he had one more tale to tell. 'Your mother and my ex-wife used to call around to our student house on Alfred Street in Roath of a Friday evening.' TT bucked up for what appeared to be a new revelation of his family's earlier life. His whole-body language changed, and he ordered two flat whites with skinny milk, to accompany the new tales. A change of story deserved a change of drink, and just like TT, it seemed that Mr. Robert Joramogi rather liked a coffee after an herbal tea. His beloved Baba always stressed they should live in the now and TT thought that was why he never told him stories about his mother. The truth was, it made his beloved Baba sad to talk about what might have been if TT's mama had lived; he never got over her and never married again.

We had to reward the young ladies for the washing and ironing they did for us on a Tuesday afternoon when we attended to our sporting duties of training and occasionally playing for our respective teams in UWIST. And let me tell you there were many teams to entertain the majority of students who wanted more than a degree certificate at the end of three or even four years academic slog. On Tuesdays I give the ladies free access to my extensive record collection. That record collection that remains part of my collection today, had mainly been built up in Cardiff from purchases made during my working semester intervals. Amid those natural academic breaks, at the end of each week, payday, cash-in-hand, tax free, saw me hunt the shelves of Spillers Records shop located in one of the old arcades in the city centre. He remembered that fortunately Spillers is still going strong unlike the Brains or Joes of this world, it's still holding its original appeal.

Similarly, to my love for music and records, your Baba and my good friend Eng. M. J. R. Tembo used his spare cash-in-hand to purchase anything photographic related that was second-hand and so good value for money. Those days there was more or less full employment and us dark fellows, as they called us back then, were seen as strong and fit, perfect short-term labourers for the little building sites popping up all around the city. The Roath area had lovely Victorian style houses, prime real estate to be converted into student flats. For your Baba and me this was fortunate as it was close to Alfred Street, both in terms of finding a job then being able to walk into work once we were employed.

Those days, unlike today in the United Kingdom, we and the general public were not aware of the racism in everyday language, like the terms used for the little black dolls called

Golliwoggs, half-casts like our Kenyan term pointy, sold down the river related to slavery and we accepted statements that today would see an arrest taking place in the United Kingdom! We were so innocent and ill-informed that we thought the Muslim man on his knees praying in the UWIST library was in-fact looking for something he may have dropped. Your Baba got down on his knees and offered to help him. All three of us ended up laughing so loudly the librarian had to give us one of her stern looks over the top of her glasses to bring the noise to an end! And that coming from someone who was aware of the call to pray in Kenya!

No, the only bad racial experience we were aware of was when someone dropped a fire bomb through our letter box in Alfred Street. The police took that very seriously even if it was never set alight. It turned out to be someone living close to us. He was a mad man often seen riding around on his bike in his white come grey vest and grey Y-front underwear in all weathers. We had burst into laughter when he cycled past and he took offence to our interest in his dress. It was the good old days, so the coppers just took him aside for a strong talking to, put him in a cell, give him a beating before releasing him the next morning; a bit like Kenya could be at times in certain places today shall we say! Word must have got out around Roath, as we never had any more trouble in the area after that!

I suspect that secretly every week the ladies were hoping for an exciting night out with us exotic fellers. What they got normally was a trip around the corner in the Roath district to see out favourite actor Clint Eastwood in one of those *spaghetti westerns*. These were shown on a regular basis in the very cheap - made for students - cinema just off the main shopping street of Albany Road. The tickets were cheap because the movies shown in our place would have worn out their welcome in the city centre cinemas which were more up market shall we say. And in those days, cinemas showed just one film, there were not those multi-screen movie houses and there were not that many films made.   Television stations were not allowed to show the latest movies for some time and of course who would have ever dreamed up Netflix or even satellite T.V.? The internet was a long way off and possibly in no one's imagination at that time - pure science fiction. Your Baba was one of the first students in UWIST to have a very expensive calculator for addition, subtraction and multiplication. It is hard to believe, but back then no scientific functions were available on this latest electronic gadget. As an engineering student he found himself using a slide rule that he tried to explain to me to no avail as my art student brain could not take it all in. Those types of things are today featured in museums. His computer course consisted of two days in the four years when he sent away cardboard cut cards made on a machine similar to a type writer. The answer to a formula would be back a week later. Maybe today that machine can also be seen in a museum along with the slide rules? Laptops, and mobile phones, please, we were lucky to have the combustion engine, let alone anyone think up the idea of an electric car driving itself like a Tesla back in the day! And today in Dubai they are already talking about flying taxi cars like large drones. Fortunately, being an art student, I did not have to bother with any of this science stuff other than in the movies like *'Back to the Future'*.

The friendly fat staff members of Albany fish bar would regularly high-jack us on our walk home and managed to pick out the last coins from our then thinly packed wallets. This was in our opinion the home of the best British traditional fish and chips in the capital city. Not up to the standard of fresh water tilapia from Lake Victoria but a good second place. The figures of the ladies who worked there would have been admired in a traditional African village, and those figures were testament to the excellent fare dished up from this highly rated culinary venue. Sadly, unlike the famous Tusker ale in Kenya, this great culinary experience would go the same way as Brains Beer & Joes Italian Ice Cream. Why oh why meddle with something so good? In Africa we leave well alone and yet these white people are never satisfied. Tusker had helped white men dance since 1922 and was still doing a great job today.

On Saturday nights the girls would treat us to a pint of SA Brains each, in one of our two preferred locals. Only the one-pint mind you, as in our fresher's year in UWIST we experienced the SA which we referred to as scull attack, a feature we experienced the next day of the aptly named local brew on drinking as many as four pints on a Saturday evening and the very early morning hours on Sunday. Those were the days we wished to forget, although sometimes, the next day, after four pints we could not remember even if we wished to recall the evening events! One particular infamous incident I do recall is when we were hungry coming back from a house party and did not even have enough cash for just chips between us. The one too many scull attacks led us to try our luck duck hunting with a homemade spear on Roath Park lake. We both got soaking wet and equally cold walking home to Alfred Street. The ducks were never in danger and that was the last evening your Baba and I took more than one pint of Brains SA each. Imagine if we behaved like that by

Lake Victoria among the hippopotami and crocodiles; we certainly would not be worrying about being cold or wet that is for sure.

On returning to Wales, and of course her capital city Cardiff, albeit infrequently these days, I very much realised the student times of when we thought anything was possible and Brains Beers from the Cardiff City Centre brewery and Joes Italian ice cream from Swansea were the best in the world; those days had long gone. Some clever young consultants had taken these local wonder products and made them available to the world. As a result, I assumed the families who brought them to the people in Cardiff and Swansea, were made wealthy in terms of money. But those clever modern thinkers had to change the way both the beer and ice cream were made in order for them to travel widely. Sadly, this made our favourite beer and ice cream, feel, look and taste different and the world became a poorer place for it.

Even our favourite Sunday Times newspaper is no longer the same. Midmorning on a Sunday was for Eng. M. J. R. Tembo and I a time to settle down with the Sunday Times and a pint of Brains scull attack accompanied with a packet of salty crisps. Eventually through the now defunct job supplement section, the seed of an idea to return to Africa came to the then qualified and newly experienced Eng. M. J. R. Tembo. A successful interview in London was followed by a Harley Street medical before a short honeymoon in Crete.

Eng. M. J. R. Tembo had found the right job in Africa less than two years after graduating and gaining experience in the United Kingdom. He of course also wanted to commit his life to the right woman, your mama Marina Tembo as she became. In their case the wedding in Zambia followed the honeymoon. Our friendship sustained beyond the distance. Marina Tembo followed her man on that two year contract to the copper belt of Zambia and never gave a second thought to the fact there was a war going on in the adjoining country at the time. Zambia was one of the so-called *'Front-Line States'* and paid a heavy price for supporting her fellow black Africans fight for freedom.

One of us would write, it would take around ten days for the letter to arrive by airmail and then the other would answer and vice-versa. I kept those letters all these years and they sit in storage in Wales with a few other personal belongings. If you would like, son of Eng. M. J. R. Tembo, I can leave those letters to you in my will. In the mean-time I can recall much of what was in them. But can I suggest we leave this for another day and firstly finish our tour of Al Hamra Village and its surrounds.

CHAPTER TEN

On safari in Al Hamra Village

Both Kenyan men delighted in a leisurely breakfast and stories anew. One of them enjoyed telling the tales to an appreciative audience of two. Yes, the second listener may have only been a big old grey cat, but even he seemed to be entertained by the speaker, his master, if a cat can have a master that is? And the other human seemed equally pleased listening to the relevant historic family tales for the first time. It was indeed a very rare treat for Titus Tembo. His beloved Baba, Eng. M. J. R. Tembo, mostly liked to live in the now and did not often talk of the past and hardly ever of his wife, TT's mama.

The plan now was for a safari, for the three of them to drive slowly through the village, taking in the sights, then follow up with a tour of the locations near-by. First order of business was to stroll across the road from their breakfast haunt to their first stop, the open beach. Pat complained loudly about the hot sand on his paws. Despite the warning from Pat the cat about the hot sand under foot, TT kicked off his beloved jandals to feel the clear white sand massage the hard skin on the soles of his feet. He dared to paddle up to his knees as the white caps splashed the bottom of his pink cotton shorts. The many crabs just off-shore lifted their pincers to protect their territory from this large intruder, but soon swam off when TT bent down to get a better look at them and the other small fish in the sea. From a distance, with their claws opened wide they shot off at such a speed that at first glance they looked like a medium sized fish. This was the time of year that brought an invasion of crabs and field like acres of sea weed in shore. The beach below the hide tide mark had a layer of green slimy fresh carpets of sea weed covering the sand and this according to the cries from Pat the cat, was no improvement from the bare hot sand. Robert Joramogi picked Pat up and gave him a stern lecture to stop his loud complaining noises.

As the seasons change, so does the temperature, along with the sea creatures on show. There are times when the beach will be littered with blue jelly fish. Other times walking as one did now at the water's edge, there be no crabs on show, but it would result in often stepping on rays of all sizes. They would be basking in the very shallow waters close to the beach. There came a time in the lagoon, just around the corner from the open beach, when the young fish were around in large shoals. This was the season when the lagoon area acted as a nursery. And Robert Joramogi added, 'if you are really lucky of an evening, you'll see a turtle on the beach or swimming alongside you.   What you do not want to come across are the five or six types of poisonous sea snakes found in this region, and take note, there is no anti-venom available for those guys. Fortunately for swimmers around these coasts, the sea serpents are not like some of our aggressive African snakes.

There was just a smattering of people around, a young woman seriously swimming just in sight, a couple of well fed middle-aged European ladies working on their tans and the obligatory Al Hamra Village dog walker watching her dog frolicking in the white caps hitting the shore line. This morning the three of them appeared to be the only contribution toward the beach population from the male species; TT assumed most people were at work given the mid-morning hour. He further speculated that Pat may be the only cat to have ventured on to the open beach at Al Hamra.

TT helped Mr. Robert Joramogi squeeze into the passenger seat before he pulled down the soft top of the silver Mini Cooper S. As the top came down, Pat the cat leapt from the walkway onto the lap of his owner and continued to shelter there out of the wind generated even at this low speed. His host, despite his old phone and lack of a maid, would be seen as a very successful man back in his African Village. Perceived as successful because in the African culture, obesity is beautiful, not that he would dare accuse Mr. Robert Joramogi of being obese. Being fat is a measure that you are wealthy enough to eat well, to drink lots of beer and not have to exert yourself working. TT's mind wandered to thinking about how the standard of beauty in Africa differs from the west, and was just as unhealthy for their women. In his culture the tradition is one of overweight or shall we more kindly say curvaceous women being considered more beautiful than those thin stick shaped women in the west who suffer just as much but in an opposite way, starving themselves at times as the emphasis was on the smaller figure being beautiful. They are complete opposites in what their cultures hold to be attractive but both as unhealthy. Mr. Robert Joramogi was lucky to have a body weight that positively determined his appeal in traditional African society. Titus

Tembo on the other hand, being younger and fitter than his passenger, had a figure that fitted better into the mzungu way of thinking of what was normal. Titus Tembo worked hard at his normality, often daily in the gymnasium, sometimes running around the tennis court making a fool of himself but nevertheless building up a sweat and finally the occasional walk hitting little white balls.

The Mini Cooper S took a sharp right behind the fancy restaurant that turned out to be the adopted yacht club for the expatriate sailors as well as a handful of locals who enjoyed a discreet beer out of sight of their Muslim peers. Robert Joramogi sat in the car and smiled to himself.   He would eat dinner in the club occasionally.   There he had observed the Nationals sitting in the far corner sipping their pints from a glass shrouded in white paper tissue. Did they think this white shield around their glass of beer meant 'out of sight out of mind?' In the bordering Emirate of Ajman, many years ago, but never forgotten, he saw one National drink too much and flip over the railings in a patio bar, to the shallow sea below. The man soon recovered from his watery seat and Mr. Robert Joramogi had to admit to himself that this was a very rare incident indeed. His countrymen or those British with their many public houses open all hours, frequently displayed far worse drunken behaviour back home than he had ever witnessed from Nationals in the Emirates.

TT left the air-conditioning running despite the top being down on the mini. He did not want to disturb his host further and delay their tour, so he abandoned the photographic opportunity presented by the boats at rest in the marina. It was just a matter of a quick dash for TT to briefly take in the sights of the stuffy old yacht club bar and its fancy eating place. What a pleasant surprise awaited him, a sports bar with large screen TVs and a pool table; all that suited Titus Tembo perfectly and if they just added karaoke, he would go there occasionally of an evening. Pat the cat welcomed him back before settling down once more to purr on the comfortable warm lap of his master.

The Mini Cooper S approached the Village at yet another entrance gate and the African security guard greeted Mr. Robert Joramogi in the open top car like a long lost relative, all smiles and waves with a shout of 'welcome Sir' as the car pulled up. On their right his host and newly adopted navigator for the Al Hamra Villa safari, pointed out the sailing club with its fenced off beach. He explained that it was fenced off at the request of some small minded official who argued it would protect the kids on the beach undergoing sailing lessons. Why it was allowed to go ahead I do not know but it means you have to go via the sailing club to enter this part of the beach - no charge of course since it's all part of our village.

Titus Tembo kept to the low speed limit sign posted within the Village. As a child the potential use of the cane and its rare occasional use on him when he was a teenager had ensured he followed the rules most of the time. The disciplinary training served him well as an adult. His current low driving speed however was nothing to do with his normal willingness to comply with the rules. There was little chance of a fine or someone pulling you over to give you a good talking to about speeding and certainly no cane at his age or in this Village at this time. No, that morning there were other very good reasons for his sedate pace in the racy Mini Cooper S. Titus Tembo was finding the sight-seeing pleasantly informative, taking in the well-kept gardens, the flame trees in bloom along the road, the pretty ladies walking dogs, and dodging various nationalities and ages peddling often on the wrong side of the road.

Coming up next was a coffee kiosk with tables and chairs placed one side of its opening, its location indicated that it catered for passing trade, maybe golfers or those dog walkers as he noticed they advertised 'free water for your dog'. The road at that point bisected the golf course so there were two golf cart paths acting as very large speed bumps hindering the advance of the low body of his Mini Cooper S. Mr. Robert Joramogi indicated to turn right first, then directly left rather than continue on to the dead end over the bridge on the island bordering the lagoon. That stretch of water was open to the sea and Mr. Robert Joramogi the navigator explained that its winding canal bordered the golf course until it eventually came full circle and ended up looking across to the sailing club beach.

TT drove along Dublin street, really Dublin Street in the Middle East! The street went past Villas of various sizes, clearly expensive homes over-looking the green of the championship style golf course, or the white sands and blue lagoon. Both, in his view probably manmade, but nevertheless magnificent. Unlike some parts of Kenya, TT noticed all the infrastructure like the roads, pavements, gardens and lighting were in very good condition. He also noted there were many electric scooters in various locations which he assumed were either free or on hire throughout the village. Garage doors were left open or were non-existent and sometimes the garage was full of items there to tempt the passing thieves who were clearly not represented in Al Hamra Village. As Mr. Robert Joramogi mentioned earlier, no need to lock your apartment door or take the ignition key out of your car.

They came to a roundabout, and his navigator indicated to go straight through, then explained the alternative routes. On the left you will come to the main gate that opens on to the public road leading you to Al Hamra Mall. The right turning is an interesting option. Today it's a bridge that is locked off from the man-made island that sits across the lagoon from the sailing club. Man-made by a company from China who, it is claimed, used prison labourers from their country. The island was intended to be an eco-friendly environment, generating all its own needs from alternative energy sources. 'I'm not sure how they were planning to be self-sufficient in water use and recycling of their garbage? The big draw I guess is that it was to provide boat owners with the opportunity to tie up their water craft on a jetty at the end of their gardens. There are rumours that the bank would not provide mortgages or loans on the properties proposed but anyway it remains a dream. That dream along with the idea of setting up to hold the America's Cup here. Lots of people must have been looking forward to viewing the oldest international sports competition that dates back to 1851 and many business people must have been rubbing their hands in anticipation of the opportunities it could bring. The rumour mill again came up with a plausible story of why it never happened. It was reported that one of the teams objected to the type of shallow waters and winds they would encounter that did not suit their boat.'

As the Mini Cooper S exited the security gate to the right, the African security guard came out of his little cabin, give a friendly wave and shouted across the road at them 'Hello my friends. Good morning Baba, may God bless you mzee.' It appeared at least to TT, that this man was yet another East African, possibly from his own country Kenya, and evidently held a deep respect for Mr. Robert Joramogi or at least an older African. At that point TT felt this Al Hamra Village maybe the place that he could hang his hat comfortably for at least the next six months that the probate could take to complete, and he hoped the courts would award him his inheritance that would give him the freedom to travel. The environment was not pretentious, yet the facilities and infrastructure provided everything you needed conveniently at hand; yes, a typical village environment but on a grander scale maybe than most villages he had experienced to-date. There was also that value for money studio to consider, on offer from that 'a bit of Yorkshire' man.

Titus Tembo would broach the subject of possibly staying in Al Hamra Village with Mr. Robert Joramogi later in the day. If he was based here, then he would also be able to check on his beloved Baba's old friend, and maybe help him decide his future whether it be in Wales with his grandkids or his own tribe back in Northern Kenya. And he would make enquires with the 'a bit of Yorkshire' man about renting that studio of his.

Wow, what a view from the road bridge across the bay and straight up the 18th Fairway towards what looks like a very large golf clubhouse. On the right the whole lagoon opened up so they could look across to the fantastic panorama that TT decided he must set his camera on later, maybe a sunset shot would do it justice. Titus Tembo's navigator for the day had seen this view many times, and was not so interested in the wow factor any longer, he was looking the other way, describing the unattractive island on their left as one destined for entertainment complexes. "Currently it seems this island is dedicated to dogs and their owners as a walking and giant dog toilet area. Behind it on the near horizon, you see a partly constructed ugly, grey, concrete high rise, this building when finished eventually is planned to be the first dedicated conference hotel in the United Arab Emirates. The same old rumour mill mentioned earlier has this investment being started by a certain long-standing Italian senior politician who is a media tycoon. Yes, it sounds like the story was based on the Italian version of Trump if you think a little deeper. Or sorry, was it a famous football team hailing from Madrid, I forget the details, '*Matatanisho*' once again!" Based on Mr. Robert Joramogi's past experience in the United Arab Emirates, once the time is right, he expected to see them building the entertainment complex on the man-made dog island, completing the conference hotel or knocking it down to replace it with something grander and similarly the residences on the eco-island. Development in the Emirate of Dubai can be much quicker than here but Mr. Robert Joramogi liked this pace in the northern-most emirate and the fact that it was rumoured the ruler is not keen on borrowing money, here it seemed there is no going into debt to speed up development.

Titus Tembo ground the Mini Cooper S to a sudden halt just past the road bridge as they got to the last of the handful of villas on their right-hand side. They sat with the last villa between them and the set of tees on the 18thhole of the Al Hamra golf course. Oh my God, TT had heard a male lion grunt and pointed out to Mr. Robert Joramogi, the end of possibly two large adolescent lion paws seen protruding out from under the gate to the property. Surely not a male lion staying here in the middle of a village? It must be a practical joke being played on people coming too close to the Villa thought TT. Yes, maybe these people like their privacy too much and it's just a ploy to scare off unwanted visitors?

Titus Tembo left the engine running for two reasons. One so the air-conditioning would keep working for both his host and Pat the cat, who were comfortable where they sat in the Mini Cooper S. The second and more important reason was they had the top down with both Mr. Robert Joramogi along with Pat the cat unprotected. As such Titus Tembo would want a quick getaway if there was a lion in this property and it made it over the boundary defences and charged at the Mini Cooper S. Mr. Robert Joramogi had never been a fan of lions since he was a youngster and did his work has a herd boy back in his village. Whether it was goats, cattle or herd boys, those lions were not picky eaters he recalled. Better safe than sorry thought Titus Tembo as he climbed on the wall and peeked over the tall fence. Well, not so tall considering what could be waiting in the garden below. The boundary fences consisted of the same inadequate 'lion defence' wrought iron railings as around all the other properties in the village but here it was backed up with some opaque glass fixed on the inside of the railings. Maybe the latter was a way of keeping the residence's privacy or, god forbid, a means of hiding the lion from his dinner walking past!

'Oh my God.' Titus Tembo said to himself aloud for a second time in just a matter of minutes. In the garden a young male lion was chasing an equally young sheep in what seemed like a surreal game with one of the creatures completely innocent of the consequences it faced. Just when TT was about to flee the scene and think about who he should report this Al Hamra Village lion to, the back door of the house opened, he froze, a mzungu lady with a beer bottle at hand, looking ready to fight off any lion, said 'yes, can I be of any help to you?' as calm as calm could be! At the sound of the door opening, a second young male lion raced around the corner of the house and what TT assumed were two brothers from the same litter, stared up at him. Titus Tembo immediately thought of the movie The Ghost and the Darkness. This block buster told the tale of another two extraordinary lions that went on a man-eating rampage that claimed over one hundred and thirty lives in his country. Those two beasts had brought Great Britain's plans for an East African railway to an end for some time at least. Certainly, these two lions below him looked potentially as capable as the older males in The Ghost and the Darkness, capable of reducing the Al Hamra Village population. Okay admittedly that was one hundred years ago in the wilderness of Kenya, but even today just across the Kenyan boarder in Tanzania, man eating lions' feast on an average of a hundred and fifty people every year. Most of those meals were of men coming home late after a few too many drinks. Man, if these two got out at night what chance would an unsuspecting golfer have under the flood lights? TT thought he could not imagine a golf club, bag or hard golf balls being sufficiently offensive weapons to keep one of these hungry lions from their meal.

To the Australian lady lion keeper, ironically named Hilda Lyons, Titus Tembo appeared more in shock rather than in thought. But he was not lost for words for very long. 'Nice lions you got their ma'am.' She smiled and took a swig of her beer out of the bottle before calling the two lions with the intention of locking them away before inviting in her visitor. 'Come boy one and you also boy two.' Looking at Titus Tembo she spoke firmly, 'please do not refer to me as ma'am as it makes me feel much older than I am, call me Hilda.' And as he came back to normality, Titus Tembo responded, 'I am TT ma'am, sorry I mean ma'am Hilda.'

'Would you like to come in?' invited Hilda as she explained the boys were away and would never hurt anyone, 'They just play a bit rough with each other and at their young age that is the worst that could happen.' Really, thought TT to himself, he did not think he'd go anywhere near those two anytime soon. 'Well, there are actually two of us human's ma'am Hilda.' Clearly, she had no problem there being two strangers at her door, TT was beckoned in and handed a cold beer which he held onto as a possible weapon if the lions came for him. It was another big effort for Mr. Robert Joramogi to drag himself out of the mini bucket seat and a disturbed Pat the cat was not over keen to join them albeit unknowingly in the lions' den.

All three visitors trooped through the unlocked gate together, two of them were on edge, as both men were still aware they were in lion territory. They were like twins in their actions as both men took a backward step as a large domestic cat came bounding towards them and greeted Pat. Ma'am Hilda Lyons told them not to be concerned as the big boys were locked away for their morning feed. TT imagined they'd be in a caged off area and he relaxed just a little. Both visitors could hear noises like *meow, hiss* and *snarl*, really just like domestic cats, but louder. Pat sniffed in great interest at the furniture and seemed to sense he may be out gunned here by the big cats that lived in this territory! He went to the door and pawed at it in his urgency to get back to the safety of the car. His behaviour became even more erratic as suddenly a mature male or female lion started off with a few long deep roars. Both African men and Pat the cat ran in unison as if their very lives depended on them reaching the speed of sound in the quickest getaway in the history of beast versus man and domestic cat. As they reached the gate, they were ready for the high jump if so required, the roars became faster ones and then suddenly silence.

Ma'am Hilda Lyons stood at the back door of the house, laughing on the top of her voice at the site of the young and old sprinting couple clawing at the gate padlock in a vain attempt to join Pat the cat in their Mini Cooper S. Pat the cat had somehow managed to sneak under the gate and left the humans to fend for themselves. The lady of the house apologised. 'Sorry guys, I always make sure the gate is locked at all times as we do not want to scare a stranger who may wander in without knowing this is big cat territory. It's also one of the reasons I play those recordings of lions in the bush so loudly. No one is going to enter over the fence when they hear those sounds. I also play it to relax the young guys. In the wild that sound could be heard up to 5 miles away, so the sound on my iPod and the amplifier is turned down when we are in the Al Hamra Village. The guys feel safe that the father of the pride roars to scare off intruders and keep them secure. Clearly it worked a treat with you two.' She giggled a little and her 'sorry' did not seem genuine. Maybe she'd played this game before with other visitors?

They calmed down, Pat nevertheless stayed in the Mini Cooper S, the humans put their embarrassment behind them and both of them made their enquiries concerning the lions. Ma'am Hilda Lyons was always delighted to entertain visitors and inform them of the work being done for the opportunity to network and possibly increase their funding. 'My husband is the driving force behind what we are trying to do. We are doing our little bit to help the domesticated lions bred in the United Arab Emirates, we are not in a position to save the lions of the world from extinction. Did you know there are only about 10,000 lions left in the wild, possibly fewer than wild rhino? In fact, there are probably more in captivity in the Republic of South Africa for their canned shooting of the poor things; yes, shocking I know that there are more lions there than in the rest of wild Africa combined. It's argued by some that the breeding in captivity may provide a buffer against wild lion exploitation.

Captive breeding is permissible under the Convention on International Trade in Endangered Wild Fauna and Flora (CITES), and we are all legal and licensed here. But we are not breeding lions and we think captive breeding is not helping towards the poaching of wild lions which isn't declining.   Lions do very well in terms of breeding in captivity, and our concern is the ethics, it's our moral duty to ensure these individual animals do not suffer. That is our role, albeit maybe an insignificant one globally, we do what we can and we are currently setting up a charity with a more suitable environment to house them outside the Al Hamra Village, to save these magnificent big cats from suffering.'

Mr. Robert Joramogi seemed very much relieved after his question was answered by Ma'am Hilda Lyons on how they envisaged the charity work. He actually had been day dreaming, thinking back to his family's Northern Kenyan village and the day he heard a cat crying pathetically in an old lady's shamba. He was concerned that the cat was so hungry it was trying hard to be noticed, so loud and pathetic were its calls, trying so hard to make his wants heard by his owner but to no avail. Please mama feed your poor cat before it starves to death. 'Mtoto' she explained to him, I just popped my cat to avoid the trouble of dealing with more little cats. He is making all this noise because he is a little sad not for food but for the other thing he'll not need in future, for all the fights and late-night outs that would be no longer part of his life. A few days later after I told my mama of the old lady and her cat popping, the same lady visited our 'nyumbani' and our once proud male cat was made sad for a short while and the household were never concerned about lots of small cats for many a year. Why didn't ma'am Hilda Lyons and her husband rather save all this trouble and provide captive male lions with a popping service?

He put that thought behind him and asked the less controversial and more polite question on what they were fed on. 'Their meals consist of raw meat and in the main that means chicken donated when it's not fit for human consumption. Indeed, that lamb you saw was not on the menu, just another rescued creature that we'll have to find a new home for here, before the lions take too much interest in her. On the other hand, our cat is more than capable of standing up to her bigger cousins and will stay, as she is certainly not on their menu.' Before they left, TT offered his contribution to their lion charity in the form of free professional photographic shoots.

The morning Al Hamra Village safari, just like the ones in Kenya, always provided a surprise or two. Ma'am Hilda Lyons was surely giving Titus Tembo a message he felt, showing TT the way by example: '*Make sure you do something you have a passion for, you will enjoy what you are doing, it will never feel like work, you'll be good at it and you will be successful; do not follow the money as the money in the end will follow you.'*

The Al Hamra Village trip for the most followed the daily rhythm of a typical African safari. After a slow start the tourists would see something of interest and then get all excited when spotting one of the big five, like a lion. As the day got warmer, interests would be more towards the views and lunchtime before more excitement late afternoon and then thoughts of home comforts. Titus Tembo's navigator was again squeezed into the bucket seat and Pat the cat was fully recovered and in his relaxed number one position laying on his back near his master's feet.

Mr. Robert Joramogi pointed out the golf club house on the right-hand side and an adjoining bistro, plus a five-star beach hotel that you travelled to by boat across the bay from the golf club car park area. There were a series of different Star Hiltons, they included sports bars, an up-market entertainment cocktail bar, buffets, karaoke English bar, seafood, Italian, Japanese, Arabic, & steak restaurants, from two star to the Seven Star of the Waldorf Astoria. There were specialised food places like mussels and beers from the Belgium Beer Café over-looking the golf range. A golf range suffering possibly from *'Matatanisho'* as the golf range catered for rugby played by men and women as well as Irish Rules Gallic football training that took place there on one evening per week.

TT thought that there were more ways to spend your time and hard-earned cash than even Nairobi offered, and all in this small area. In his opinion enough entertainment surely to cover all the different nationalities of the village and beyond. For the tea lovers there was the TWG tea shop in the Waldorf Astoria. There was even an outdoor BBQ area with live music on the beach at the White Bar. His host Mr. Robert Joramogi had tried all of them, and a lot of them like the tea shop, on many occasions. Over the years Mr. Robert Joramogi admitted he had also attended the ladies' nights in the bars for observation reasons only he insisted; Mr. Robert Joramogi grinned as TT gave him a strange look following his last remark.

Mr. Robert Joramogi was warming to his task as entertainer as well as navigator. Further down the road he explained there is a conference centre next to the beach where, when you are ready, you can get married a fourth time! Next along the coast road Mr. Robert Joramogi described where there was a small beach resort with a spa and tennis court. Closely following on from the quaint beach resort, the Mini Cooper S approached the Ras Al Khaimah equivalent of the Dubai man-made island but on a slightly smaller scale than the Palm Jumeirah. It's ironic but the mountains moved to build both islands came right here from the Northern Emirates. Maybe, son of Eng. M. J. R. Tembo, you would feel more at home on our island? Or if we travel north on this same coastal road, you may like to live in a similar complex to Al Hamra Village but without the bars, golf course, and winter sporting venues.

No Mr. Robert Joramogi, it all came spilling out from Titus Tembo, 'if I do decide to live anywhere it would be in the village environment, not the one in Northern Kenya for clarification, but here in the Northern Emirates. To be frank, the way I feel right now, I'd be more comfortable and ready to live in Al Hamra Village when probate is underway than anywhere else in the United Arab Emirates. Can you please help me Mr. Robert Joramogi? Should I look at what the 'a bit of Yorkshire' man has in mind or look in the same complex as you or the marina or what other recommendation you may have?'

That's wonderful to hear, thought Robert Joramogi. He would support the son of his best friend Eng. M. J. R. Tembo and one of the first things to do was to check out the proposal from 'the taste of Yorkshire' or was it 'a bit of Yorkshire'? That place on offer and compare it against market values in the three Village complexes. Or possibly let's put that second on the list and first a good lunch and more shared memories. 'So, TT, lets drive on to Al Hamra Mall and we'll kill three birds with one stone; you can see the golf apartments which are very conveniently located near the mall with all its services, try out the popular Arabic eatery, and chat over what we can do to assist you in your quest for a temporary home.'

CHAPTER ELEVEN

The lesson of Ubuntu

The lunchtime eatery Mr. Robert Joramogi selected provided an ambiance that transported you out of the mall to somewhere exotic and old worldly Arabic. Mr. Robert Joramogi had heard that this chain of United Arab Emirates eateries had first been established by a Lebanese couple who started off with just a kiosk in Beirut on the sidewalk corner of a busy intersection. Their kitchen, like those Kenyan street vendors preparing maize corn for the hungry on their way to and from work, had basic cooking facilities in the form of a charcoal fire. When they first started, the eatery consisted of a few tables and comfortable chairs on the pavement. He cooked and she served. Shishir was soon added and the infamous clear white liquor tasting of aniseed was issued as a gratuity to regular customers.

The eatery in the Lebanese capital proved very successful and Mr. Robert Joramogi suspected they surely were thinking about what level to take their business to next, just as one of those regular Lebanese wars broke out and the decision was made for them. The once busy intersection where they located their outdoor restaurant turned into a battle zone. The middle-aged couple packed all their precious belongings in the form of United States Dollar notes, they managed to fill one suit case with their life savings, another with their essentials and memorabilia to start a new life when they fled to Dubai. The decision to leave was not easy, but they had no children as their business and clients acted as their family. As a consequence, today in the United Arab Emirates many people are benefiting from one of those far too frequently fought Lebanese wars.

This eatery in Al Hamra was a place to relax and enjoy, yet it was situated in the middle of a busy modern shopping Mall, old world eclectic surrounds, healthy Lebanese food with its French influence, the finest Arabic coffee, and from an adjoining area facing the road came that sickly yet sweet smell wafting from the Shishir to fill the air. Young waiters and waitresses in long starched stiff clean white smart aprons, ensured your table was never neglected. In the United Arab Emirates, they were not at liberty to provide the special white liquor to loosen people's tongues but it nevertheless was a place to take your time, fill the table with tasty refreshments and take the opportunity to communicate with everyone around your table. This was a favourite pastime for many well-off families in the United Arab Emirates on a Friday afternoon.

'Son of Eng. M. J. R. Tembo, I promised to tell you more about your Mama. She was a good friend of my ex-wife. But I can do better than tell you about her, rather I will tell you what your Baba said about your Mama. Your Baba wrote to me many letters when he first departed the United Kingdom for the copper mines in Central Africa. In one of those letters, he explained to me about the first hiccup of your Mama's journey to Africa, following checking in of her luggage for the Zambian Airways overnight flight from London to Lusaka. It took off with her suitcase and she was left with her wedding hat, the wedding cake and her yet to be blessed gold wedding ring at Heathrow. Your Mama was a little hard of hearing so may have not have heard the departure announcements. But then Zambian Airways should have off loaded her suitcase if she did not go through to the plane after check-in. Your Mama sat and relaxed in the Heathrow departure lounge as all her other goods were in the suitcase and unknown to your Mama it was jetting its way to Lusaka and onwards to Kitwe without her.

It was hours later your Mama realised there may be something seriously wrong. Possibly the incoming flight had not landed from Lusaka as yet? Your Mama at the time did not know she had a problem of hypermetropia; so, without glasses she may not have seen the departure board saying the flight had left. I always recall puzzling over how she struggled to see the numbers on those big red double-decker buses in Cardiff until it was right on top of the bus stop. Years later in Africa when she finally got her eyes tested and wore glasses, your Baba said, she remarked how it was the first time in her life she realised from a distance trees like the Acacia had individual leaves rather than one green mass! Although her eyes could see no sign of the departure on the information boards, the lounge area was starting to not only empty of fellow passengers, all the outlets were winding down for the night, and many were closing the shutters on the front of the establishments. No planes would be coming in or out at this late hour due to the restrictions that give local residence some respite from the harrowing sounds of the jet engines. Your Mama eventually decided to return without her suit case by train to the City of Swansea, then onwards by bus up the Swansea

Valley the next morning. All her family seemed shocked apparently, thinking she had second thoughts about going through with the marriage to your Baba.

All these years later, I can tell you many more stories of your Mama and Baba in great detail. This apparently super human power I have is simply down to the content of your Baba's letters stored in my memory banks. Maybe those memory banks are full and that is why I sometimes struggle today to remember little things like where I left my phone, or reading glasses, or that you are left or is it right-handed? Anyway, to put your mind at rest about my memory, these stories are all recorded and available for you in the letters your Baba sent me over the weeks and years we communicated with each other. I would read those letters several times before I would consider writing back to Eng. M. J. R. Tembo. My ex-wife would read them once I was done with them. She missed her friend, your Mama, very much. It seemed like she absorbed every detail about her before she lent the letters to your grandmother to read. She in turn tied the letters with some ribbon and stored them in a cardboard shoe box that today sits in her home, close to the village your Mama was born in. So, if you want the letters, they are located half way up the Swansea Valley in Wales the United Kingdom, in the village of Clydach where my ex-wife hails from.

Clydach is in the next village along from Glais where your Mama was born. Unlike your adventurous Mama, my ex-wife never left the Swansea Valley, never left the village of Clydach other than to do her teacher training in Cardiff. Ended up in Clydach teaching the next generations in the same village she was brought up in and being very content with that connection. They were in Pontardawe Grammar School together but as far as I know, were not friends until they met at teacher training in Cardiff together. Indeed, my ex-wife would support Vardre Rugby Football Club where her father captained the local team and her brother and cousins played. Your Mama as an only child would support their arch rivals Glais Rugby Football Club where her father and uncles played. Do not get fooled that they were just watching sport, no, this was very serious indeed my friend; in Wales rugby is considered by many as far more important than religion. What united those two in the end was that they both married African men from Kenya.

As your Mama struggled with the start of her African adventure in the United Kingdom and made a second attempt to fly to Zambia, your Baba was in a state of shock in Lusaka, the capital city of Zambia and its main and only international airport. He'd made special arrangements, taken the couple of days leave he had accumulated, to greet Marina his wife to be, on her landing in Africa for the first time. This was not your Baba being purely romantic, no, it was partly done as your Baba Eng. M. J. R. Tembo on landing in Lusaka for the first time, had seen the trials and tribulations of some of the mzungu new arrivals. Some poorer or dishonest Africans, both in Kenya and Zambia and maybe other countries, looked at a mzungu as if they were a money tree or ATM machine in today's terms! No doubt there were wealthy travellers, but not every mzungu was rich and in your Baba's eyes it was no reason to be dishonest whether they were wealthy or not. These victims included people who had all the necessary documents and vaccinations. However, the array of bureaucrats at the entry port could find some reason to bother and fleece innocents of their hard currencies. Your Baba did not want your Mama facing this on her arrival.

Well, in the end your Mama was not subject to any of that bother on entry when she arrived a few days later. A mine company administration official had checked the manifest after missing her on the earlier flight at the end of the previous week. It was a mystery to the mine company administration official why Ms. M. Davies did not come the first time as she was a listed passenger. This time around he made certain she was whisked through arrivals and taken to the internal flight in good time. With his duty completed successfully, the official wished Ms. Davies a safe onward journey. With his job done in Lusaka, he failed to inform anyone in the Kitwe regional office a Ms. Marina Davies or even a Ms. M. Davies was on her way at last, better late than never.

A few days earlier your Baba was downcast as there was no sign of his bride to be and no more passengers were coming through to the exit at Lusaka international airport. Eng. M. J. R. Tembo accepted his fate after talking to the flight crew. There was a Ms. Mary Davies but no Ms. Marina Davies on the passenger list and he or she must have cleared the gate as there were no more passengers behind the crew and certainly no Miss Marina Davies, was listed as a passenger. A naturally despondent Eng. M. J. R. Tembo tried to put a brave face on for the various people who were in Kitwe and expecting him to come around and show of his new love and bride to be. They all sympathised openly with your Baba but he suspected some of the older women secretly felt for the unknown brave young woman who clearly came to her senses at the twelfth hour!

Eng. M. J. R. Tembo wrote to me that he was not sure how he would react to the loneliness without the potential of having your Mama with him. Eng. M. J. R. Tembo put it to me clearly that he no longer could take the likes of filling his time of an evening playing stupid games like that mindless bingo with the crowd of expatriates who had arrived in the mining town on the same day as him. They meant well, your Baba stated and clearly, they had taken the young man under their wings but most of them were of a different culture and also new to this experience. At least your Baba was African and bush wise. He had no problem with the fact that butter would only be in the shops for a short while once a shipment from Ireland arrived. On the other hand, the experienced expatriates would buy it up and hoard it so they could live normally with one of their essential foods for at least the next six months.

Eng. M. J. R. Tembo would not be pushing people aside and as he had already witnessed, pushing them into open fridges in the super market to ensure he was clear of his rival shoppers and therefore had flour in his pantry to bake bread. Your Baba as an African, despite the British university education, could get by on paw-paw fruit or other local fruit the expatriates referred to as exotic tropical stuff. It was the same for the local veggies. He did not need weekly supplies of refrigerated apples flown in from the apartheid Republic of South Africa every month. The rest of the world were not buying the white regime's goods so why should he. And if there was no milk, he'd drink water. If there was no chocolate coming in from the rebels in Rhodesia that became Zimbabwe, he would suck on the sugar cane sticks that were growing next to the railway lines. There were lots of beans to be had, fruits and vegetables in season, and ugali maze despite the different name, they liked to call it mealie pap in that part of the world, it tasted just as good as in Kenya despite the new name.

Your Baba did face some challenges during the early days in Kitwe. In their wisdom the mine company's human resources team forgot he was due to get married soon. They housed your Baba with who they thought would be a like-minded British man. He was a roughneck rigger called Frank Gifford, who was single and of a similar age to your Baba. This is where their similarities ended. The problem was the human resources administration had not thought enough about the situation of the unmarried Eng. M. J. R. Tembo. Housing him with Frank Gifford was not the best idea. Frank Gifford had no intention to waste his hard-earned money on a car. So, they were billeted together in a house close to the mine and in fact walking distance away from work. Frank Gifford was not going to spend money on fencing the compound and feeding guard dogs to protect his property as he had nothing worth stealing anyway. Work or home was no different to Frank, just that one was a place to sleep. He did not see the point of spending on luxuries like curtains and carpets. This was a real bachelor pad where clothes would be dried in the oven of the electric cooker, so saving on the need to press them. Frank's main meals would be eaten in the works canteen to save on the washing up of dishes at home.

The young Frank became your Baba's choice of best man for the big day. Admittedly they saw very little of each other after that, as your Baba got to know a whole lot of, shall we say a better class of people, or better still different type of people. Frank was selected as Best Man as your father had no one else at the time. The fact that your Baba moved out as soon as he could to share in a flat where he was more secure and comfortable, only came shortly before your Mama arrived in Zambia. So, there was no going back on the plan for Frank Gifford acting as best man. Rough Frank took up the job for the day under the understanding his speech would be short, your Baba would provide him a suit, a tie and he got as much free beer to drink on the day as he liked, even if he no longer could stand up or talk clearly. Rough Frank had bought himself a motor bike by the time the wedding day arrived and your Baba had got an old VW Beetle.

Unlike your Baba, Rough Frank had learned to drink and drive. In those days the police were of very little danger as there was no law against drink driving in Zambia, and anyway there was no such thing as a test for drink driving in that part of the world at that time. The police vehicles were mostly in the repair shop awaiting foreign currency to buy parts from South African distributors. The result was that at night the streets would be more or less devoid of any police vehicle and the police enjoyed the security of their comfortable stations where they no doubt sat relaxing and drinking sweet tea. How rough Frank Gifford did it, no one could believe but apparently, he managed to drive regularly at the weekend on his bike when he could hardly walk straight. Rough Frank Gifford wasted none of his hard-earned money on anything with the exception of beer, cards and an occasional loose woman.

On landing in Kitwe unannounced, your Mama, poor young untravelled mzungu, found herself it seemed to her, in the middle of the African bush and far from civilization. The closest she had come to seeing sights like these previously was in documentaries on black and white television in the United Kingdom. She was concerned about what lay out there beyond the airport fence. It was here in some corrugated sheeted tin shack she found her suitcase secured in a lock-up designed for this very purpose. It had travelled alone from London Heathrow and waited patiently for her to arrive - it seemed as if it had a life of its own! The cabin crew and the handful of ground staff were ready to depart in a minivan provided by the airline. The group of workers had done their duty for the day and wanted to quickly close up and leave the airport for the comfort of home and family. All of them were talking in the local dialects which all sounded the same to your Mama, untranslatable into English. They were at least looking in her direction. They were however likely wondering what this young white girl would do, stuck out here for the night? Okay she'd be safe enough, but possibly uncomfortable and her people would pick her up at some time, or would they?

Fortunately for your parents they were to experience the Ubuntu of Southern Africa. This is a similar concept to what Titus Tembo son of Eng. M. J. R. Tembo that we Kenyans understand as 'Harambee', all pull together, in an unwritten law of generosity. This, Mr. Robert Joramogi explained simply in a story he heard from a mzungu friend back in Cardiff. 'Ann Williams went to Kenya on a gap year after teacher training college. She was lucky to have experienced the delights of Kenya for a year and never forgets it. Ann Williams became a friend of my ex-wife and so for a time a friend of our family and therefore me also. One day in her second term of teaching her class of young kids, she offered a bag of sweets, this was big enough for the whole class. Her offer however of the big bag of sweets was for the one child who could answer three questions correctly. They were to write the answers along with their names on a sheet of paper she handed out to each child. Although she set three very challenging questions, they had covered the answers in class that year. To her surprise and initial disappointment, only one sheet was handed back, she hoped for more of the children to have a go and encourage the competition, with the winner enjoying the reward. She unfolded the one piece of paper handed in, to find the right answers, but all the kids names were also written on the one sheet. When she questioned the class over this mind-boggling response, all she got were smiles at first. Later some of her brighter kids explained how they would have not felt right somehow; when others lost out to them, and that would make the winner with their sweets unhappy. The majority of the class would be looking on hungrily and leaving the winning child with their big bag of sweets feeling sad.

And so, it was the same for your Mama, the Zambia Airways staff were all in a happy mood to go home to their families but how could they be happy if they left this young mzungu lady behind in a sad mood. Mind you your mother was not sure what she'd let herself in for and when a few of the staff were dropped off at their traditional village homes, the mini bus was surrounded by kids banging on the windows, waving at her and shouting friendly greetings she could not understand. On top of this your Mama must have been exhausted by her to-ing and fro-ing in the United Kingdom between the Swansea Valley and London Heathrow, the long sleepless night flight to Lusaka and her short bumpy flight in the light aircraft from Lusaka to Kitwe. Sleepless on the flight to Lusaka, as she sat next to a lovely talkative African lady who should have booked an additional seat for her large frame rather than sharing the seat with your mother. You can imagine I am sure the traditional African figure of a mature lovely lady from Zambia!

The cabin crew ended up dropping your exhausted Mama at what was regarded as by far the best hotel in town. The Edinburgh Hotel staff on duty were keen to solve your Mama's problems, as your Baba's employers were their top clients. The government mine basically owned and ran the town of Kitwe. First it was tea for the lady, that ended up being complimentary. Fortunately, no bill was presented as your Mama had no local money, only British Pounds, worth their weight in gold on the black market. She knew nothing at that time of the black-market rate for Sterling Pounds exchanged for the local worthless Kwatcha, so it could have ended as a very expensive tea indeed.

After a number of phone calls, your Mama was taken by the hotel staff car to the mine administration office to await the grand arrival of your Baba. Grand indeed it was not. Eng. M. J. R. Tembo had been working underground with his team. He was leading them testing and commissioning some electrical power installation deep underground. It was hot and it was dirty and this was reflected in his condition and appearance. Nevertheless, your Baba was so glad to be called back from the depths of the earth to finally welcome his wife to be. He did not have the mind-set to shower, change his dirty clothes or prepare his appearance for your Mama; he just wanted to make sure she had arrived safely. It was a further shock to her that even an African could look dirty. There was, however, no mistaking that big white grin of your Baba lighting up the room when he set eyes on your Mama.

Your Baba wrote me that it took him three refills of the bath tub to get him presentable, and his house boy probably took just as long washing his filthy work wear in the same tub the next day. Your Mama had to wait some time before she could wash her skin and no doubt was happy just to lie on their single bed resting. Yes, a single bed, as they had not been awarded a house of their own as yet - that would only be ratified on the marriage arrangements being confirmed to the mine administration officers. In fact, they were still to share a single flat with a young British engineer. The few days of leave your Baba had accumulated were used up when he took the trip to Lusaka to welcome his soon to be bride. As such your Mama, come the next morning, would be left to her own devices while Eng. M. J. R. Tembo attended to his work duties. It gave your Mama time to rest up a little more and unpack the few things she had brought in the one suit case.

It was a nice time of year weather wise as the rains were long gone and the hot October weather was yet to hail the on-set of the next long rains. It had been a good growing season and the local veggie market was full of seasonal offerings. This was not the United States of America nor Western Europe, and you were offered and cooked whatever was in season, be it just peas, runner beans or cabbage. Other times it could be carrots, potatoes, and corn mealies. Fruit was a similar in-season tropical offering, so no apples except when flown in from South Africa, no strawberries and pears from cooler parts other than those from Rhodesia, breaking the sanctions. Those sanctions meant there were very little or no imports as Zambia bordered the now Zimbabwe but the then Rhodesia.

Zambia was known as Northern Rhodesia, until it gained its own independence from Britain in 1964. The White ruled Rhodesia had declared its own independence with the support of apartheid South Africa. As a result, at that time they were going through a civil war that lasted 14 years plus, one when a black elected majority government under Bishop Abel Muzorewa failed to hold on to power against the forces of Robert Mugabe and Joshua Nkomo. The settlers had many times suppressed a series of rebellions or what was locally referred to as a Chimurenga. And in this latest and final Chimurenga the Rhodesian air force ruled the sky and warned the Zambian forces by radio not to interfere when they attacked the freedom fighters based in Zambia.

One of the other side effects of the Chimurenga was felt by the residence in the city of Kitwe. Like the rest of Zambia people in Kitwe were facing a dusk to dawn curfew after it was rumoured amongst the expat community that the Rhodesians had blown up every road bridge in Zambia overnight. I digress, but we'll get back to that bit of your Baba's story at the end of his two-year contract in Zambia.

Your Baba was puzzled why your Mama was not exploring the Kitwe Town. She was tired from her recent travels for starters, and your Baba had experienced for himself the effects of high altitude when he first arrived on the copper belt. Life here was exhausting in the first few weeks of becoming accustomed to the heat, and most importantly the high altitude. However, the main obstacle keeping your Mama in the house turned out to be partly due to her tour round the townships thanks to the kind hearts at Zambia Airways, after that experience she was scared. Scared to be a rare white face in a sea of black. Your Baba should have been more sensitive to be perfectly frank; we'd faced the same thing when first studying in UWIST Cardiff. There was that time we feared for our lives when that mad man posted the fire bomb in Alfred Street. So, your Mama was sent out under the guard of the house boy who in fact was no boy but an old man. This eased your Mama into being out an about in a strange environment that felt threatening to her.

On moving to their own house, the old man house boy decided to stay where he was and your parents went through a number of unreliable house boys. Your Mama now had the opportunity to visit Kitwe Town in a two-seater red Sprite sports car with an English lady who lived in the next house. Elsie was married to an Australian mechanic Stan. She left England and went to live in Perth Australia where she met Stan, but she failed to settle in the lucky continent. They returned to England where Stan failed to settle due to the grey sky and incessant rain. So here they were, trying together on a third continent in Zambia to find themselves at an age where they should have been relaxing with their grandkids. It was a simple case of '*Matatanisho*' for white folks.

Your Mamas' network of friends expanded as everyone liked the young innocent Welsh girl who was due to be married soon. There was also Pauline, married to Slimy Phil. They part time ran an illegal casino, mainly for the Italians. Phil worked at the mine but loved money and took this big risk of illegal gambling to enhance their lifestyle. At the back of their garden your Baba installed a small set of steps to allow them entry to converse with the recently married young British couple. Sue Jones was a very attractive lady and Martin was a squat front row rugby player. Your Mama and Baba guessed there was an attraction between them that was not obvious to the likes of the outside world, and your parents were never rude enough to ask the question. They had three very nasty dogs patrolling their garden 24/7 and as such your parents always called from the top of the steps, ensuring the guard dogs were locked away before venturing into their territory. Your Baba wrote to me that he only made the mistake once of thinking all dogs liked him and to be honest most dogs do. You may have seen the scar left on his right ankle that one of those beasts' bit as your Baba climbed back to safe ground.

Across the road was another English family with a couple of kids but your Mama did little with them, as sadly the father was home on sick leave due to chronic hepatitis C. His liver was in a bad way, he was a yellow colour, very unhealthy, weak and everyone sadly expected him to pass on. I specifically mention this as in the end it also killed your Mama some years later. There were friends of friends who were also part of the British expat network your Mama hooked into. This ensured that as a couple, your parents knew what was going on, did not miss out on whatever was on the grapevine, which could be just the latest shipment of Irish butter in the shops, or that South African wine had just arrived, or a party at, etc. It was that simple when there was no WhatsApp, no texting, no email, or mobile phones or laptops, just telegrams and landlines which your parents could not afford.

Zambia and the mines were no cake-walk for your Baba. The day he arrived all the expats were on strike following the shooting of one of them as the police let off their guns in a nearby copper mine town one evening earlier that week. The dead man was unlucky to have found any police out at night. They mistook his car for one they thought was involved in an earlier crime. One of the bullets that the police indiscriminately fired bounced off the road and through the back of the poor man's car before hitting him and striking him dead instantly.

Transport was in itself a challenge and your Baba, who had learned to drive in Cardiff, obtaining a United Kingdom driving license to go with his British passport, never got his Zambian driving license and he never mentioned car inspections or insurance in his letters to me. The only car your Baba found to buy on his budget, even with black market exchange rates, was an ancient VW Beetle that needed one front brake pad and a new starter motor that were not available on the copper belt. As a result, on slowing down, the car would always pull sharply to the left. Then occasionally, well - like every third time your Baba started the car, he'd have to crawl under the car with a long screw driver that had an insulated handle to protect him as he sparked the old beetle into action. Sorry to say, how your Baba ever found this way of starting the car is beyond me as an arts graduate who knows nothing about car electrics. What I do know is that it must have been an inconvenient method of starting the car, particularly during the rainy season! Your Baba's budget was stretched to the limit, even after selling Sterling Pounds at the attractive black-market rate. Your Baba wrote me once that the local currency seemed to fall in value every month before the expatriate miners lined up in Barclays bank to send a chunk of their monthly salary home

Your Baba's work initially was a disappointment to him as all the newly arrived younger engineering graduates reported to Slimy Phil to do a time and study report on the railways carrying raw materials between the mine and the refinery. Then he was put on power station duty in the control room where the most exciting event was when one of the large rats would show itself under the control room main desk. Your Baba had guessed that maybe one of the operators had fed the rat as it turned up daily about the same time of day, sniffing around for food and unconcerned that he was sitting right above him or her? Eventually he was lucky enough to take over responsibility as the man in charge of the electrical testing and commissioning team. And that was one of the reasons he was underground the day your Mama landed in Kitwe.

Despite all the new challenges there were also some perks. Your Baba's role as man in charge of the electrical testing and commissioning team came with benefits. He had the electrical test sections rations of sugar, tea and coffee to issue and win favour from his team. I understood that my friend Eng. M.J. R. Tembo was not sure if these goodies were just for consumption on the premises, but if that was the case, he would have to increase the breaks for his team, which could reduce the working day by some two hours - he wrote me in jest. In the case of the electrical testing and commissioning section there was also a need for large quantities of industrial salt to soak the ground with a salt water mix on testing earth conductivity. Once again, the stores had issued far more than they would need in the work environment. So, your Baba put that Zambian Ubuntu into practice with the issue of tea, coffee and especially sugar and salt aplenty, so each man went home happy at month end.

Your Mama had perks of her own. Through the Italian friend they had made, one particular older man took a great interest in her. Your Baba and your Mama had the sugar cane concession and both were clear of the limits to be set. Let me explain the sugar cane logic to you, it is what us old fellows would describe as temptation between men and women. Could you have a woman as a friend to a man or the other way around? Well could you use a sugar cane stick as a walking aid or eventually would you nibble at the sugar cane? I think that is clear, enough don't you Titus Tembo son of Eng. M. J. R. Tembo?

The older Italian fellow, as was their culture in Italy, would tap your Baba on his shoulder when dancing and ask him to move over so he could dance with your Mama. Discreetly, he would manoeuvre just out of sight of your Baba and into a crowd, then pinch your Mama's bottom. It was common practice by Italian men in those days, and given the name *'pacca sul sedere'*, a slap on the bottom. Though it could be a pinch or a brush but too precisely located to be accidental and today less likely to happen or for that matter be accepted. The older Italian man would repeat this practice after dropping your future parents' off in their home driveway as your Mama exited the car following your Baba getting out - so he would not see this inappropriate action. The older Italian fellow assumed wrongly your Mama did not tell your Baba about his strange habit. Well strange in their cultures.

The old Italian kindly left them with some quality coffee or cheese as a parting gift each time they met up together. They cut their ties with the Italian when the older man suggested to your Mama having lunch alone and he would give her a personal gift of perfume or sun glasses in return. Both of your parents decided they did not need to play the sugar cane stick game. It proved to be a very wise decision as those Italians were caught dealing in illegally poached leopard skin and ivory bracelets.

CHAPTER TWELVE

The wedding

Your Mama and Baba were setting up a new home and planning their wedding at the same time. Two tea chests arrived from Wales with some precious goods your Mama had helped pick out in Swansea. First among the list of these important arrivals was the bedding, naturally for a double bed. Maybe because mature Zambians were traditionally built on the larger side, the mine's human resource department issued the soon to be married couple, two single beds. This was not seen as a problem as together they would act as a King size bed, but in this case, they were of dissimilar heights and proved a challenge in more ways than one. Difficult to sleep on, and somewhat untidy looking even after making the bed afresh each morning.

The curtains bought in Swansea market were more successful than the bedding as one large curtain was sufficient for each of the small windows in the house, and hung nearly to the floor. It turned out they had sufficient curtain cover for their bedroom windows and all but one of the lounge windows. The large partly curtained lounge looked a bit odd with one window left bare, but was sufficient to give your Mama and Baba the privacy they needed. The two wooden old fashioned Indian tea chests that had come from Wales, doubled up with a bamboo Zambia-made carpet from the local tourist market, on top, as a modern kitchen built in table top; albeit a bit lower than normal!

The mine's human resources administration department provided an electric cooker which challenged your Mama at first as she had only previously used natural gas. There were a few flat sponge cakes and partly baked vegetable pies to start off until your Baba explained that the electric oven had to warm up a while and was not instant heat like natural gas. He'd told your Mama in simple terms to watch the thermostat light go off before she started baking! From then on, reading between the lines, I believe your Mama had no further problems converting from natural gas to electricity.   The mine's human resource administration people also provided the basic pots and pans along with crockery and the other essential materials to help your Mama and Baba start their domestic bliss in Kitwe. The one item that left them a little challenged was the tropical freezer your Baba shipped directly from the factory in the United Kingdom to save on the value added tax. It had arrived with no compressor or possibly someone had stolen the compressor on route! So, until this was resolved they had that extra kitchen storage space but with few items to store and a pressing need for a functioning freezer.

Being at altitude near the tropics provided a very pleasant climate most of the year with the exceptions of the warmer sticky weather around November before the rains brought relief toward Christmas time. This warmer weather also meant there were weevils in their food stuffs like flour and pasta. This they got over at first by sieving all their food before cooking, which was laborious and time consuming. It would have been such a waste to throw the food stuff away, expensive and very hard or near impossible to find replacements in good time; replacements likely also full of weevils. So, your Baba got your Mama to adapt to the African way and they cooked the weevils along with the pasta and flour as extra protein that neither of them noticed in terms of colour, taste or stomach upsets.

What they could not deal with themselves were the fleas the warm weather brought to their uncut grass in their yard. It was only a matter of time before the dogs would be infested and then their home furniture. The mine vermin control team came to the rescue as the fleas were an infestation spreading along the street gardens. There was a mass spraying in the area and at that time the two guard dogs were locked in the house enjoying all the comforts of home.

There were ceiling fans but your father had complained in his letters to me that one of the fans that was in the main bedroom seemed to cry out at night for human company. It was not the noise of the ceiling fan or the two uneven single beds that kept your Baba awake most nights. The garden was blessed with a large avocado tree and two mango trees. Occasionally fruits would get so mature they'd leave their home on the tree. The heavy fruits would crash to the ground and made a loud thud on doing so. It was for the first time in his life your Baba admitted to me in his mail, that he experienced fear of the dark. There were armed thugs targeting the relatively wealthy found on the copper belt. People like the Italian business men and those Italian smugglers had money. All expats were as a result seen as targets for some very profitable break-ins. Even the likes of your poor Mama and Baba may have been seen as potentially very lucrative opportunities in a weakly policed residential area such as in Kitwe. The fact was that these police were ill equipped and inadequately trained for dealing with armed robberies.

Your Baba became a very light sleeper and heard nearly every heavy fruit that fell to earth. Each of those happenings set off a series of events where the man of the house got out of bed, did his rounds of checking on the doors and windows, switching on the outside lights to peer out while the two sleeping guard dogs remained undisturbed. The benefits of such productive trees, was their two large dogs never went hungry as the avocados were mixed with maize meal porridge in large plastic washing up bowls. The large guard dogs had big appetites and were most appreciative of what your Baba dished up. They never put on weight but then never looked thin.

So, the evidence was in favour of the dogs being sufficiently fed and yet there was that time when the bigger of the two dogs ate most of a hard-backed library book. Your father wrote it was probably from boredom when your parents were out, as they locked the dogs in the house when they were going out; but possibly he was hungry and as such their diet portions were increased from that day onwards. No more books were left out to tempt either dog just in-case. The dogs were put out in the garden when your parents were at home, except when your folks tried to sleep at night and they wanted the dogs inside to deter any attempted break-in. When the rains came the guard dogs, became home loving pets and were never too keen to go out in the cool wet weather. That action however did not explain to the librarian the damage dished out to that book, so your Mama had to discreetly pay over some money for them to continue as library members. Your Mama and Baba both agreed that was an essential investment as they could not afford a television set and remember this was before the days of computers, the internet, Netflix, DVDs or even the old-fashioned Betamax tape players. Sadly, your Baba never got to replace that book and as such never found out the end of the story.

As with the majority of expatriates, the house had a six-foot wire mesh fenced yard. This kept their two large dogs in the garden to do their patrol duty. In addition, your Baba had designed a safe room using scrap metal parts he welded to guard the internal bedroom door and a means of electrifying the window burglar bars. Finally, if all else failed, there was a siren at the ready to alert all around when they were in need of help. For the balance of the two-year contract, I know my good friend Eng. M. J. R. Tembo did his duty; there was never a robbery or a good nights' sleep at your parent's home in Kitwe. This excellent safety record may have been down to one of the dogs named Eric. He looked like a kindly Golden Labrador but acted like a Rhodesian Ridge-back military police dog. The school kids helped to train both dogs as each morning they ran along the outside of the fence dragging a stick against it in plain sight of Eric. He charged, gave a menacing growl and barked to let the kids know to never dare step across the threshold. His big black companion named Shaka, ambled along-side wagging his tail.

Eric was eventually recruited by the mine police when your Baba give notice at the end of his two-year contract in the Zambia copper mines. Your Baba informed me, but not your Mama, he thought the big friendly Shaka the second of their dogs may have been taken and eaten by the newly recruited Filipinos. It was rumoured that some of these Asians ate dogs but your Baba hoped and prayed their Shaka was a bit on the larger size so as to make him unattractive enough to serve up as a home meal.

Your parents kept the dogs as long as they could for protection until a few days before they pulled out and just the one day after the yard fence was sold off. The very next day the school kids at first seemed puzzled when they ran along the non-existent yard fence with their sticks. Shaka bounded towards them wagging his tail, showing his large teeth grinning and slobbering; little did they realise he was smiling and wanted to play. All of them bounded down Princess Street, screaming on the top of their voices in fear with Shaka loving the feel of freedom and their company. The big black dog was having fun and barking loudly in the joy of it all, while Eric, luckily for the school kids, was locked inside protecting the house. Shaka returned under his own steam on that occasion. Days later as your folks prepared to leave Kitwe, possibly for the last time, Eric was away as he was signed up for his future security duties and Shaka sadly had disappeared two days after the fence came down.

Going back a little in the time sequence for this story; soon after your Mama and Baba relocated to their detached house on Princess Street from their shared bachelor flat, one of their old Italian acquaintances helped them. Little did their Italian contact know then that his assistance would impact on their family not just for then, but it would last a lifetime. The Kitwe Meat Market was a place of plenty. The population in Zambia is relatively small yet growing very quickly. It is one of the most urbanized countries in sub-Saharan Africa. So, butcheries are big business in Zambia. If you have the right connections and plenty of money, there is all the meat you want.

Tribes such as the Tongas, Lozis, Cewas, Namwangas and Mambwes were traditional cattle keepers and the majority of cattle remained with them. Cattle, like in Kenya, were traditionally used as a means of trade and in marriage ceremonies, a symbol of wealth and even used to pay court fines. The days of paying war reparations by the losing tribe may have been over, but cattle in Zambia still played a very important role like the tractor in the western world; farming in Zambia depended very much on an ox-drawn plough. The traditional cattle keepers used the cattle dung as both fertilizer and as a source of fuel. Kitwe and the copper belt in general were not an area where people would rather go fishing, so meat was one of the cornerstones of the food needs of these people.

In the face of these pressures from pre-colonial days, add the other typical business challenges in Africa, corruption and nepotism. Little did your Mama realise, her appointment was meant to address all this baggage. What the appointment meant to your Mama and Baba in an instant was the wedding reception was taken care of meat wise and of course your Mama had already the wedding cake brought safely from Wales. Your Mama's salary was partly paid in a large chunk of meat cuts at the end of every month. By then your Baba had sourced a compressor for his United Kingdom delivered freezer and the monthly meat salary was stored safely.

The Kitwe Meat Market would do their reception proud and they needed to design the wedding feast accordingly. Ubuntu came from their network of friends; they were provided the perfect venue for the wedding reception feast in the form of a lovely private garden set around a swimming pool on Princess Street. Slimy Phil kindly appointed his Zambian house boy-come chef, to manage the Braai. Steaks were cooked to order, rare, medium rare to medium, and well done plus very well done or burnt, by the newly appointed chef. The chef also put to one side a pile of pre-cooked sausages to accompany the various steaks on order. Phil had instructed his cook not to kill the meat twice by over doing the exposure of the steaks to the flames of the Braai.

It was planned that the meat feast would be accompanied by Southern African maize meal pap that Eric and Shaka enjoyed daily. The minor difference between dog food and the wedding reception menu, was that avocado was included as a fancy starter rather than mashed in with the pap. The pap at the wedding reception was to be served with a rich tomato gravy. The quality of the steaks was good enough as it had served the needs of Prince Philip and the Queen when they visited the copper belt. This was done as part of the commonwealth conference a few weeks earlier. Eng. M. J. R. Tembo had dug through his treasure trove of goods that came in the two United Kingdom tea chests. A car lock from that trove was bartered to provide much needed, hard to get sparkling wine for the reception. I was of course invited, but it was a little too far and expensive for us to attend from the Welsh Valleys you understand.

At that stage your folks were putting the cart before the horse or rather the plough before the cattle. Your Baba accepted that this wedding was considered one of the most significant events in the life of a Luo and ranked high for his British blood also, but the decision in his own head was that it would not be a Luo society ceremony as that would be far too complicated and they could therefore avoid several steps. They were doing this away from the meddling parents, and he already asked the parents of the bride to be, your grandparents, who I understand you've never met, for their agreement and there was no discussion of the bride price and therefore no Ayie ceremony, no deal involving a neutral intermediary, no payment to the mother of the bride. T

Thank goodness your Baba had wrote to me, thank goodness there be no Meko with the kidnapping of his bride by his friends and relatives. If the Meko was done seriously, peoples' courage would be tested, noisy skirmishes would take place using sticks. He also did not want to put your Mama through the deflowering of his bride with witnesses! His bride's parents would not need to slaughter an ox, as Kitwe Meat Market would provide. Your Baba decided, with my approval that he would join the modern Christian Luo and have the wedding take place in a church and avoid the practice of polygamy even if he got to the point of owning enough cattle to pay the dowry for up to five wives. He told me he meant for this one to be is only wedding ever, and as you know that became the reality.

So now they'd organised the reception, the cart per say, they now had to find a horse for that cart in the form of a church to hold the wedding. As luck happens there was a second hand book and cake sale at Saint Luke's Church on the last Saturday of every month. This was the starting point of their search as your Mama being a member of the Anglican Church would prefer that choice of church. Eng. M. J. R. Tembo had started off as a youngster being brought up in ancestral worship. His Luo brothers and sisters recognized a supreme being whose common name was Nyakalaga, the one who dwells everywhere, and just like the Christian God, and the little green man seen in old British churches, one who supports the universe he created. The underlaying difference was the Luo worship of ancestral spirits. Mr. Robert Joramogi so an opportunity at this point to remark that there may have been some conflict in terms of your Baba's ancestral worship - if there was a death and the burial were not honourable, then the spirit would become a jachien and haunt the living relatives. And Titus Tembo you need to be aware of this for the body of your Baba. The wedding posed no such problems and as such Saint Luke's Church was to serve their needs admirably.

Kitwe was founded as far back as 1936 and had grown into a small city and as such there were many Anglican Churches. But not any Anglican Church in Kitwe would do, no, there was a specific need for this wedding in terms of the English language that Saint Luke's Church could provide once your parents had tracked down the ordained clergy responsible. There were lay people a plenty but people qualified to carry out the marriage on the dates your Mama and Baba wanted was not such an easy question to get the right answer that your Mama and Baba needed.

The key man to officiate at the marriage had broken his leg recently while showing his paces alongside no less a footballer than Rainford Kalaba the Chipolopolo captain. On that fateful day for your parents to be, there were other Kitwe football stars in the form of goalkeeper Kennedy Mween and the main Zambian striker Jacob Mulenga a friend of the Saint Luke's minister who was also a star footballer in his younger days before he found his real calling. He had turned out for a charity match and paid a heavy price for his good intensions when he broke his leg.

The other choice for the wedding day minister happened to be out in the villages doing his good work on the edge of Kitwe city. Your Mama and Baba could not wait for his return without delaying the wedding. They took their sturdy charger in the form of the old red VW Beetle, and headed out the following Sunday in search of the Irish minister. There was in those days, no smart phone, internet or google maps, in fact not any form of map, just a compass to give some comfort. Directions from the few villagers who spoke some words of English, consisted of *'drive to the big tree and ask there'*. Big trees stood out as much of the surrounding area had been cut down for firewood. The compass led your Mama and Baba to believe they were heading in the right direction, and clearly the kindly white man with red hair was well known to many people in this rural area.

The villages may have been on the edge of a city, but this was a whole new world for your Mama as a young woman coming from the Welsh Valleys. The people in the city were relatively well off due to the copper mines. In the rural areas it was clear to your Mama that the population lived in poverty. There was a challenge just for access to the basic services, water, sanitation and decent housing. Your Baba wrote to me that there is an abundance of fertile land yet there were so many kids that looked hungry. They found their red headed minister dressed in his everyday clothes helping out organising the building of a small church come child care clinic.

The minister was happy for the visit from two outsiders and the opportunity to take a well-earned break. This was a serious matter, he made it clear to your parents over a cup of strong sugarless black tea out of a chipped white enamel mug. Their new found minister friend explained that this was a wedding different to one held in Europe. It's a contract through the church. He made them aware that in Zambia religious marriages have no provision for divorce. It was lucky your parents found the right man, as for anyone to carry out a religious marriage they must be registered with the government to solemnise the big event. The church itself must also be gazetted, which Saint Luke's Church definitely was. What they needed to do was book the date for the church and read the banns. Both your parents hoped the date they wanted was free, but it did not matter, as the minister insisted they attend the three Sundays the banns were read out in the services. Everything was moved back by a week from the Saturday they had in mind.

Later that week, on returning to civilization your parents met with the lovely lady who played the organ at Saint Luke's. The lady wanted to hear from the happy couple what hymns they'd like played at the ceremony. She first posed this question to your Baba who had not prepared himself well for the meeting. His limited knowledge of English hymns forced him to blurt out the idea that 'Bringing in the Sheave's was a nice lively tune. He remembered this English song so well as it reminded him of good times when he was a boy. The headmistress at his village school was a committed Protestant Christian, A Seventh Day Adventist, and loved this particular up beat gospel song, so much so that she used it in her teaching of English literature even if it was American, well it did go back to 1874. As her role of head teacher involved leading the whole school in assembly, she had every child learn the words and got them singing this during the times of good rains. She said this was to encourage nature to provide her bounties to the people of this land who had worked hard, sowed their tears and who now should reap in joy. I must say to you son of Eng. M. J. R. Tembo, I'd like to have gone to the school this lady ran.

Sowing in the morning, sowing seeds of kindness,
Sowing in the noontide and the dewy eve;
Waiting for the harvest, and the time of reaping,
We shall come rejoicing, bringing in the sheaves.
Bringing in the sheaves, bringing in the sheaves,
We shall come rejoicing, bringing in the sheaves;
Bringing in the sheaves, bringing in the sheaves,
We shall come rejoicing, bringing in the sheaves.

The organist turned away from your Baba and looked to appeal to your Mama. And your Baba managed to record the exact words in this letter to me. *'Yes, it's a very nice Psalm my dear, but do we think it's the best tune for a wedding?'* After that the lovely lady focused all her efforts on your Mama. The flowers she would bring from her garden earlier on the Saturday morning and the wedding service that would start by ten thirty as they usually did for Saturday weddings, would be moved to early afternoon to accommodate the mine working hours that included working Saturday mornings.

Yes, your Baba could get away early that day and they never went underground on a Saturday in case of delaying their weekend. There was no danger of your Baba being late as there would be no need to take several baths to clean off the dust. The team in his section would clean up the workshop and keep themselves busy organizing the stores and equipment for the week to come. To the relief of your Baba that was that his contribution on the planning front completed, he was left to contemplate life after the big wedding day. Your Baba pondered, could they afford some time off to celebrate the event together on a proper honeymoon? Yes, he wrote me that the cost of the wedding and the reception must have been well under what people in somewhere like Nairobi would spend, and I guess the same in Wales even if all their family and friends were to attend. Your Baba had got off relatively cheaply, so he would see what could be arranged for a honeymoon in the short time left before the wedding day.

Both your Mama and Baba attended church that first Sunday. That in itself was a great achievement for they worked hard all week and as young people do, they craved some relaxation and entertainment on Saturday night. The following Sunday they drew lots to see which one of them would be there when the Banns were read. The plan was for your Mama to walk to church alone the following Sunday as your Baba snoozed on. But as no one took the opportunity on the first two Sundays to object to their marriage, both your parents agreed they'd stay in bed the Sunday before the wedding was set to take place.

On the day of the wedding your Mama was very nervous. Slimy Phil was due to give her away and before that, drive her to church, and even before that she had to get ready in Slimy Phil's home while his wife Pauline helped with hair preparation, did the makeup and encouraged your Mama by saying many times how perfect she looked. Slimy Phil naturally was a smoker and your Mama took a few from him for herself to calm her nerves. Her nerves but not her head ache, this was further helped with half a bottle of sherry.

The wedding was to be just like any service in tying the knot, be it religious as your Mama and Baba planned, or a civil one. Two Zambian church members led people to their seats as there was no differentiation on either side of the isle where guests of the groom sat, and opposite, guests and family of the bride. They were all in this together supporting the couple to be wed. Your Baba who never touched a cigarette in his life, was outside calming Rough Frank Gifford down as he chained smoked several cigarettes. The Best Man led the way and they entered together and stood one side at the front of the church once word came of your Mama approaching in the Slimy Phil wedding limo.

The lovely organist did a fine job of the 'Here comes the bride'. Both your parents said the service went in a blur, words of welcome, opening remarks and introduction, next the Irish officiant offered a few of his thoughts on marriage. There were readings before the exchange of vows that they both learned very well, everything went as expected. The kiss came, then a unity ceremony followed by the final blessings. Paper work was signed in the church, both of them assumed the wedding was registered in Zambia and they need not worry about that, and the only thing that remained was to reflect the change on your mother's passport.'

Mr. Robert Joramogi was enjoying tapping into these memories of his best friend and sharing them with his only son. But he needed some tea to quench his mouth before continuing with the events of the celebrations after the wedding that he could recall vividly from those letters of some thirty-seven years ago. Just a sip was sufficient for him to refuel and he looked at Titus Tembo with a gentle smile on his face. 'Your Baba's letter highlighted that there was a moment of hesitation outside the church when your Mama considered what came first, the bouquet toss, or the cake-cutting? Your Mama guessed correctly that every couple did it slightly differently and the wedding party headed for photographs that your Baba supervised. Some of those photographs can also be found with his letters back in Clydach. There was no grand entrance to the reception, but there was the traditional bouquets and garter tosses before the cutting of the Swansea wedding cake. Dinner was taken standing, with the main course being handed out from the black Zambian stranger burning the steaks on the BBQ, or Braai as they learned to call it there in Southern Africa.

The first dance took place in the strong sunlight next to the garden swimming pool. I am not sure if the smoking and the half a bottle of Sherry your Mama drunk before-hand, helped her in any way for the church service. It certainly cut short the wedding reception where according to what your Baba put in his letter, the minister and organist seemed to be enjoying letting their hair down as the newlywed couple provided hospitality for friends but sadly no family. Neither of your parents was in the mood to receive society as yet as a married couple, with one of them suffering the after effects of the wedding preparations that morning! Your Mama by then was exhausted and was ready for an early night to the disappointment of everyone at the party. This was taken particularly badly by the best man Rough Frank who was leading the drinking frenzy, and was worried the celebrations would be closed down too soon for his liking.

An early night fitted in well with your Baba's plan, as next day he had arranged a surprise - that they would fly to South Luangwa National Park. The bush lodge your parents were to stay at for two nights was outside the National Park and was open to visitors only during the dry season, come the rains it would be broken down and left to return to nature. No, not a typical honeymoon destination, but nevertheless a very exciting prospect for your animal loving Mama. Your Baba wrote me that they landed in the light four-seater aircraft on the uneven runway of a bush airstrip. There was a lot of room in the Cessna for them, it was just them, the pilot and a few bags. Not only did they have decent room but also there was great visibility with the high wing. Your Baba was unsure if the pilot was showing off to your Mama but he certainly made flying look easy.

The commentary from the bush pilot flowed as easily as his plane took to the sky. What was clear from the air is that South Luangwa was incredibly beautiful and your Baba expected it would also be memorable. It was the first time your Mama had experienced the bush. Sadly, it would be her first and one of her last times due to illness, as it turned out the sherry and cigarettes were not the reason for her exhaustion the previous day. After a quick check and refuelling, the pilot went to pick up the other two guests who would be staying with your parents at the same lodge. One of those Zambian guests had won a competition to stay for two nights and she was going to bring her sister along. Just like your Mama, these ladies would be in the bush for a first experience.

Your Mama was thrilled but a little concerned to be driven back from the air strip in an open sided vehicle in the middle of that wilderness. The Land Rover Defender had been adapted for safari work. The second row of seats had been slightly elevated and a third-row had been installed in the long wheel base defender, those seats were like sitting in a grandstand with the animals to view as if on a stage. The first thing your Mama commented on was the fact that the breeze was one of warm air a sensation that never came across watching those wildlife programs on black and white television. Your Mama commented that she had always wondered, on watching those wildlife documentaries, why people were not wearing coats like in Swansea when the wind came up! The driver, the ranger and your Baba had looked at each other and laughed at the remarks as they had never heard of anyone making such an observation before.

On the drive to the lodge your Baba wrote that they could immediately see a lot of wildlife, but it was always partly hidden by the thick bush and game viewing was difficult. The ranger however talked to your parents about the afternoon drive planned in the National Park where they would drive along the fertile areas near the Luangwa River. He told them they were going to see pure Africa, wildlife and birds in a stunningly beautiful land. But first they were to settle your Mama and Baba into the camp, to let them rest before they went out for a sun-downer. Around the camp there were lots of herbivores feasting on juicy green vegetation.

The camp may have been seasonal but nothing could have prepared your Mama for such a site. It was truly romantic being under canvas in a four-poster bed with the African bush sounds piping all around. A short walk away was a separate shower area but, on this occasion, there were no other guests to share it with. Your Mama was honest with your Baba when she explained it would be difficult to settle back into Princess Street after the luxury of the bush!

Your parents had their own guard to escort them to the shower area and the lounge come dining area, or to the traditional camp fire set out each night. Your Mama told your Baba that she hoped that man with his stick was ready to lay his life down and defend her against any of the big five or for that matter any wild animals with intent of putting her on their menu. A drum sounded for afternoon tea in the dining area where they met the other two Zambian ladies who would be with them on the afternoon drive. The ladies jumped into the last row of seats which was the luck of the draw.

An elderly white-haired man of European origin took the guide's seat next to the man who drove your parents from the airport. This older gentleman looked as if he taken a lot of sun over the years as his skin was nearly as dark as your Baba's. Both your parents thought him a bit long in the tooth for this type of adventure, and probably struggling to spot the road ahead never mind the game in the distance. It was a case of never judge a book by its cover, your Baba wrote later.

Norman Vehicle introduced himself and gave your folks a bit of a safety talk. He told them there would be definitely no leaving the Defender unless he approved. There should be no standing up to break the silhouette of the Defender that the animals were used to. He requested no loud talking please or any sudden movements. He had requested all this for good reason that became obvious to all of them later that day. That was about it, and they travelled into what your Mama thought at the time could be certain death with no seat belts and in the knowledge their two guards from their private lodge were not allowed to carry rifles in the National Park.

Norman Vehicle had far better eyesight than apparent on first impressions and possibly a sixth sense for spotting the smallest of birds hiding in the bush and an uncanny knowledge of all their names and habits. He even pointed out a snake that none of them saw at first but were all very happy enough in the end to be safely distanced from this dangerous evil reptile. Soon after they entered the National Park, the Defender sped up in response to a radio call. They were in for the treat of seeing a couple of dominant male lions of the local pride relaxing on a concrete river bridge a short distance away. Your Baba had never seen such big lions in such good condition. One confidently lounged and the other moved off lazily into the longer grass as they approached in the Defender.

As the four tourists focused on the bridge and the display of this magnificent beast, your Baba occasionally snapping the beast yawning, Norman Vehicle was watching the brother lion coming around the back end of the defender, it appeared to cut them off or wanted to drive them into the jaws of his partner in crime. Norman Vehicle was thankfully one step ahead of them and instructed the driver to take the Defender on a U turn towards an open area where the river broadened out and large crocodiles were basking in the last of the afternoon heat. Your Baba pointed out to me in his letter that all three ladies in the Land Rover were oblivious of any danger, as if they were in a city zoo or in the case of your Mama watching the events on black and white television.

The vehicle was driven across the low waters but soon on the other side it entered a dry gully and for some reason the driver just left the engine revving slowly. Close bye, out of the thick tree cover, four mature female tusked elephants emerged very relaxed with what appeared like a neutral attitude towards the humans sitting so close. Norman Vehicle slowly turned his head towards his guests, he whispered, *'stay very still and make no sound whatever happens'*. What happened was that those four grey massive gentle ladies brushed past the Defender in silence with their trunks sniffing at your parents' heads. Your Baba was frozen to the spot, unable to move even if he wanted to take a photograph. The ladies burst into chatter as soon as the elephants had moved off. Mr. Norman Vehicle, instructed the driver to get under the bonnet and fix that loose clutch cable once and for all! On a kopje well out of reach of those lions, the obligatory gin and tonic was issued, less the gin in three of the four glasses, as the sun plopped out of the sky; then the Defender took the satisfied four home for dinner and camp fire side stories.

Your Baba always said there is nothing like a bush shower after a dusty afternoon in an open 4 x 4. He also claimed the camp fire in the bush came a very close second place to the shower. So, he was a very satisfied groom enjoying the delights of his honeymoon in the most relaxing environment he could wish for. To top it all Norman Vehicle told the tale of two lions he had adopted when he found them as rejected cubs in the bush and certain to die. They were the animal actors in the Born Free movie. Those two appeared in the film about a lion in Kenya that was returned to the wild after being rescued and initially brought up in a domestic environment. The letters themselves were exciting, wow what more would they tell of the experiences on this short safari? The wedding party would not have to wait long according to Mr. Robert Joramogi as your Baba was to write about a night drive where they would have another unusual experience.

The morning drum called everyone for coffee and some very sweet cake. This certainly was a place you could build a traditional African figure like mine; your Baba wrote me. At the time your Baba visited Zambia they had one of Africa's highest rhino populations with four thousand alone in the Luangwa valley region. So, no surprise then that they got charged by a black rhino protecting her calf.

Getting away from your Baba's story for a minute, forty years on if you visit the same area, they talk of the big four no longer the big five. Sadly in 1998 the rhino in Zambia was declared extinct. The rhino had been poached out of existence in Zambia during the 1970s and 1980s all to meet the demands of Arabs wanting dagger- handles and the Chinese medicine trade. Their horns are believed to help fevers and disorders of the blood. Not as an aphrodisiac as the myth in the Western press keeps on reporting. As your Baba would say today if he were here, it's not about what the rhino horn does, it's about the perception of people. Unlike when your parents visited the park, today it is full of just the big four, nevertheless it still has a very high hippo and Nile crocodile density. It has such a high density of animals that Hollywood stars love to visit it more than any other African location for real adventure.

Your Mama and Baba were told to close their eyes and expected on opening them to be gazing on their breakfast with Champagne as advertised, all this being set out below the canopy of an acacia tree. The surprises kept on coming in the form of animal experiences, and that's what they paid for. On opening their eyes as per the command, the Defender, was sitting in the middle of a herd of more than a hundred buffalo. Just like the close encounter with the elephants the day before, these potential killers seemed unaware and certainly unconcerned about the humans sitting in the Defender just meters away from them and their young.

The night drive was another special experience, first picked up from your mother's good sense of smell. They followed their noses and came across those two dominant males doing what comes best to them after a heavy meal. Their wind carried for some distance in the natural wind!   Some eighteen lionesses lined up to take the seconds from an old bull buffalo. Even by the best of Kenya luxury safari standards this was up there with the best. And the honeymoon in Crete a memory relegated to being just another summer holiday replaced by an unforgettable African Utopia honeymoon.

There is a little bit more to tell before the letters from your Baba dried up as your Mama became ill.' Titus Tembo was thrilled to be enlightened about his parents and their activities by his Baba's letters through Mr. Robert **Joramogi**. Memories never touched on before and he was so grateful for this opportunity that Mr. Robert Joramogi so generously shared.

CHAPTER THIRTEEN

A time of contemplation

One morning Titus Tembo woke from his planned twenty minutes transcendental meditation session an hour after he had sat in his normal spot on a comfortable leather chair in the bedroom offered to him by Robert Joramogi. He sat down and started at 7.00 am, but suddenly his mobile showed it was 08.00 am. The night before TT had enjoyed the bliss of his regular twenty-minute meditation, then he'd walked Pat the cat on their local beach in the relative cool before the sun dipped over the horizon. TT completed a thirty-minute gentle evening pilates session and read a relaxing self-improvement book. Even sharing the home of Robert Joramogi did not put TT off keeping to his regular habits, one of them was ticking off the 'must do' events on his daily check list. This was TT's routine most nights and these days he would fall into a peaceful eight hours of undisturbed sleep.

The only exception to this good night's sleep of eight hours was if TT missed his early evening twenty-minute meditation session. This disturbance of his regular sleep pattern was particularly noticeable if he tried to do this missed twenty-minute session just before his regular bed time. Then it became like TT's teenage years of disturbed sleep. That evening it was a perfect sleep. This had become the norm for TT after he started regularly practicing transcendental meditation for several months. Before that he was lucky to get six hours sleep at best, he would always struggle to drop off and looking at the state of his bedding come morning, it seemed he had been in a war zone. This had been Titus Tembo's normal nightly experience since a teenager when he listened to radio programmes, normally music late into the early hours and in his twenties listening, he'd be tuned into current affairs on the World Service of the BBC, sometimes this went on until the sun came up.

He had no excuse these days to fall asleep for that length of time during his meditation other than if his mind and/or body needed it. Titus Tembo awoke energized from his morning meditation session and with the clear thinking that he needed his own place in Al Hamra Village and the male companionship that Mr. Robert Joramogi would provide and his friendship that had been missing in his life since his beloved Baba Eng. M. J. R. Tembo left this earth.

Mr. Robert Joramogi was ready with the breakfast table set for his left-handed friend and Pat the cat made loud sounds as if to request his own breakfast. Mr. Robert Joramogi was preparing omena from his stash that someone had caught in Lake Victoria on a moonless night. This special breakfast was to honour his guest who he knew was leaving today, as per the note on the back of his front door.

A lot of people shy away from this fish delicacy due to an overpowering smell that it produces if prepared wrongly but Mr. Robert Joramogi was an expert after years of practice. When the boys were out on their morning walk, he had soaked any of the remaining dirt away then boiled the omena to remove its bitter taste and odour. This was the second time of boiling as he always did this prior to storing the fish for future use usually to mark a special occasion as of this morning. Mr. Robert Joramogi decked in his full chef's white outfit, slipped the omena into a saucepan to dry them over a low heat. In another pan he'd prepared a tomato puree and added cooking oil before putting the omena in the pan. As the fish turned from silver to a golden brown, Mr. Robert Joramogi, Master African Chef, added lots of salt the way all Kenyans liked it, then a little spice. Three minutes on low heat, then both men and cat could enjoy the treat from home. A little crispy toast on the side with Kahawa Chungu muddy black coffee and they were good to go or in TT's case, he was ready to spill the beans.

Titus Tembo shared his vision of the next six months with his beloved Baba's best friend Mr. Robert Joramogi. TT was going to eat the elephant a bit at a time. First move out of Dubai and at least short term rent that studio from 'a bit of Yorkshire' who he had phoned on his walk back from the beach. Titus Tembo explained to Mr. Robert Joramogi that the man soon woke up when I agreed to his proposal on a one-month trial and pay him later today in cash on my return from Ras Al-Khaimah and him being available after his golf in Dubai.

The studio apartment was fully furnished and even had Wi-Fi and satellite television, so it met TT's short-term needs perfectly. That evening would only be a matter of TT packing the last few personal things he had in his bedroom and his clothing he had left in Dubai that would just fill the Mini Cooper S. Hopefully, fingers crossed, Mr. Robert Joramogi was okay with him leaving his stuff, well, a lot of photographic equipment related stuff and a few clothes, with him for now and then he'd collect them when he moved into the studio. In the evening tomorrow, TT's plan was to go shopping in Al Hamra Mall for essentials like groceries. Mr. Robert Joramogi was delighted that Titus Tembo son of Eng. M. J. R. Tembo was to join him in Al Hamra Village and so soon. And TT was delighted he had his male muse to advise him when needed and he'd do his best to look after the mzee.

'A bit of Yorkshire' or his alternative name of DJ from his time on the radio in the United Arab Emirates, had some surprises up his sleeve that convinced TT it would only be just the one month's stay. To the agreed price was added, a not previously mentioned safety deposit, albeit refundable under certain conditions, a charge for one entry card to be used at any of the Village security gates, a bill to clean the apartment after he left even before he moved in, a bill for one month's Wi-Fi connection and satellite television. All these additional charges, 'a bit of Yorkshire' off set with the offer of two games of free golf with him at one of the up-market golf courses in Dubai or Abu Dhabi.

'A bit of Yorkshire' had done this out of the goodness of his heart for TT. No, his new landlord had made the offer as he needed to honour the terms of his free credit card golf in order to ensure he had a tee time booking and would not miss out on his monthly free allocation of golf. Thus, 'a bit of Yorkshire' got paid the various extras and off-set them for TT by arranging free golf for his new tenant at no cost to himself. However, when they did play TT had to go by the name Johnny Jones as 'a bit of Yorkshire' had already booked the two balls for the coming month before agreeing the financial arrangements with TT. And so it was that DJ arranged for TT to become JJ for two days of golf! TT had little choice at such short notice but to dish out the extra money with no other place to hang his hat as he would not further impose on Mr. Robert Joramogi and his kind hospitality. In reality there were two winners here as TT very much looked forward to both rounds of golf on the Five Star courses in Dubai.

With the death of his beloved Baba, TT had survived this relatively short time alone before he met with Mr. Robert Joramogi. Of course, it may be some months yet before the Dubai courts came very close to nearing a decision with respect to the probate and therefore a decision on all of Eng. M. J. R. Tembo's assets that were in the United Arab Emirates. For Titus Tembo at this time, transcendental meditation was a great help. However, TT remained unsure; was he a mzungu dressed in an African body? Or did he want to be a real Mwafrika to truly photograph Africa, its people, landscape and wildlife in a way that outsiders could feel the real Africa?

Time would tell as he decided he would just be himself for now. Did he want to end up in a place where Titus Tembo would be called brother by all around him and be comfortable also, in turn call other Africans his brothers and sisters? For every African in Kenya, all brothers of the father were called father and all sisters of the mother were called mother. Titus Tembo did not have to worry just yet about that as Eng. M. J. R. Tembo had joined his Mama. Titus Tembo currently knew of no other living relatives but that might yet change?

What he did know was that if he was really African, the accepted practice of polygamy in Kenya would have seen his three wives remain under his roof! Right now, there were more urgent issues in eating the elephant, like where he would live in a month from now, and then where to live after the probate was settled? What about the funeral for his beloved Baba who died holding a visa from what emirate? As that would determine where he could be buried if he was to be buried in the United Arab Emirates? How would he live beyond the next six months without further income if the probate was delayed? What did he need to do to survive on the cash he had currently?

Titus Tembo did not feel too concerned about his future as he packed up the last of his photographic equipment. The house on the Dubai island no longer felt like home with his beloved Baba gone and no Trixie keeping it clean and fresh. Titus Tembo had handed over a considerable sum for a key entry card to Al Hamra Village and the keys to the studio in the Marina apartments that was owned by 'a bit of Yorkshire'. The Northern Emirates provided TT with the possibility of starting afresh with the support of mzee Mr. Robert Joramogi to fall back on for advice. Titus Tembo's circle of friends was also changing as he now had a golfing buddy in DJ even if he was also to be his landlord for just the next month. TT had a pal to walk the beach of a morning and that was company he could enjoy even if he could not understand what Pat the cat had to say. When arriving in his new home, TT was successful with the new entry key card and confidently drove in as a village resident as if he was someone who had lived there forever. There was no permanent under cover parking unlike the Royal Breeze blocks of apartments; some type of shade was provided but not a great barrier for the United Arab Emirates summer sun beating down from the clear blue sky. Another good reason to look for alternative accommodation thought TT. The studio apartment was uninviting with no balcony and a view of what appeared to be a boat yard. Yet another motivation for a quick relocation. On the credit side of the equation, the studio was spacious and peaceful. Titus Tembo had paid to stay for a month and it was a great base to search for something a little more his style. In the mean-time Titus Tembo needed to head out for that essential shopping.

Titus Tembo's intentions were to scout around Al Hamra Mall and fill his car to ensure he'd be comfortable and would not go hungry in his new place at least for a few days, as he envisaged that no doubt there would be short falls in his first Al Hamra Mall shopping expedition. TT intended to put a comprehensive list together once he had settled in and found out exactly what was needed. The exit gate at the rear of Royal Breeze provides the uninitiated with the intriguing prospect of going back in time. The main road lay to the right but straight ahead at the roundabout was a more interesting path.

Titus Tembo was in no hurry and in a mood to explore. TT headed towards the Red Island, Al Jazeera, which was no longer an Island or even the colour red. The place did appear completely different to anything Titus Tembo had seen in the United Arab Emirates in the short time he'd lived there. The place reminded TT of the older parts of Mombasa on the Kenyan coast. Indeed, this was also a historic old town that had survived the vagaries of time. Later on, talking to 'a bit of Yorkshire' he found out his landlord was some kind of history buff when it came to the Northern Emirates. He told TT some interesting stuff and TT could see for himself the great photographic opportunities Al Jazeera had to offer.

He smiled to himself when he pictured his art work of the old buildings in monochrome. TT saw the similarities in the architecture to Mombasa's use of blocks of coral in the buildings. What he learnt from his landlord was that the place was an old fishing and pearling centre, that became a major trading post dating back hundreds of years. He'd added an interesting fact as if it was just an afterthought, the inhabitants in the middle of the 20th century up sticks to move to the expanding city of Abu Dhabi but locally people say everyone moved out overnight and today it's referred to as the ghost town!

TT could see that although many of the buildings had become ruins, some had even been cannibalised and modernized for use by the new, possibly poorer, Asian and African inhabitants. Titus Tembo saw this as an interesting spectacle for a camera in the right hands. The buildings that survived and built of coral displayed decorative designs on their walls and around the windows that reminded TT of the historical ruins at Gedi on the Northern coast of Kenya. No attempt, unlike here, had been made in Kenya to reconstruct, restore and rehabilitate the key buildings. Here it looked as if the powers to be were gearing up for an outside museum to attract in the tourists from Dubai. And TT was well placed with his camera to beat many of these tourists to their prize.

A little further down the track the road turned to tarmac and then back to sand with a number of large local residences on the one side of the road that headed towards the small sea port. On the tarmac lanes leading off the stretch of the sand highway, were smaller modern residences with flat roofs. The newly made road was prepared for the tourist influx and already was lined with all sorts of small shops just as if they'd been transported from Mombasa. Titus Tembo was intrigued to explore further.

First appeared a grimy little shop in the long line of commercial offerings. The grime was all-purpose white flour dust as the men worked the dough with their hands in a traditional bakery. Two men sweated away in sight of their potential clients and a third man baked their output of oval shaped grand efforts in a tandoor, a cylindrical oven, the primary cooking equipment of the sub-continent region that reminded TT of the Italian pizza ovens he witnessed being used in the Kenyan coastal holiday town of Malindi.

Cheek by jowl the shops lined up like those terraced houses the British seemed so fond of, but here with large glass fronts. The exception were the several car cleaning establishments swarming with activity. Many little grocery stores came close to Titus Tembo's experience of Kenya, where if one lady made a success of selling then many more ladies with the same offers would set up along the street. Maybe TT was wrong, he thought and on a second view saw that these grocery places targeted specific nationalities and the goods for their cultures and taste buds?

There were ironmongers, repair shops for all types of machinery, a handful of car workshops with tyres and batteries stacked high, and where there was all this human activity there had to be tea and coffee sellers. What came to mind was an old-fashioned Mall, a Market, a Bazaar or Souk. But Titus Tembo felt none of these words did this place justice, it was more than the sum of the parts! Here you could fill your car with fuel, send a letter at the post office, call in at the friendly police station, enter a money exchange, eat authentic food from many parts of the world. In fact, TT was welcomed most humbly into a Pakistani restaurant where he sat among the usual customers who all had table service. There was some confusion when paying as they asked TT for a grand sum that came to less than half of what TT paid in Dubai for a coffee the previous week. And that was the correct bill for his two-course meal and a cup of tea.

TT, like a winning gambler, was on a roll and keen to try to win again. Next stop was a traditional barber shop that was conveniently located next to Super Shine, where over the next few months he would become a regular, getting his silver Mini Cooper S washed, vacuumed, shined and tyres polished. While this was taking place, TT was scouting the offers for his hair in the barber shop. The wash and cut were followed by a free head, shoulder and back massage. TT was so impressed that he had a shave before a facial that came to a tenth of the price of the Dubai equivalent and much cheaper than he could even hope for in Nairobi. At these low rates TT could afford to improve his life style compared to the one he had in Dubai and might even consider a permanent move to the tax-free Northern Emirates!

With no list at hand to guide his actions, TT failed to reach the grocery store of choice in good time. It seemed like he'd never arrive since a series of phone shops provided Titus Tembo with the opportunity to bring his phone back to a good standard, a new glass screen and holder for his iPhone was obtained at a ridiculously cheap price. And there was a photographer's shop which dared TT hope for a repeat of his experiences so far in the Red Island terraces. Indeed, when TT would need photographic prints, this would be his first port of call. He checked out the prices, equipment and quality which he was happy with.

All this positive experience in such a short time, what more was out there Titus Tembo could not imagine. He had to post a letter home and the Emirati in the post office was a gentleman of the first order and provided good advice. Another pleasant surprise was that Mpesa phone money was easy to buy across the road from the post office for his Kenyan number. The exchange rate and value for money charges, TT was more than happy with. The good experience was repeated as his Mini Cooper S car was filled with fuel and the clean windscreen washed, and unlike in Dubai with no expectation of a tip. He called in the local book shop for his first disappointment, no books for sale, it should have been renamed the administration supply shop with everything you'll need or we'll get it for you. TT noticed a handful of bike repair shops also selling many different models of reasonably priced bikes that he might consider buying once he settled into the village. TT's final stop was the first thing on his non-existent list, a large grocery shop at the end of the terrace bazaar, a standalone building a few hundred meters away and boasting its own car park.

When TT recounted his visit to the Red Island, Mr. Robert Jaramogi concurred fully with his feelings of it being much like Mombasa, even down to the midday closing of all the outlets until the cool of the evening. In fact, Mr. Robert Joramogi admitted that when he was driving himself, he spent a great deal of time on the Red Island, eating there, shopping there and playing cards with the locals outside a coffee shop near the post office. Mr. Robert Joramogi now spent his time in the Al Hamra Mall for the central air-conditioning with its taxi rank next to the main entrance that allowed him the ease of running back and forth in his later years.

Mr. Robert Joramogi admitted to TT that he missed meeting with Africans in the Red Island, even those who asked for a helping hand occasionally to buy gas or pay their rent. In return for helping out a poor man or two, one of those friends delivered to Mr. Robert Joramogi Swahili food. This from the Red Island that he had researched on social media to find just such a delicacy but unsuccessfully. Let this be a lesson to you son of Eng. M. J. R. Tembo, a lesson of karma, it is always good to give to those in need when you can afford it, and you can afford it. Mr. Robert Joramogi also admitted that he had not seen that a posh Titus Tembo from Jumeriah Island would be so taken by the Red Island in the Northern Emirates. TT smiled and said '*I guess it's like Marmite, Red Island that is, you either love it like us mzee, or avoid it like the plague to enjoy a clinical Al Hamra Mall and its various more expensive offerings.*'

Al Hamra Mall was not going to see much of Titus Tembo in the short term thought Mr. Robert Joramogi, and he also expected the search would be intensified by his young friend Titus Tembo for an alternative to his studio along the road in Royal Breeze. Indeed, the search soon turned up a suitable large one-bedroom apartment for rent or sale, partly furnished. Titus Tembo had walked in and loved his potential new home at first sight. He mulled over his quick decision. Was he in touch with his artistic side or was he spending too much time alone to make such comments to himself?

White minimalistic décor, white leather comfortable sofa, modernised simple kitchen, walk in shower room, single bedroom with lots of storage space. Unlike the similar few places TT had seen to date, in this apartment each room had a door with glass panels to clearly demarcate the designated space, stop smells drifting through the whole apartment and isolate a cooler bedroom over a warmer more comfortable lounge area. The balcony had a sun shaded area of a tiled roof that not many other apartments enjoyed in the block.

As you walked into the apartment the large sliding glass doors framed a picture of the highest range of mountains in the United Arab Emirates. No snow to be seen this time of year but he had read on-line that it happens come a cold winter. Once your gaze was over the mountain scenery and dropped a little, the 180-degree view took in an interesting vista of a green golf course, blue lagoons with palm tree borders, and the ocean view was tucked around the side of the balcony. The other apartments Titus Tembo had viewed to date could not compare. The boasted views of the beach he'd seen earlier in other apartments were great over a holiday weekend, yes, but then only in the daylight hours.

This apartment faced east for the best of sun come morning time and cool shade come a summer afternoon. Under-cover parking was in the building, a gymnasium on the second floor with the large swimming pool looking over the beach area. So, there were no further questions to be answered and Titus Tembo signed the lease agreement that afternoon at the estate agent's office, made a non-refundable down payment and set his moving date for the start of the following month.

There was still quite a lot of that elephant to eat but TT was keen to play those landlord's earned rounds of golf in Dubai before he broke the news to the 'a bit of Yorkshire' of his imminent departure from the Marina Buildings to that of Royal Breeze. TT had to phone his landlord as the man never had any credit or data pack on his phone. As such 'a bit of Yorkshire' would only pick up WhatsApp's when he had free Wi-Fi anywhere or when he was at his home. It was September and as such their golf would best start very early in the morning or just in time for 18 holes before the sun set. TT, given a choice of tee time he would pick the former, but his short-term landlord was flabbergasted at the thought of getting out of his bed before 10.00am. 'A bit of Yorkshire' explained clearly to TT that city life involved late nights and relaxing mornings.

TT was getting to build an understanding and friendship with this unusual character. He discovered 'a bit of Yorkshire' actually hailed from the city of London and not the North of England. This was his nick name given to him by members of a Dubai golf society for his support of what he referred to as the *'Mighty Owls'*. 'A bit of Yorkshire' selected Sheffield

Wednesday as his soccer team of choice while his parents continually argued over their family rivalry of Arsenal and West Ham United that had come down the generations of either side of his parents' families. And this was the only thing his loving parents ever disagreed on. Ironically his uncontroversial team selection came back to bite him years later. His sister went to study in Manchester, did her teachers training and met her Yorkshire husband; his family supported the rival team across the city, yes, Sheffield United. So, DJ, as he was known from his early days on the radio, would argue about soccer with his brother-in-law on his visits to see his younger sister in Sheffield.

The September golfing tour they set themselves took in TT's thirty fifth birthday due on the fateful never to be forgotten day the 11th of September. This was a special day in that TT not only had to follow the normal routine laid down by DJ, pick him up and drop him back home, pay for the coffee or tea on the course; today in addition he needed to buy the birthday drinks and DJ was insistent as he liked a few ciders. DJ must have been a wealthy man as he played golf nearly every day other than when he was busy dealing with his rental properties in London twice a week.

It appeared DJ ran a second-hand golf business on the side from his home in Dubai. This is where TT purchased his left-handed set of second hand nearly-new irons, well nearly new according to 'a bit of Yorkshire,' along with a bag to house his newly acquired irons. The shopping continued for his nearly new shoes and a nearly new set of woods. Nothing was free from 'a bit of Yorkshire,' except those games that came with a catch attached. To top it all off there were small bags of recovered golf balls on sale.

This was a wealthy man clearly down to his ability to sell as well as his aversion to spending his own money. Free golf for himself and the occasional partner like TT came via the number of credit cards he signed up for and the running of his golf society. TT had met his long-suffering Asian wife who held down a full-time managerial job but still also managed the household without the assistance of a maid or any input from DJ. The lady not only put up with the golf shop in her front room but his collecting of lost golf balls when they played together over a weekend. TT witnessed this when they played together one weekend and the Asian lady hurried DJ along as he did his normal search along the water's edge for lost balls that would end up in his sales.

The first two rounds were tied to the property contract but more free rounds followed. As they played the Els, the Trump, and Dubai Hills twice, TT got to know the man and his game. The golf was social and the scores could no way be fairly entered toward their handicaps. Much talking took place and TT was getting an introduction to, or rather the gossip revolving around the British business world of Dubai. He suspected that part of this gossip was based on some truth, and that likely came first hand from the Asian lady who held down a good job. But DJ must have been fed some third hand information from this network driving the rumour mill.

Towards the end of the month TT felt confident enough that their newly formed friendship would stand the news that he'd be moving out. TT came to like 'a bit of Yorkshire', his old English humour and the business tales he shared. DJ was very comfortable with the chauffeur and waiter service TT provided him on golf days and the decision was that they would play together at least once a month in the future with no green fees to be paid, and with the occasional game on the courses in the Northern Emirates that they would shell out for. It was a shame, speculated TT, that this golfing arrangement of 'I'll scratch your back if you'll scratch mine,' may come to an end within the next six months if he moved on from the United Arab Emirates.

CHAPTER FOURTEEN

Business friends of a feather

The next name provided to Titus Tembo on Eng. M. J. Tambo's list of helpful gentlemen was in fact an Emirati Lady! His first point of contact, Mr. Robert Joramogi, had proved very helpful but the second, a local lady, why? A name of a lady after all that his father had warned him about the risks of friendships with the opposite sex! He had said these relationships were like using sugar cane as a walking stick, eventually you would be tempted to eat the sugar cane! Anyway, I am sure my beloved Baba had good reason to recommend this local lady as a source that could be of assistance to me if needed; but in what way?

Possibly this was the Wasata he needed down the road? One aspect he thought about where she could help was delaying the decision he had to make about the body of his beloved Baba? Possibly buying him some time with the authorities before he needed to take action over the body of his beloved Baba? Titus Tembo had a lot of thinking to do over what option to take for the funeral, or even if a funeral without a body could be arranged?

After an initial guarded response over the phone, the whole tempo of their discussion changed once Titus Tembo explained his situation to the good lady. Ma'am Naila the Emirati lady invited him to visit her home in Dubai, where Titus Tembo and ma'am Naila sat on the floor with all five children, her husband and father to enjoy dinner. The lady of the house was a little surprised when TT told her he was a vegetarian after she'd or rather one of her maids had especially prepared khuzi. There were however some vegetables, rice and hazelnuts amongst the rice if you had young eyes and it was easy enough to avoid the lamb. The whole roasted lamb was made in the honour of the visit of Titus Tembo, and it reminded him a little of East African culture that was clearly an influence in this household, or was it the other way around that the Arabs influenced East African culture? Whatever the answer, Titus Tembo was right in his feelings, as it turned out the father still had a house in Stone Town, the old capital on the Island of Zanzibar.

The connection with Eng. M. J. R. Tembo came from a young Ms. Naila at that time meeting His Baba in Cardiff. She smiled broadly and her eyes sparkled when she recalled the reason for her being in Cardiff. Mrs. Naila clearly was a clever woman, bringing up five kids and holding down a challenging job as a human resources manager in a multinational company with offices in Dubai and the Northern Emirates. Ma'am Naila did admit to having a cook, a maid and two nannies who helped her greatly. This assisted her with all the domestic chores, took pressure off child minding, and prepared her for managing people in the work place. Titus Tembo wondered if that latter experience was included on many a resume put together by women returning to the workplace?

Mrs. Naila explained all this to Titus Tembo in the open family forum so her children could hear the lesson. As a young girl she'd not been doing so well at school and spoke to her mother. Will God help me with my school work, sure her mother advised her and yet her results were even worse next time around. On checking back with her mother and complaining that she'd messed up her exams once again; her mother questioned her on what studying she'd done. 'Oh, none' she responded, I was too busy praying to God to help me.' That is when her parents decided to send her to the international school just outside Cardiff in Wales.

At that time Eng. M. J. R. Tembo was revisiting the capital where he had studied twenty years previously. Some company had brought Eng. M. J. R. Tembo to London for a job interview so he'd taken the opportunity to travel for the day to see how Cardiff was doing. He had also told Mr. Robert Joramogi about this visit to Cardiff in one of his letters. Eng. M. J. R. Tembo was disappointed in the Brains Beer, and told Ms. Naila the same, but he also told Ms. Naila how excited he was about all the great ongoing developments both in the City centre and the adjoining town of Penarth or was it, Cardiff Bay?

Anyway, ma'am Naila got off the subject of beer and back to the matter at hand. Mrs. Naila had met his beloved Baba when eating Pizza. She was enjoying lunch with a friend and they were wondering what was the topping on their Pizza, when this African gentleman (your father) pointed out to us young Arab Women, 'you are eating pork!' We were so happy Eng. M. J. R. Tembo kept our secret as we went on to finish the whole pizza and we kept in touch with each other from that day. We caught up face to face once your father settled in Dubai. Eng. M. J. R. Tembo became a family friend and took our family portraits over the years as the kids grew older and some departed the nest. This is why Titus Tembo got a very rare invite to an Emirati home. The African gentlemen and the well-educated young Emirate lady had helped each other in business over the years and hoped she might assist Titus Tembo also?

Clearly the family was relaxed with this first-time visitor as Ma'am Naila's husband humorously teased his wife with reference to her as the *'English One'* because of her education in Wales. And added he was also there to assist if needed by the son of Eng. M. J. R. Tembo, who was a very good man, he was pleased to confirm. The old man and head of the family offered the use of his house in Stone Town anytime TT would be in Zanzibar. Titus Tembo really felt blest, so proud of his beloved Baba that he had made such a good impact on this lovely local family. They all came to the garden gate, even the five children, to wave him off on his journey back North. He might come back to ma'am Naila in the months ahead as he possibly could use her Wasata if his elephant was to be completely eaten in good time.

TT took a detour to Ikea in Festival City, where he ticked off all the items on his shopping list. His complete list of all items needed in his partially furnished one-bedroom Royal Breeze apartment were not that extensive. He made a total of what he bought and for how much. This made him think a minute or two about his failed Nairobi ceramic business and he felt it must be very challenging for any Western manufacturer to compete on price with their Chinese competitors on these everyday household goods. He was assuming, of course, that a lot of these goods were manufactured in China as most things seemed to come from there these days? There were exceptions of course and he turned over the saucer he was drinking green tea from. Yes, here is the proof, where the likes of the Stoke-On-Trent Steelite brand of tableware still sold their hard-wearing ceramics world-wide to hotels, restaurants and airlines. They had a product that competed on cost, as it stood up much longer to the robust commercial environment it was living in, its life expectancy was much greater than those cheaper Chinese copies. But their Nairobi Hi-Five ceramic business had not built that difference into their goods as sadly for him anyway and likely many others he guessed, the Chinese can copy any cute design and sell it at a much lower price to win the day.

TT took a call on his mobile from a 04 number, a Dubai landline and a lady on the other end was giving yet another polite reminder of his responsibilities. Pressure was being put on TT from the authorities to deal with the body of his beloved Baba. The easy way out, but maybe not the best solution would be cremation in the emirate of his Baba's visa if they had a crematorium. Alternatively, in that same Emirate a local burial could be arranged at a Christian cemetery, and if Dubai, that would be in Jebel Ali, on land provided by the government in the charity-financed cemetery. None of those solutions would be in accordance to his beloved Baba's dreams and he may need the influence and guidance of his Baba's local lady friend to achieve a suitable solution. Mr. Robert Joramogi was hinting broadly at TT that these options or putting the ashes next to his Mama would not be the acceptable alternatives to following tribal traditions. So maybe if ma'am Naila could not help, then it was time to visit the lawyer appointed by Eng. M. J. R. Tembo to deal with all his legal matters including the reading of the Final Will and Testimony and the matter of his beloved Baba's body.

His beloved Baba's Scottish lawyer had practiced in the United Arab Emirates for more years than TT had been on earth. The Scot had a very relaxed manner and an easy way of explaining what could have been a very complex legal issue into their simple essence. The estate of Eng. M. J. R. Tembo with permission of the Dubai courts was paying the expenses to keep the body in the morgue until the decision was most likely to be made on its future after the probate was finalized. The probate was taking longer than the average expatriate cases due to the matter of the investment in the eco business.

The Scottish lawyer saw no point in reading the Will to the concerned parties, namely TT he assumed, until the Dubai court announced their decision with respect to the probate. In fact, this was a relief to TT as it bought him some more time to think over what he would do with his father's body, and where the body or ashes would eventually be put to rest. Mr. Robert Joramogi was not so easily ignored, he was his beloved Baba's best friend, he knew the traditions of the Luo tribe while, TT was all at sea with where he hailed from, what his duties were and how to move forward, yes 'Matatanisho' once again. TT was not stressing about it, he did expect to make the right decision after the probate, he still had time as well as cultural and traditional input from Mr. Robert Joramogi and the clear logical and calm actions coming as a result of his transcendental meditation.

There was a new revelation disclosed at this first meeting with the legal representative that His Baba failed to discuss at any previous time or even communicate in writing in the notes he left for his mtoto. TT had assumed all would be his to do what he liked with but no, it was just like his assumptions with regards coming to the United Arab Emirates and being presented with a position at his beloved Baba's business. Much of his inheritance sat in a trust that was not subject to the probate and as such TT in theory would not have to wait for the Dubai courts to rule on all the assets. However, the lawyer had been instructed to await the outcome of the probate before releasing any funds to TT. Thus, the reasoning not to read the full will at this time and the Scotsman stressed to TT not to make arrangements for the funeral until the will was read.

There was a standard application form, partly designed by Eng. M. J. R. Tembo, for allocating funds to TT, that naturally TT would need to complete. What TT was not aware of, and would not be made aware of, is the guidance notes his beloved Baba had given the trustees of the fund. The guidance notes would dictate what money could be released for what purposes at what times. This was in the interest of TT and made little difference that he did not know what the guidelines contained, as he still used the yard stick of 'would it make Eng. M. J. R. Tembo happy, if yes then go for it'. Eng. M. J. R. Tembo did not want easy quick money stopping the growth of his mtoto as a good person. That is why Eng. M. J. R. Tembo appointed his Scottish lawyer of many years standing and his best and wise friend Mr. Robert Joramogi as trustees. Mr. Robert Joramogi had explained to TT prior to his visit to the lawyer that day, his Baba wanted TT to make his own way in the world and understand good values not corrupt him with easy money. As such TT, left the lawyers office with nothing but positive thoughts.

As it stood currently, TT was settled in a very comfortable one-bedroom apartment in a great location. He had sufficient funds to pick and choose or reject some of the paying video and photo shoots that came his way by word of mouth and social media. He had his contacts, be they Kenyan, British or Emirati, they were all vital at times. He had his free leisure time to improve his golf, fitness and maybe also tennis. His transcendental meditation and regular 'get togethers' with the transcendental meditation group and his teacher on the palm in Dubai were helping him think clearly and be calm. He was off the booze and meat, which both helped with his new healthy lifestyle. Pat the cat kept him company on his morning beach walks. TT felt good, and time was on his side in the devouring of his elephant.

THE EPILOGUE

A journey of discovery

In keeping with the theme of 'Matatanisho', one can consider this section the prologue to Part 2 of Africa's Second-Best Photographer; A Journey of Enlightenment. There is a big chunk of elephant for Titus Tembo to eat just yet. The United Arab Emirates has turned into a home where TT is more than just surviving, but how will he maintain his new healthy lifestyle? The Dubai Court has yet to rule on the probate and the estate was locked up in the trust fund until the ruling was made to trigger the trustees to accept applications from TT for cash. What will the Dubai courts rule and when, so TT could move on with his life? He was keen to give back if funds were to come to him after the probate was complete and start exploring a good cause he could support for life. Will he return to the continent of his birth and do what? And will his beloved Baba be cremated, his body returned to his tribal land or will it find a home in the United Arab Emirates or even next to his mama in the Swansea Valley? Or did TT have something else in mind to satisfy his Baba's dreams for his body?

GLOSSARY

Ayie	Stage one Luo agreement to the wedding
Baba	Father
Chai	Traditional brewed black tea, full fat milk & sugar
Chizungu	Bantu word for behaving rich
Harambee	All pull together, an unwritten law of generosity
Hongo	Bribe
Jachien	the spirit of a dead person
Kahawa Chungu	Special Kenyan coffee
Kopje	A small hill in a generally flat area
Kundi	Crowd
Maa–	Maasai Language
Mama	Mother
Matatanisho or **Hiraeth**	Confusion
Matatus	Privately owned minibuses use as shared taxis.
Mbu	Mosquito
Meko	Bride kidnapping tradition
Mtoto	Son
Mwafrika	African
Mzee	Old or wise
Mzungu	White person
Ningojee	Wait for me
Nyumbani	Home
Ouma	Afrikaans grandmother
Pole Pole	Slowly
Potjies	A three-legged cast-iron cooking pot
Safari	Journey
Tell me	East African greeting
Wasata	Arabic name for influence